# ESCAPING GRACE

# J. Q. DAVIS

Published: J.Q. Davis 2015, 2019
jq.davis@yahoo.com

Editing: Precy Larkins
Cover Design: Murphy Rae, Indie Solutions by Murphy Rae
www.murphyrae.net
Formatting: Elaine York, Allusion Graphics, LLC
www.allusiongraphics.com

# ESCAPING GRACE

*To my protector, my Casanova,*
*my Biggie, my Cassie.*

12 YEARS EARLIER...

DAMN IT. MY PHONE was really a piece of work. I needed to remember to find the time to get a new one.

I kept one eye on the road and one on the stupid phone, hoping that somehow it would just magically fix itself. But that was the problem with technology these days. People had become so reliant on it and used it constantly, until that one day they needed it the most. Then it didn't work.

I was never big on the technological era the world seemed to be embarking upon. I was an old-fashioned doctor. If it were up to me, I would probably just use my hospital pager. But my wife, Eve, had always been pretty good at making sure we were up to date. She handled all of that stuff, including the upgrade of a new phone. Unfortunately, I'd been working so much that I haven't had a chance to even have a normal conversation with her. If I did have the time, we'd argue about how I never had the time. It was a vicious cycle.

I missed Eve and Gracie so much.

It was sad that over the past few months, I hadn't been able to watch Gracie grow. It was almost unbelievable that she was already five years old. It seemed like only yesterday when Eve and I were in the hallway of the maternity ward, watching our newborn baby girl through a glass window. She was the only one in the row of wailing newborns who lay quietly in her bassinet, smiling. She was so tiny.

And that full head of hair! I just knew she'd have gorgeous hair when she got older—just like her mom.

The roads were pretty clear. Usually, Los Angles traffic began an hour away from the city itself, which was about how far I was from home. But it was four in the morning and the city seemed to be sleeping.

A few days ago, Eve had called to inform me of Grace's illness. We spoke briefly and only long enough for her to tell me that Grace had come down with some kind of flu. We got into a massive fight before my phone shut off on its own, mid-conversation. I couldn't even remember what the fight was about.

She frustrated me sometimes. I loved her so much, but she didn't give me enough credit. I was working hard for our family. Should there be a balance? Absolutely. But at this moment in our lives, my career demanded all the attention.

I tried to tell her that it wouldn't always be this way. It was only temporary. But the conversation always ended badly. And I always ended up saying things I'd regret later. The D word was one of them, but I didn't want to divorce Eve. I'd never wanted that.

Eve was an amazing doctor and mother—the best I'd ever known. I knew that she could take care of our little Gracie, even if I wasn't there.

Her voice did seem a little frantic this morning, though. At least my stupid phone allowed her to leave a voicemail message. If it hadn't, I wouldn't even had known that she'd taken Gracie to the hospital. Had this have happened a week ago, I would have dropped all of these ridiculous seminars and classes to be with my family. But it was a requirement for the position that was offered to me—head of the Orthopedics Department and a seat on the Board of Directors. It was an offer I'd been wanting for a long time.

The hospital was in Palo Alto, but it didn't take much convincing to sway Eve's decision to move there. She loved California but hated L.A. It was too noisy. Too dirty. She wanted a quieter place to live. A place where she could enjoy the mountainous views without spotting a filthy homeless man on every corner.

I threw the phone into the passenger's seat, frustrated as all hell that it wouldn't allow me to call her. I wanted to let her know that I was almost home. She probably thought I was avoiding her. Or worse, seeing another woman. If you asked me, that would be a complete waste. I was in love with Eve from the moment I met her. From the moment we walked into the same patient's room.

The poor patient had been in a terrible motorcycle accident. He was a young man. Still in his teens. He was racing motorcycles with his buddies—something I used to do in my own youth. His sports bike drifted on a turn and he lost control, colliding into a tree. The kid was lucky to be alive, but his injuries were critical. Broke almost every bone in his body, which required him to have multiple surgeries.

Eve and I had both entered into the room at the same time to assess his injures. She was new to the hospital. I was new to the city. We had never seen each other before but all it took was one look. One look into her stunning brown eyes and I was hooked.

She stood at his bedside, wearing heels, a dress perfectly tailored to her body, and a white lab coat. She was so professional, yet so unbelievably sexy. Her confidence radiated off her as she concentrated deeply on examining the poor boy's surgical wounds.

Eve worked on his back and spine. I worked on all of the other broken bones and torn ligaments. We were great together, and we were able to fix him up pretty nicely. And Eve...well, she performed a miracle. Made the kid walk again. Made me fall in love.

It took days before I could muster up enough guts to ask her out. She was so intimidating.

A few raindrops hit the windshield. I hoped and prayed it wouldn't rain. It was enough that I'd been speeding. Wet roads wouldn't be good a thing.

I was desperate to get home. Or get to the hospital. If Eve brought Grace there, I knew it had to be serious. And believe it or not, I needed Eve. I'd always needed Eve. I vowed to myself that I would fix all the problems we had. After all, she was the love of my life.

Feeling the need to hear her voice, I reached over to grab my useless phone from the passenger seat. It probably wouldn't work anyway, but I had to at least try.

I couldn't feel the phone. I glanced over, just for a second, to find it. The dim, green light illuminating the dashboard was not enough to light up the seat.

My peripheral vision spotted headlights heading directly toward me like a train. I was confused. Why would a car be in my lane going in the wrong direction?

Thanks to my reflexes, I immediately turned my attention back to the road. I swerved to the right, trying to dodge the car heading straight for mine. My car spun. I turned the wheel to the left, then back to the right, hoping to straighten it out. But the tires weren't even screeching, and I knew it was the first rain sliding me all over the road.

I was on a highway. The opposing traffic was on one side, a ditch on the other. I knew I was going to end up on one of those sides because I couldn't get a handle on my vehicle. It now had a mind of its own.

I wasn't even sure exactly where I was. My mind was clouded with so many thoughts, and I found it hard to pay attention. While I was trying to figure it out, my body suddenly felt like it was coming up out of my seat. I closed my eyes, preparing for the fall. It felt like I would never land—as if I was flying and there was no ground underneath me. I tried to think of Eve's face. Of Gracie's face. I tried to remember all of the good and happiness they brought into my life. I tried to remember what it felt like to kiss Eve's lips and to see Gracie smile and—

My eyelids felt like bricks. I couldn't open them all the way. Only enough for a little sliver of light to sting my retinas. My body felt horrible—like it was being weighed down by an 18-wheeler. I was lying down on something soft and there was a beeping nearby. I tried to move my head but couldn't. A terrible spasm shot down from my neck to my lower back, forcing a pained moan to escape my throat.

"You're awake."

I knew that voice.

I fought against my heavy eyelids and pried them open with every muscle my face would allow me to use. After several rapid blinks, a blurred silhouette came into view.

"How are you feeling?"

That voice sounded so familiar.

My eyelids were threatening to close, but I managed to somehow keep them open. I focused on the figure standing beside me. His face began to refine out of the blurriness, like the pixels of a digital picture uploading on a computer. My mind was slowly registering who it was.

"You must be thirsty." He lowered a cup with a straw down to my face. He read my mind. I was as thirsty as a fish out of water.

After taking a large gulp, I swallowed a few times to clear the dryness. "Mark?"

"Yeah, buddy. It's me." It was Dr. Mark Walker.

"Where's Eve?" My voice was hoarse.

"Boy, you are one lucky guy. You got banged up pretty good."

"Is she coming?" I needed my Eve. I knew I got banged up pretty good because I couldn't move. I needed to know if my wife was on her way.

Mark's expression changed. "Sorry, Jack. She has to stay home and take care of Grace."

A small burst of energy suddenly rose up in my stomach. "Grace. How is she? Is she okay?"

"Oh, yes. You don't have to worry about her. She's recovering nicely, pal." He set a hand on my shoulder. "You just relax and focus on getting better. You need to get back to her."

Now that I knew Grace was safe and well and at home with Eve, I needed to know what my injuries were. "How bad is it?"

He glanced over my body before answering. "Got a few broken bones. You fell down a ravine and straight into a tree. You have some broken ribs and a distal radius fracture of the right hand, probably from holding on to the steering wheel when you hit. Your left shoulder has been dislocated. Your legs were crushed into the dashboard, which caused an incomplete fracture of your left knee. But the worst is the compound fracture of the right tibia."

Shit.

"External fixator?"

"Yes, sir. And a free lap. We're going to have to apply an internal fixator as soon as we can. It's a wonder that leg didn't snap off completely."

I closed my eyes, taking in everything Mark had just told me. "What about my head?"

"Got some stitches from hitting the driver-side window. Your face is bruised up quite a bit from the airbags."

"How about internal?"

"CT says your brain is in intact. No bleeding confirmed," Mark answered.

"Anything else?" I was trying to be funny, but it was hard to smile.

"Not that I can see, Doc. Like I said, you're pretty banged up. But at least you've got your looks." He grinned.

I couldn't care less about my looks. What I needed to do was get back to my wife and child, but with this external fixator, that would probably not be possible anytime soon. What that meant was that a metal device with pins would hold my bones together until the tissue around it was strong enough to withstand surgery.

But with all the rest of my fractures and broken bones, there was no way I was going home to make Eve take care of me. It was enough she had Gracie to worry about. I would just have to stay here, wherever it was.

"Where am I, Mark?" I didn't think I was at my hospital. I was still about an hour away from home when the accident happened. I had to be at Baptist or Memorial.

Mark wrote something down in my chart before answering. "You're at my place."

"Your place? You mean your office?" Maybe I heard him wrong. I still felt a bit out of focus and groggy.

"Oh, Eve didn't tell you? I opened my own clinic. We're not a full-functioning hospital, but we have the necessary equipment."

Mark was an old friend and colleague of Eve's. They met in college and ended up doing their residency together. It had been a couple of years since I'd seen him, but Eve still kept in contact. His specialty was general medicine, but he was a highly intelligent individual. He dabbled in many different areas of the medical field, including emergency medicine, microbiology, and even my field of orthopedics.

He was a good man and a great physician. I trusted I was in good hands, but I didn't understand how I ended up under his care.

"Were you the one who found me?"

He set the chart down and came over to my side. "Yes and no. I sort of intercepted you. I was in the ER at Memorial when you came in. After making sure your injuries weren't dire, I had you transported to my place. I figured you would be more comfortable here. And this way, Eve can focus on Grace without having to worry too much about you. She knows I'll call her with updates," he explained.

It made sense. And if Eve was okay with this, then I was, too.

Mark pulled up a chair next to my bed.

"Jack, I need to tell you something," he said in a low voice. This made me nervous. His face fell and things suddenly felt serious.

I braced myself for horrible news. Did he find something in my scans? As a physician, I'd like to think that I took good care of myself. I exercised, ate healthy meals, had my annual checkups.

But sometimes none of that mattered. Was Mark going to tell me he found cancer somewhere in my body?

"There were some complications with your daughter."

This was worse than cancer.

"What do you mean?"

"She suffered from so much dehydration from the virus that it was too much for her little heart."

No.

"Eve called me when she couldn't get a hold of you. I rushed over to them, but it was too late. The virus had already taken over."

I couldn't breathe.

"We performed CPR and tried defibrillation, but her little heart didn't respond."

I suddenly wished I had died in the car accident.

"Mark, what are you saying?" I tried to maneuver my body into an upright position. It hurt, but I managed to sit up. "Are you saying Grace is gone? Because you just said she was recovering."

"It's okay, Jack," he soothed as he gently pushed me back down onto the bed. "Grace is alive and well."

Relief washed over me. "I...I don't understand. You just said CPR and defib didn't work."

"It didn't. But I had the solution." His eyes glistened and he smiled. It was obvious he was proud of this, but I still needed more information.

"You have to explain this to me, Mark."

"Yes, it's true. Grace could not overcome her illness. She expired on the table for twenty-three minutes."

My heart shattered into pieces.

"However, I created a serum to replace those methods of revival. When injected, it restarts the heart and all functions of the body. Jack, this discovery is revolutionary."

"So, you injected Grace with this? Is this how she's alive?"

"Yes, Jack. She's alive because of Serum Z. Do you realize how valuable this method could be?"

"But what about the side effects? What were her chemistries? How is her mental status now? And what about long term?" I was worried. Part of me wanted to kiss Mark for bringing my daughter back. The other part of me was in doctor mode.

"We've done the diagnostics. Of course, she's still in need of some more observation. There was an episode the other night, but Eve called me immediately and we are working to figure it out," he said, as if it were no big deal.

"What episode?"

"No need for concern right now, Jack. She's doing fine. And Eve is taking great care of her. She'll fill you in once you are well enough."

I allowed myself to relax again. Hearing that Eve was with her sent a tranquil ease through my body.

"Serum Z. Does the Z stand for your son?"

Mark glanced down at his hands. His son's death was obviously still painful to him. "It is. Unfortunately, I couldn't come up with this sooner. He might be alive today. But his death is the reason why Grace is alive now. It's what pushed me to create it."

"He would be proud, Mark."

"Indeed he would," he agreed. "But there's something else I would like to bring up. Serum Z has remarkable capabilities of restoring and re-stimulating the body. Not only was Grace revived, but she was almost immediately free of the virus that riddled her body. Now, I wonder if maybe you would be interested in allowing me to inject you with the serum."

"Me?"

"Yes, you. Don't you want to get back home to your wife, and more importantly, don't you want to get back to Grace? You don't want her to see you this way. And you don't want to add more stress onto what Eve has already been through. What if we eliminate all of that, and at the same time, fix your body?"

There was eagerness in his tone. He was excited about this idea.

I, on the other hand, was not. Sure, it sounded perfect—a medication that would just magically heal me. I could get up and walk out of here as if there was no accident. But nothing was perfect in this world. Everything came with a price. Everything had a consequence.

Dr. Mark Walker might have been a smart man, and he might have just altered the field of medicine as we knew it with this serum, but I needed more than that. God forbid something happened to me because of this serum. I could have easily died in that car. I was given a second chance at life. What if my body didn't respond well to this new drug and I die because of it?

"Mark, I don't think I can do it."

He inhaled deeply. "I figured you would say that. But I must point out that you have a daughter and a wife who need you right now. Eve may be a strong woman, but she's under a lot of stress. Knowing that her husband is seriously injured and that her young daughter had to be brought back to life has been hard for her. She's not doing well emotionally."

Eve *was* an extremely strong woman, and hearing that she was stressed and emotionally distraught was actually surprising.

I closed my eyes, imagining what going home would be like. Holding Grace after everything she had been through was going to feel different, I just knew it. Knowing that I could have lost her makes me want to cherish her existence even more.

I imagined holding Eve. I needed to see her. I needed to see my wife.

"How much time are we talking for surgery and recovery? You've seen my leg. How much time before this is fixed, without the serum?"

Mark searched the air for numbers. "We have to wait a couple of weeks to have the surgery. And then once the surgery is done, we've got to rehabilitate you."

"Okay. I'd say about a month before I'm out of a wheelchair and walking with a crutch." I was really talking to myself. After all,

I was the orthopedic here. "What about with the serum? What are we talking?"

"Jack, we're talking minutes. Once the serum is in your bloodstream, it immediately does its job. You could be up and walking out of here by the morning."

By morning? That took me off guard and made the decision more difficult. Mark must have noticed my deep contemplation.

"Jack, we will monitor you every step of the way. My team is here and ready to react if need be."

"What's the worst that could happen?"

"The worst thing?" He shrugged his shoulders. "Well, you know what the worst thing is."

This was a difficult decision to make. If it worked, I could be home with my family by tomorrow. But if it didn't work and I had a bad reaction, I could die.

I glanced at Mark, who was sitting patiently, awaiting my response. A good full two minutes passed before I made a final decision.

"Okay."

He sat motionless, and then grinned. "That's great, Jack. That's really great. Okay, I'm going to get the serum ready. You just stay right where you are."

"I don't plan on going for a jog, Mark."

He laughed. "Well, you'll feel like you can by tomorrow. You'll be ready to run a marathon soon. I'll be right back."

I stared up at the ceiling when Mark left the room. I went over our conversation and tried to determine if the decision I'd made was a good one. My Gracie died. She literally died, and I wasn't there to be with her. To hold her.

I made the decision, right then, to change. I was going to take what happened to Gracie and what happened to me as a sign. I wasn't a very religious man, but I thought God was trying to tell me something. I needed to stop working so much. I needed to stop being away from home so much. I needed to spend more time with my family and show them that I cared. Grace would be easy to win over, but Eve had been neglected for far too long. It was time to rekindle what we once had, which was a love that nothing could break.

Mark entered the room, this time with a nurse following close behind him and wheeling a tray.

"Okay, Jack. Are you ready to feel better?" he asked enthusiastically.

I didn't feel as confident. I was afraid. Afraid that this decision may be the wrong one.

As a physician, I worked really hard to give my patients the best treatment I could possibly give them. I answered all questions honestly and tried to give them any and all information I could regarding their condition. But now, this was about me. I was the patient. The shoe was officially on the other foot.

I had no idea what this experimental drug was. We doctors always warn our patients about taking medications that weren't FDA-approved. And even then, pills were always being recalled. It was enough that I was now worrying about what side effects Gracie could have from the serum. Did I want to put myself in the same situation? I was her father. I was supposed to live and grow older to watch her journey through life. I was supposed to be there for her every step of the way. Should I be risking that just to have the chance of recovering more quickly?

Mark must have noticed my hesitation. "Jack, don't be worried."

The nurse handed him the large needle. You'd think that because I was a doctor, I wouldn't be afraid of needles. And usually, I wasn't. But not today.

Mark lifted the sleeve of my hospital gown. I tried to remain relaxed, but I could already feel my arm tensing. He swabbed the inside of my elbow with an alcohol pad. My heart raced.

"I'm going to inject the vein now. It's going to be okay," he assured me. "Just take a deep breath, and it'll be over soon."

I took a long, deep breath and held it. The tip of the needle pinched my skin and slid inside. He pushed the top of the syringe down, injecting the serum into my bloodstream. A cold sensation spread below and above my elbow, traveling to my fingers and my shoulder.

Mark didn't mention what I would feel after, which was probably something I should have asked him because I instantly felt fatigued. My eyelids felt heavier. A kind of euphoria filled my head, almost as if my mind was there but it wasn't.

As the serum coursed through my veins, my surroundings slowly began to change. The fluorescent light above me became brighter. The sound of the machines in the room grew louder. I glanced at Mark, who was now spinning in slow circles. My extremities started to feel restless, and for some reason, I wanted to get up and start running. My face became flushed, and I could feel the heat burning my ears.

I tried to focus on Mark long enough to inform him that something wasn't right. I didn't feel right. My heartbeat was speeding up faster and faster, and somehow, I felt both exhausted and exhilarated at the same time.

"Jack? Jack!"

The beeping from the machine next to me became a constant noise instead of a steady, pulsating throb. My head began shaking uncontrollably, and soon after, my body began convulsing.

"Irene! Go get Dr. Charles! Jack, hold on buddy!"

I couldn't stop. I wanted so badly to relax, but my heart kept pounding harder and harder inside my chest as if it was going to pop right out of me. My eyes rolled and everything darkened.

Another man's voice filled my ears. "What's happening, Mark?"

I couldn't see anything. I couldn't say anything.

"I'm not sure. I injected him, but something isn't right."

"He's seizing! His heartrate is through the roof! Irene, propranolol and fosphenytoin. Now!"

The convulsions were getting stronger and more intense. I had no control over my body any longer. My mind was slipping into darkness. The room had closed in around me. I fought hard against the shadows.

Eve. I thought of Eve's face. Her smile. The way her soft skin felt against mine. I loved her so much.

Gracie, my baby girl. My sweet angel. Her kinky curls hung just below her tiny little face. She looked just like her mother.

*I love you, Grace. I'm so sorry.*

A single tear escaped my left eye and rolled down my cheek, and it was the last time I could feel anything.

# THE TRIP
*Present Day*

ALONE.

In my seventeen years, loneliness wasn't something that I'd felt often. Sure, I was an only child. I really didn't have much family—just my mother. And recently, I found out that I had an aunt. But I never really felt *lonely*.

I had made friends along the way. I always had someone to talk to. Phoebe was around for the majority of my life. She was my best friend from the moment we met in grade school. And when we realized that we were soul buddies, there was no question that she would be around forever.

When Tristen Miles came into the picture, our relationship was short-lived. But it was so good. I could honestly look into his eyes and see a future with him. Crazy, I know! We had only been whatever we were for a total of...what? Three days?

Okay, maybe I was too young to even grasp seeing a future with only one person. But I didn't care. The fact that it was a possibility was enough. But those sweet thoughts of Tristen and my best friend were now tainted. They were beginning to feel like distant memories. And now, I felt so alone.

I sat on a brown leather couch in the yacht, staring out into the ocean. I slept for most of the thirty-two hours we had been in the middle of what seemed like nowhere. The traveling took it all out of me; it took forever to get to this point. But the scenery was stunning. Miles and miles of water, until it looked like it could be dropping off the Earth where the sun met the horizon.

I glanced down at my hands. The wire from my earbuds was tangled between my fingers. My iPod rested on the vacant spot next to me. I had taken the earbuds off about thirty minutes ago, feeling the need to think without the sound of Lorde belting melodramatic lyrics in my ear. Her brittle voice was perfect when I was in a thinking, self-loathing kind of mood.

I felt a hand on my shoulder. "Grace, we're going to be docking in about twenty minutes. If you look over that way, you can see the bay."

I nodded and turned in the direction of where Dr. Walker pointed. I didn't respond. I didn't talk to him much at all throughout our travels—not that I was upset with him. I just didn't know how to feel about any of this just yet.

Two days ago, I was told that I was a zombie. Well, Dr. Mark Walker said I wasn't. But I ate a stray domestic animal right off the street. I bit a girl's arm almost clear off her body and ate it. I actually ate my best friend. Literally. Ate.My.Best.Friend

I was a zombie.

But according to Dr. Walker, that term was from the movies and he didn't like to use it. Instead, I was Patient Zero.

When I first heard that name, we had just boarded the transit van in San Jose, Costa Rica and were headed to our next destination. Dr. Walker was on his satellite phone, probably talking with his personnel, and I had heard him state, "We'll be there with Patient Zero in another day or so."

I instantly hated the title. For some reason, the name made me feel like I wasn't even a person—like I was some kind of *thing*. Or, like I wasn't human. But I guess I really wasn't human. Not completely, anyway. Half of me was human, functioning in all the ways it should be. The other half was zombie, dead and constantly demanding food.

Unfortunately, the fact that I decided to keep to myself and hardly speak a word to anyone around me during the trip caused my mind to wander off into all of the dark and secluded parts hidden within. I thought about the days before I left. The horrible scenes replayed over and over in a constant loop. The cat. Sonny Westwood's arm. Phoebe.

The fresh smell of blood and flesh still lingered in my nose. I could feel little Fluffy's neck shattering in my fingertips. I could clearly see Sonny's pained expression and the look on my friend's faces when they witnessed me eat human flesh. I could hear Phoebe's boyfriend, Eric, sobbing in the corner of his bedroom for his girlfriend while I straddled her lifeless body and held her guts in my hands. Those memories would be seared into my brain for as long as I lived. Or didn't. Or whatever.

I could feel the waves under the boat, carrying it to the dock. Everyone inside the cabin began shuffling around, packing all of their belongings. There were only five of us, two of which were Dr. Walker's secret agent-like bodyguards and the other was a woman named Kate who spoke to Dr. Walker the entire time we were traveling. Every chance they had, they were going over folders of documents and discussing God knew what. I didn't care to eavesdrop.

Dr. Walker came over to me again. "Are you about ready to finally get off this boat?" he asked with a chuckle.

I nodded and stood up.

"Are you hungry?"

"No, not really," I mumbled.

"Okay, well, I'll ask you that question again once we get to the facility. I'm sure your mind will have changed by then."

I nodded again, completely agreeing with him. I knew I would be hungry soon. But I wasn't as worried about it as I was back home. Since the moment we began our journey, Dr. Walker kept to his word and made sure I was fed. As soon as we boarded the first private plane from New Orleans to Miami, a flight attendant brought out plates and plates of food to me before we even left the runway. I wasn't quite hungry because of the...meal...I had the night before, but I was curious about what he had to offer.

Apparently, I had been eating human meat since I was a little girl. Mom confessed to me, before I departed, that she was secretly cooking with it. Even her famous pomegranate juice was made out of human fluids.

After giving it a whole lot of thought, the pieces of the puzzle began to fit perfectly. Everything she said and did was a lie. She worked as an assistant to a forensic pathologist only to be in contact with the deceased bodies. She stole their flesh! She never wanted me to eat anywhere else except at home, and she always had a simmering pot of something cooking on the stove. She claimed to be using recipes she found online, but it wasn't as innocent as she had made it sound.

Dr. Walker's food didn't taste or look much different than my mother's. This was worrisome. I didn't want to have to eat human meat. Don't get me wrong, it was so deliciously satisfying, but the idea of eating humans didn't seem right.

When the pretty stewardess handed me the food, I inspected it thoroughly. In my mind, I was expecting to actually see brains and body parts covered in a bloody sauce and lined with hair. That was what zombies ate, right? But it all looked like the same food as my mother's. Just like her chicken pot pie and bacon-wrapped fritters and roast beef and fried chicken. And when I decided to taste a cocktail meatball, I was pleasantly surprised. It was almost exactly like Mom's!

What was even better was that Dr. Walker ensured me that it was not human meat at all. It was an animal. He said that it was important to transition slowly into changing my food more toward the...fresher side, and once we got to the island, he would explain how the "feeding" schedule worked. I expressed concern over animal meat not being enough to appease my starving belly. I didn't want to eat people, but I also didn't want to feel like crap. However, he said I should be okay, as long as the animal meat was fresh and eaten very often. And that we would discuss what my future meals would be, human or not, soon. This made me feel a little better about being so far from home alone.

The boat halted, which meant we were docking. Anxiety crept through me, similar to what I felt when I was boarding the plane in New Orleans. I was getting ready to embark on something new. Something unknown. And I was scared out of my mind.

The raindrops felt nice on my skin. I stepped off the boat and my gaze instantly darted to the beautiful waterfall that cascaded down the side of a cliff. I squinted as I looked up, trying to keep the rain from getting into my eyes.

"Miss Shelley!" Secret Agent Number One came rushing to my side with an umbrella, but a part of me didn't want him to. The cool beads of rain were refreshing.

"Thank you," I said.

I didn't know their names. Like I said, I kept to myself and my earbuds the entire trip. I could tell the two bodyguards apart simply because Number One was bald, the other wasn't. Also, Number One seemed to be quite kind to me. He stuck by my side through most of the short time I'd known him. He opened doors for me, asked me if I was hungry, and sat near me most of the way here. I wondered if maybe he was assigned to me or something like that.

We walked together down the pier, reaching two Jeep Wranglers with a driver in each, ready to go. Dr. Walker, Kate, and Number Two hopped into the first one. Number One laid a hand on the small of my back, leading me toward the second Jeep. He opened the door for me, and I took a seat in the back. He walked around to the other side, opening the door and sitting beside me.

I glanced at the driver. He was dark-skinned and thin, wearing a hat that reminded me of something an archaeologist doing an excavation would wear. He kept quiet and started the car once we were inside. We began our drive, following Dr. Walker's Jeep down a muddy trail.

I realized that this was the first time I had ever seen a waterfall in real life, so I admired it again before it was out of view. As we drove closer, I leaned toward it, hoping that I could hear the sound of the water crashing at the bottom. But the window on Number One's side was closed and the rain was drowning out any other sounds.

Number One noticed almost immediately what I was trying to do and pressed the button on the door. He powered the window all the way down, allowing the tranquil sound of rushing water to fill the inside of the Jeep. I hadn't smiled in days, but this moment changed that.

I glanced at him while he continued to face forward. Raindrops were colliding with his face, but he kept his serious composure.

"You can roll it back up," I said, feeling a little bit guilty. His face was now wet. I reached down into my bag to find my travel-sized baggie of tissues and handed him one.

"Thank you, Miss Shelley."

"You can call me Grace."

He blotted his face. I turned to look out of my window. We were entering what seemed to be the beginning of a vast forest. Everything was green.

"So, are you assigned to me or something?" I asked without turning in his direction. I decided to just come out with it already. Maybe I should get to know at least one person while I was here.

"I guess you could say that," Number One responded.

I was right. I had my own personal bodyguard. This made me wonder. Was there a need for me to have a bodyguard? What exactly was he guarding me from?

The rain seemed to be coming down harder, making it more difficult for me to sightsee. I turned my attention to Number

One and examine him while he looked ahead. He sat stiffly in a well-fitted navy suit. He was a really big guy, and it seemed like he could barely fit inside the Jeep. I obviously couldn't see what was underneath the suit, but his chest jutted outward and his arms looked as though they could be about the size of both my thighs put together. I made a bet with myself that he had to be some sort of body builder. His bald head glistened from the rain that came in through the window. His facial features were strong and very masculine, almost like a sculpture made of stone.

He turned and glanced at me, probably because I was staring at him. His eyes were as blue as the ocean we were just sailing across. I quickly turned away, feeling a bit awkward that he caught me watching him. I thought about asking him what his name was but decided not to. I was sure I'd find out sooner or later.

We drove for another twenty minutes before we finally came to a halt in front of a large steel gate. *Jurassic Park* style. Dr. Walker's Jeep pulled up to a tollbooth. After about a minute, the steel gate opened, and an arm reached out of the booth's window to wave the Jeep through.

Ours rolled forward, stopping next to the booth. "¿Cómo estás, Jose?" our driver asked.

"Muy bueno, Carlos. La lluvia es malo hoy, ¿eh?"

"Los mismo que cualquier otro día." Our driver chuckled.

Jose gestured for us to proceed. "¡Que tengas un buen día!"

Crap! I needed to learn Spanish. Number One must have caught sight of the confusion on my face because he translated.

"They were just talking about the weather."

I nodded and smiled.

We drove through the gate and pulled to a stop in front of what I assumed to be our destination. My nerves were killing me, but I was very happy to finally be somewhere.

I peeked out of the window as Number One stepped out and opened an umbrella. I couldn't see much due to the dark gloomy weather and rain that was bearing down on us. But I could make out a small one-story brick building with an arched entryway. Above the arch, large, red letters protruded out of the brick wall that read: EVERLASTING PARADISE.

# THE OASIS

A CHILL ROLLED DOWN my spine and I couldn't fight the fear, and maybe a little suspicion, of the unknown.

Number One opened my door. "Are you ready, Grace?"

I grabbed my bag and we followed Dr. Walker up to the arched doorway and through the building's doors.

"Welcome to Everlasting Paradise, Grace," Dr. Walker said, opening his arms wide as if I'd won something on the *The Price is Right*.

I glanced around the foyer. There was no one in sight. To be honest, it didn't seem like much of a paradise. It reminded me of the inside of an office building with the fluorescent lighting and white walls. A single, tall plant leaned against a corner. It was four walls of drab. To the left was a room with only a desk, a chair, and a bookshelf. Maybe this was the place where people came to check in.

Number One, Number Two, and Dr. Walker's assistant-person, Kate, all stood staring at me, awaiting a response.

"Um...it's nice?"

"I know this part doesn't look like much," he said, detecting that I wasn't impressed. "Follow me."

He walked ahead, and the other three waited for me to follow. I did so, hesitantly. I wasn't sure what he was going to show me. I kept expecting to see a zombie pop out from somewhere, stumbling about and groaning "braaaiiinnnsss." Just like the haunted houses back home.

We walked down a long hallway. At the end, Dr. Walker hooked a left through a door that led outside. I held open the door and turned to find Number One directly behind me. He gave me a slight smile, showing no teeth. Slight may not have been the right word. It was barely a smile. Or maybe he wasn't smiling at all and I was just imagining it. It could have even been a frown.

I spun back toward where Dr. Walker stood, and my jaw dropped.

We were on the balcony of a cliff overlooking an...island oasis! The beach was a short distance away, where the water matched the color of the gray skies. The rain had subsided to a drizzle, so I walked out from under the awning to the railing of the balcony to get a better view.

There were four beach-style huts. A two-story structure that looked as if it were made out of stone or concrete or something of that nature stood all alone in a far corner to the left, away from the others. Another two-story building similar to the beachy huts stood alone in the far corner to the right. Palm trees and grass and flowers lined what seemed to be one large courtyard in the middle. There were picnic tables and benches scattered about, reminding me a bit of home and Middleton High School.

The weather was a bit depressing, but it was still beautiful. With the beach as a backdrop and the forest surrounding the place, it could have easily passed for a resort.

"So, what do you think?" Dr. Walker asked behind me.

I thought hard about what I wanted my answer to be. I didn't want to tell him the truth, which was that it didn't matter how beautiful or interesting this island retreat was, I would rather be home. A part of me was curious, but I didn't want to tell him that I was interested or thought it was spectacular. I didn't want him to think I was happy in the least bit about being here.

"It's big." I settled on a vaguely true statement.

His expression did not falter. He maintained the same creepily excited composure he managed to keep the entire time I've known him. I noticed Number Two bring his hand up to his ear and press down, exactly how a secret agent would do.

"You are on Cocos Island. Have you ever heard of it?"

I shook my head.

"As you know, we're off the coast of Costa Rica. About three hundred miles or so. This island is a national park and a popular destination for professional divers."

"Divers?"

"Yes. It's home to sharks, rays, dolphins, and a large number of marine species. If you're interested, we have diving professionals who can teach you."

I didn't respond. I never really thought about diving. And something about the sharks just didn't strike my interest.

"Besides the ocean, there are plenty of trails and hikes that we do on a daily basis. There is much to see on this island," he said with enthusiasm.

"Where is everyone?" I asked, suddenly realizing that I hadn't seen anyone besides our drivers and the tollbooth guy.

"Our facility functions as any kind of business would. People are in class and working. It also just rained. But it's let up quite a bit, so you'll see everyone heading out into the courtyard before too long."

"What about other people? Are there locals? I didn't see much of anyone on the dock." Paranoia began to set in for some reason. I just needed to feel like I wasn't completely alone.

"This island is mostly uninhabited. Besides the subjects and my colleagues on the facility grounds, you won't see much of anyone else around here. No one actually lives here except maybe a handful of natives, and permission is needed to visit Cocos Island. And even then, visitors aren't allowed to stay on the island overnight. I guess you can say we're VIP." He chuckled.

I didn't think it was very funny.

"Sir, you're needed in the Z lab," Number Two interrupted.

Dr. Walker didn't turn away. Instead, he peered out onto the compound with me. "Grace, I know that you're worried and maybe a little bit afraid to be here all alone. But I want you to know, this is good for you. We're going to make you feel as comfortable as we can."

I didn't look at him.

"I know this isn't home, but I can only hope that you'll see it that way one day."

"How long will I be here?" I asked, realizing that no one had told me this.

"Well, it really depends on your treatment. But time will fly. You'll see. You'll be having too much fun to even notice."

I doubted that.

"Sir?"

"Yes. Okay, Grace. I must go." He looked at Number One. "Will you please escort Grace to her suite?"

"Yes, sir."

Dr. Walker headed toward the door, Kate and Number Two mimicking his exit.

"Grace," Number One called.

The breeze from the ocean found its way through my loose curls. It felt incredible, but not much different than New Orleans. Humidity was in the air, and I silently thanked God I knew how to handle it for my hair's sake.

I suddenly remembered my luggage. "Are my bags here?"

"Yes, they should be in your suite now," he responded. "Please follow me."

Number One was assertive, but I felt I could trust him for some reason. Maybe it was because he had been attached to my hip the whole journey here. But I was sure he got paid really, really well to do so.

I tagged along close behind him as he led me down a long and narrow flight of stairs off the balcony—basically down the side of the cliff. It was incredible! The steps seemed to be cut out of the side of the mountain, and as we climbed down, the stairs curved. My fingers grazed the exposed rock, feeling the warmth of the smooth stones as we made our descent.

We reached the bottom and were immediately in the courtyard of the compound. We walked toward the first building on the right. They looked like huts or cabanas from far away, but they were actually much more sophisticated up close. Transparent white sheaths draped over the sides and bellowed in the breeze. The structure seemed to be well-built and sturdy and made out of some kind of thick wood. Bamboo, maybe? The roof was covered in thatch, but I was sure it was much tougher than it looked.

The building was larger than when viewed from above. There was a sign dangling above the open door that read: VENICE. We continued walking to the next building, almost identical to the first one. Except this one read: LAGUNA.

I followed Number One up the porch steps and through the entrance. Once inside, he led me down a long, wide hallway. The walls were bright white, and my flip-flops smacked against my heels and the hardwood floor.

I normally wore my *Chuck Taylors*. I had a million pairs in all different colors, but I knew I was coming to an island. I didn't want a farmer's tan on my ankles.

We passed multiple doorways, some closed and some slightly ajar. I caught glimpses of beds and dressers, which confirmed that they were bedrooms. We finally reached the end of the hallway, my "suite" I presumed. Number One opened the door inward and gestured for me to go in. I stepped in slowly, not sure of what I was going to find. But I didn't know why I had any hesitations. It was beautiful! And rather spacious.

There was a queen-sized bed and a wooden dresser on one side. A desk and an armoire aligned the other wall with a door leading to what I assumed was my very own bathroom. Straight ahead was a sliding glass door that led to a tiny screened-in patio. It was open, allowing the warm breeze to flow freely through the white translucent curtains.

Half of the view from the patio was the Venice hut, the other half was of the white sand and waves crashing on the beach. It wasn't attached to the room next to mine, but I could easily see my neighbor's patio.

"Your things are on the bed," Number One informed me.

"Yeah, thank you. Um...so does everyone's room look like this?"

"Yes. Pretty similar. I'll leave you to get settled in. I'm right outside the door if you need me."

"Well, don't you have other things to do?" I asked. I mean, he didn't have to be with me all the time.

"No." And with that, he shut the door.

I stood in the middle of my room with only the sound of the ocean. I had been on a plane, in a van, and on a boat for about three days at this point, but it all suddenly seemed to be happening so quickly. And it all seemed to finally feel real.

# THE SPY

I GLANCED AROUND MY room. It was very bright, even with the gloomy weather. There was nothing on the walls—definitely something I would have to change. Even a calendar would make it feel more homey. And necessary to keep track of how long I was here.

I sat on the bed, sinking into the delightful mush of down comforter and memory foam. That was definitely a plus. I might even sleep better than I did back home. I stood up and walked the length of the room. The dresser and armoire were a matching set of espresso-colored wood. I opened the armoire doors. It was very beautiful and detailed with tribal-like carvings. I grazed my fingers over the smooth texture and admired the artistry.

As I outlined the armoire doors with my fingertips, the bouncing screensaver on the computer caught my eye. Messages.

I sat down on the ridiculously comfortable office chair and moved the mouse to awaken the hibernating modem. After logging into my Facebook account, I waited patiently for the unread messages to load. I hadn't checked anything computer related since we left. Internet connection was at one bar—no bars for most of the time. My heart raced at the thought of reading a message from Tristen. I had only been gone for three days, but I was desperate to know what he was doing. What was he thinking? Did he even miss me? The thought of him not missing me actually hurt. I missed him, and I didn't want to be alone in my feelings.

There were no new messages. I backed out and signed into my email account. My unread messages loaded, and I scanned through the junk emails. There were about fifty of them, though it seemed like a million. All emails encouraging me to sign up for a credit card, check my Instagram notifications, and other crap I cared nothing about.

When I finally reached the last bolded heading, my heart sank. Nothing from Tristen.

At that moment, a faint sound of laughter resonated in my ears. I peered over to the patio door and saw people walking toward the beach. I stood up and got closer to get a better view. There was one guy and two girls, one of which seemed to be pretty young. The little girl's red pigtails dangled below her shoulders as she skipped through the sand, holding a boogie board. The older girl had short black hair and was also holding a boogie board, smiling at the little girl. The blond-haired guy looked like a walking *Abercrombie and Fitch* ad, wearing a wet suit and clutching onto a neon yellow surfboard.

I stared for another minute before the guy turned around. He looked straight at me. I quickly moved over and away from his glance, almost as if I was caught spying.

*Get a grip, Grace! They're just people.*

I shook my head and chuckled. There was a low rumble in my belly. It was time.

I found Number One standing in the hallway, facing away from me. He quickly turned around. "Everything okay?"

"Um...yeah. I'm just getting hungry. Do you know where I can get some food?"

"Would you like it sent here, or would you like to go to the mess hall?"

"I have room service?" I asked, a little shocked. I'd never had room service before. The thought of eating in my own room did sound better than going to the mess hall, whatever that was. I wasn't quite ready to meet other people, which was obviously showcased a few moments ago by my amateur attempt of going unnoticed.

"I'll eat it in my room, if that's okay."

"Absolutely." Number One began walking down the hall with his finger on his ear. Poor guy. He had to stand in front of my room all day? Why didn't those other people have bodyguards with them?

I left my door open and began unpacking my things. I heard a chirp from my cellphone and immediately dove into my bag for it. It could be Tristen.

But, of course, it wasn't. It was a text message from my mother. I should at least let her know I was safe. Well...as safe as I thought I was.

**Mom:** *Grace, I just wanted to tell you that I love you.*

I stared at my phone. I didn't even know her real name until just the other day. Who doesn't know their mother's real name? It pissed me off to even think about it. How could she lie to me for so long?

I blacked out my phone and threw it back on the bed. There was no way I was going to respond. Not now. Not anytime soon.

Over the many hours of traveling, I had thought long and hard about the last thing I said to her. *I will never forgive you...* At the time I was furious! I was just told, after seventeen years of my life, that when I was a child, I had died for twenty-three minutes and was brought back to life by some experimental serum. That my body only worked halfway and that my mother was feeding me dead people without my knowledge. My life was based on a lie. Even my own mother's name was a lie. How else was I supposed to react?

*What is that smell?*

But the point was that she lied to me, and I didn't understand why. Why couldn't she be honest with me? Why did she make me find out on my own? And in the worst way possible! I had to eat my best friend before I could get any answers.

*God, that smells so good!*

My face flushed, and I could feel that I was getting angry...and hungrier. Thinking about her made me infuriated.

A knock at my door prompted me to turn around, and the smell of something delicious made my stomach growl loudly. A short, tan woman wearing a floral uniform walked in, wheeling a cart full of food. My hunger levels rose, and I began to sweat.

"Miss Grace, you lunch," she said softly in a deep Latin accent. Words couldn't form in my throat. I was feeling faint and pretty surprised at how quick the service was.

I didn't see her leave the room or even hear the door shut. My eyes darted to the plates full of hamburgers, French fries, chicken tenders, pasta, cupcakes, and brownies. I didn't think. My legs involuntarily moved my body over to the cart. My arms involuntarily reached out. My hands involuntarily dug into the steaming hot wonderment of the only thing that mattered most at that moment.

I scooped the pasta up with my fingers, smashing it into my mouth. I had to chew violently and quickly to get the food down my esophagus, to feed the unholy desire for nourishment. My body gradually needed and wanted more and more as the days passed. And when I finally had it, nothing else mattered.

My eyes closed in satisfaction as I shoveled every last morsel into my mouth. This food was incredible, but anytime I was hungry, the thought of what I'd eaten the night before I came to the island entered my mind. Nothing could compare since then. And I often wondered if I would ever be able to taste it again.

I finally opened my eyes to the empty plates in front of me. Apparently, I didn't even bother to move from where I was; I was still standing at the cart. My stomach rumbled a bit before letting out a small growl. This food just wasn't enough.

A knock at my door broke me out of my grub trance. I opened it to a serious look from Number One.

"Grace, Dr. Walker would like to see you now."

"Okay."

"Please follow me."

I trailed after Number One across the courtyard to the other side. Here, there were two more huts that looked exactly like mine from the outside. One was labeled MALIBU and the other, NEWPORT. I could see movement in the Newport hut through the front open windows and focused real hard to get a better view. I wasn't ready to meet anyone just yet, but I still wanted to see what the other people looked like. I was still half-expecting to see a horde of zombies shuffling aimlessly through the courtyard with backpacks on, as if it were an ordinary day at school.

I quick-stepped to match Number One's pace when I realized my nosiness made me fall behind. "What are these huts for?"

"Malibu is the common area. Newport is the mess hall," he answered firmly.

We approached the two-story structure that I had seen from the balcony. As we walked closer, I confirmed that this building was definitely made out of concrete. A large, silver Z was etched into the glass door. Number One swiped a card on the door, and we entered a tiny enclosed foyer. This led to another door, which was clearly steel. He then typed on a keypad nearby and stood stiffly, facing forward and looking up at a small round camera embedded into the wall. A low buzz rang out, and Number One opened the door. Lots of precautions just to enter this place. There must be important things in here.

Once inside, we walked over to a receptionist sitting at a desk. "Good afternoon, Robin," Number One greeted without a smile. "This is Grace Shelley. Dr. Walker requested the appointment be moved up sooner."

The petite woman wearing glasses smiled sweetly at Number One. "It's nice to see you again." She batted her long eyelashes at him before glancing at me. "Hello, Grace. Welcome to Everlasting Paradise."

I smiled back and fought the urge to shudder. The name of this place just did not sit well with me.

She picked up her phone and dialed one number. "Grace is in." After a short pause, she responded, "Yes, sir," and then hung up the phone. "Okay, Grace. He's ready to see you."

Number One nodded at the receptionist. She gave him another coy smile and nodded back, her eyes looking up over her glasses at him. I wasn't an expert on flirting, but by the way her eyes twinkled when she gazed into his, I thought that maybe there could be some kind of love connection there. But when I glanced at Number One, he kept true to his serious demeanor and didn't seem to give her another thought. He led the way past what seemed to be a waiting room, then down a hall, and toward an elevator.

When we stepped in, he pressed the button for the second floor.

"I think she likes you."

He didn't say anything. Instead, there was silence until the elevator door opened into another waiting room area, with another receptionist sitting at a desk directly in front of us. This receptionist was quite a bit older than the first. She was wearing glasses too, but ones with a chain dangling on each side. Her hair was white and wrapped in a neat French twist. She looked up at us.

"Hello, Grace. Please have a seat and Dr. Walker will be out to get you shortly," she said with a bit of disdain in her tone. She sounded a little grumpy. I wondered how long she had worked for Dr. Walker. She seemed to be a seasoned employee. Not because she was older, but because she had this kind of seniority and authority about her. Maybe it was her attitude. Whatever it was, you could tell she took her job seriously. I watched as she hastily thumbed through papers and files and typed away on the keyboard in front of her.

I sat down in one of the chairs in the waiting area and Number One stood by the elevator doors. Did he ever sit down? Moments later, Dr. Walker appeared from behind a wall.

"Ahh, Grace! Welcome to the Z lab!"

I stood up. He leaned over the receptionist's desk and laid a hand on the woman's back, setting down a folder with the other.

"Beverly, will you please have Dr. Charles look over these?"

She nodded.

"Thank you." He turned toward Number one and gave him a quick nod before waltzing over to me and wrapping his arm around my shoulder. "Come. Come with me so we can get these pesky tests out of the way."

"Tests?" I mumbled. Anxiety instantly flooded me.

# THE TESTING

HE LED ME BEHIND the wall and through a glass door. Holy science lab! It was like another world—glass doors, desks, computers, lab equipment, white lab coats.

I peered around as much as I could and caught glimpses of people in each individual room, standing around and talking, sitting at computers, pouring green substances into beakers, talking on phones, writing in folders... Everyone seemed to be doing something. Things that looked important. Things that reminded me of something you'd see on TV. It was a scene straight out of a Sci-Fi movie. Like in my comic books!

We walked past each room, all of which were walled by floor-to-ceiling windows. At the end of the hall, Dr. Walker opened a door to a small, hospital-like room that wasn't see-through. Probably for privacy. There was a desk with a computer and a stool. Next to it was a long chair, cushioned from top to bottom. I had never been to a doctor because my mother was one and always examined me herself, but I assumed this was the basic examining room at a run-of-the-mill doctor's office. Actually, now that I thought about it, she never took me to a doctor because I was half-dead. Duh!

Damn her lies!

"Okay, Grace. Hop up on the table and we'll get started."

"Um...what exactly are you starting?" I asked as I took a seat.

"Oh, you don't have to worry. We're going to start out with some simple tests. We'll give you a hearing test, an eye exam, check your blood pressure, your reflexes, and get some bloodwork. Things like that. It's all just routine procedures for us to get a better understanding of what we're working with."

He started up his computer and began typing.

"Are you looking for anything in particular?"

"Not necessarily, no."

"Is any of it going to hurt?" I asked, feeling my anxiety levels elevate higher and higher as he spoke to me. Dr. Walker turned and glanced at me above the rim of his gold-framed glasses. Before answering, he wheeled his stool closer, giving me all of his attention.

"Grace, as you know, your situation is very complex." He placed a hand on my knee. "Every single person before you who has sat on this examining table for the first time was frightened. But when you meet the others, you'll see that they are well and healthy, and that we take very great care of our subjects. We are here to help you. Our goal—my goal—is to permanently stop your hunger and pains and fatigue and everything you were feeling before."

"But what about what I did? What I did to Sonny...and Phoebe?" I asked, fighting back the tears that were now stinging the corner of my eyes. I didn't really want to talk about it, and I hadn't since it happened. But for some reason, sitting on this table made me feel very vulnerable. I desperately needed to know what happened to them.

"Oh, Grace. Sonny is going to be fine."

My heart skipped. He was telling me this, but I still didn't know if I should believe it.

"Phoebe Morgan's body was recovered and given to her family so that they can give her a proper burial. We have also compensated her family and taken care of all the finances for her funeral services." His tone was sincere.

I could no longer fight back the tears. Hearing the words "Phoebe" and "funeral" in the same sentence was just too hard.

The question of what he said happened to her crossed my mind. How could he possibly come up with a story for her death? Her body was...what I did to her was... I couldn't even come up with something on my own! The last sight I had of her body was too hard to think about, but it looked like it was something a wild animal would do. A wild, vicious, starving animal.

I decided I didn't want to ask. I didn't want to know. I knew what really happened and hearing lies about it would never change that.

Dr. Walker reached over to his desk for a tissue and handed it to me.

"And Eric?" I asked after blowing my nose. I didn't even know his last name.

"Eric was also recovered and delivered to his family for a proper burial," he answered. "I know what happened was unfortunate. And although you don't see it now, what happened to Sonny and Phoebe and Eric led you here, to a place where we can help your sudden and uncontrollable urges so that it doesn't happen again."

I couldn't look at him. My eyes stared down at my fidgeting fingers.

"Grace," he said in a low tone. "You are in good hands now. You just have to trust me. Can you do that?"

I looked him in the eyes. I scanned them, as I had done in the past in a desperate search to find some reason to trust him. I could never find it before. But I was here now. This was home now. And what else did I have to lose? Looking into his eyes and trying to find some sign to justify my presence here was no use.

After a long pause, I gave in to my deep hesitations. I nodded and gave him the answer he was looking for.

His lips turned up into a wide smile, showing his gloriously white teeth. "Wonderful. Now, let's get this over with, shall we?"

He wheeled back over to his desk, and I took a deep breath.

The tests were performed, just as Dr. Walker explained. The first was an eye exam. Standing away at a distance, I was told to read the letters on a chart, covering one eye at a time. The second test was a hearing exam. I was sent into a tiny room where I wore headphones and was told to raise my hand in the air every time I could hear high and low beeps in each ear, separately and together.

Next was the reflex test. While sitting on the examining table, Dr. Walker used a metal triangular-shaped tool to repeatedly tap my kneecaps. Each time he tapped, my leg would involuntarily flinch. This was followed by the blood tests. I was surprised to see Dr. Walker's assistant, Kate, enter the examining room with a small cart. I didn't think she was a doctor because she wasn't wearing a lab coat like all of the other ones. Maybe she was just helping out.

Kate gently lifted the sleeve of my T-shirt and tied a rubber tourniquet around the upper portion of my arm.

"Can you make a fist for me?"

I opened and closed my hand. Before reaching for an alcohol wipe and the needle in her cart, she searched for a proper vein. Once she found it, she wiped my skin clean.

"You're going to feel a big stick, but it'll be done before you know it."

I looked away. If I watched the needle enter my skin, it might hurt worse.

I felt a pinch.

"Okay, you can relax your hand."

I could hear the suction of every tube that she attached and pulled from the needle. There were about thirteen total. When she was done, she pulled the needle from my arm and wrapped it with a sort of sticky, rubbery, nude-colored type of tape.

"All done." She smiled kindly. I watched her for a beat, getting a really good look at her. She actually looked kind of familiar, like maybe I had seen her before back home. But before I could ask her if we might have known each other before all of this, she left the room.

Next, Dr. Walker checked my blood pressure by using a cuff on my arm and my heartbeat by using some kind of clip with a red light that attached to my finger. I looked over at the monitor for this one, remembering when he and my mother tried to explain to me that my heart rate was lower than it should be due to my condition. I did some research on this while we were traveling, and apparently, a normal heart rate for a girl my age was sixty to a hundred beats per minute.

The number next to the little heart symbol read twenty-seven.

He then instructed me to breathe in and out while he listened to my chest with his stethoscope. After taking in a few deep breaths, I was told to lie back on the table, where he proceeded to tap on my belly and gently press down on my throat.

"Okay, Grace. You can sit back up."

"Is that it?" I asked, hoping that it would be.

Without looking up from his computer, he answered, "Not quite." He stood up from the stool and walked over to me. "Everything seems to be right on track, but there is one last thing we have to do."

The number on the heart monitor changed to twenty-eight, then twenty-nine.

Dr. Walker glanced over at it. "No, no, Grace. No need for alarm. For this part of the test, you'll be asleep."

"Asleep?"

"Yes. You won't feel a thing. When you wake up, you might feel a bit groggy. But that's simply because of the medication we will give you to help you sleep." He was speaking slowly, as if he were explaining this to a five-year-old.

"Why do I need to be asleep? What are you going to do?"

"Well, we need to check your sleep patterns. We're going to give you something to help you fall asleep. When you finally do, I and a couple of my colleagues will monitor your heartrate and your brain waves. You'll keep this clip on your finger, and we'll attach little stickers to your head. Once we're done, you'll be awake. It's as simple as that."

My nerves were going crazy. *It's only a test, Grace. Be brave.*

I took a deep breath. "Okay."

"Great!" He turned around and reached into the drawer of the desk, pulling out a needle. "I'm going to give you a shot in the neck. You'll feel a slight sting."

He moved my hair out of the way and quickly stuck me. I didn't even have time to prepare myself.

"Go ahead and lie back for me," he said softly, gently guiding my shoulder down toward the table. Right as I began to move, the room seemed to be caving in. I allowed myself to fall into the cushion of the table, feeling as though I would never reach it.

Once I finally did, my body relaxed, and I felt almost paralyzed. I stared up at the ceiling, my vision slowly beginning to tunnel into darkness. My eyelids grew heavier and heavier, and before I could think another thought, I—

My eyes fluttered open. I was lying on my side, covered with a fluffy down comforter. I rolled onto my back, feeling a twinge of pain on the right side of my abdomen. I winced and lifted my shirt to see if I could find the source, but the room was dark. I rubbed the area with my hand but felt nothing. I slowly maneuvered myself into a sitting position. The movements made me feel dizzy. Dr. Walker said I would still feel a little groggy.

I stood up slowly and tried to focus my eyes into the darkness. When they finally did, I reached over to the floor lamp in the far corner of the room. With one flick, the room illuminated, and I suddenly realized that I was in my suite.

How did I get here?

I rubbed my face, hoping it would somehow help me remember. I was still in my clothes from earlier, since the journey to the island. A shower seemed like a good idea.

As I walked past the sliding glass door, the thought of some fresh air actually seemed like a better idea. I unlocked the door and slid it open. A cool, salty draft of the night air instantly sent a chill through my body before I stepped out. There was a lit tiki torch beside my patio and a row of them leading down to the beach. I sat down on a wicker bench and rested my head back, closing my eyes.

I was exhausted. The last three days were a rollercoaster of dark thoughts, anxiety, sadness, doubt, and worry. Basically, a thesaurus of emotions. The entire trip consisted of thinking about what happened the night before I left and of Tristen and the fact that he hadn't sent any messages or emails. I was beginning to feel heartbroken. Stupid even. I guess I should have expected it. I did tell him not to wait for me. Maybe he was doing just that.

"You must be Grace."

I opened my eyes and quickly glanced around to see who was speaking to me. A guy was standing on the opposite side of the screened-in patio. I couldn't see his face all that well. The flame from the tiki torch created a kind of shadow around his body, and the screen and darkness of the night obscured my view.

"Sorry. I didn't mean to startle you. I was just on my way back to my room. It's late. I didn't think anyone else would be awake," he said in a low voice. He had an accent. European?

"How did you...know my name?" My voice was hoarse, my throat sore.

He chuckled and looked down at his feet. "Well, you are very popular here. Everyone has been waiting for you."

"For me? Why?"

"You're Patient Zero, right?"

Gross. I hated that name so much.

"Yes," I muttered.

"Everyone's been dying to meet you. No pun intended."

I forced myself not to smile.

"So, did you just finish all of your tests? You look kind of rough."

"Um...thanks?" Seriously? Who was this guy?

He smiled. "I didn't mean it that way. I just know how it feels afterward. And your voice seems a bit scratchy."

I brought my hand up to my throat and gently rubbed.

"It's okay. It's normal. You'll feel one hundred percent better once you eat."

A familiar pain shot across my stomach right as he said that. I wasn't sure if it was an ache from the tests or if it was the hunger coming back.

"Well, I'll let you recover. It was nice to finally meet you, Grace. We'll see each other around," he said, then turned to walk toward the Venice hut. He didn't tell me his name.

I kept my eyes on him, trying to focus them into the night to see if maybe I could get a better view of what he looked like. But all I could see was the back of his head and the silhouette of his shorts and flip-flops.

Another sharp pain rippled through my stomach. I stood up slowly from the wicker bench and walked back inside my room to the door. It was pretty late, but Number One had to be somewhere, if not right outside my room. I had to check.

When I opened my door there was no Number One, but there was a cart full of covered plates.

Well, that was convenient.

My eyelids were beginning to weigh down and lethargy from the hunger set in. I wheeled the cart into my room and uncovered every plate, finding slices of pink meat underneath. Not just pieces. Slabs. Slabs of pink and red *undercooked* meat. It seemed to be drizzled in some kind of red sauce. I poked my finger into one of the slices, only to find that it was cool—warm at best. I normally preferred my meat cooked well-done, but the smell of it was now engulfing the entire room and my stomach started to think for me.

I took the first bite, and that was all I could remember before I realized every single piece was completely gone in a matter of minutes. It was all gone, but I could still taste it on my tongue. It was so familiar. So luscious. So incredibly amazing. Flashes of the night I bit off Sonny's arm and the taste of Phoebe whirled around my head.

Was this the same thing? Did I just eat someone? Did I just eat human meat?

Panic coursed through me and I pushed the cart out of the way, rushing for my door. I wasn't sure where I was going, but I had to talk to someone. How could I have eaten another human?

I swung open my door and jumped at the sight of Number One standing before me.

"Grace! Is everything okay?" he asked, alarmed.

I was breathing heavily. "I...I need to see Dr. Walker! Someone...someone just left this cart in front of my door and...it was...human...and I ate it and..."

Number One grabbed my shoulders to stop me from squeezing past him. "Grace, calm down! Nothing's wrong."

"But I just ate a human!"

"No, you didn't. That was boar. You ate boar."

I looked up at him. "Boar?" I exhaled.

"Yes. The chef left it in front of your door because we knew you would be hungry when you woke up. Boar is one of the main sources of food for the patients here on the island," he explained.

"But it wasn't even cooked."

"I know. It's how it is eaten. It looks like Dr. Walker decided to change up your meal." He twisted me around and gently eased me into my room. "Everything is okay. Dr. Walker will explain this to you tomorrow. I'm going to take the cart. You should get some sleep."

I wasn't tired at all. I was completely energized. And any grogginess or pain that I felt earlier from the testing was completely gone.

Number One wheeled the cart out and shut the door behind him. I stood in the middle of my room feeling a little embarrassed by my overreaction.

It wasn't a human. It was boar. Just boar.

# THE
# IMMORTALITY

THE BOAR SEEMED TO get tastier and tastier over the next seven days. And I seemed to get more and more depressed. The days kept passing by with no word from Tristen. I tried my best to refrain from holding on to hope, but I couldn't help myself. I was sure that he truly did like me as much as I liked him—at least that was what he made me believe, anyway. The dark cloud loomed right over my head all day and all night. There was really no one to talk to about everything I felt. Mom had tried texting me a few times, but I ignored all of her apologetic messages and desperate attempts to get back on her daughter's good side. It might have been a little harsh, but I honestly had no idea how to forgive her.

My only other option to open up to someone about my shattered spirit was Phoebe. But it actually wasn't an option anymore because I killed her, and this just added to my misery. I could possibly talk to Number One, but just looking at the hard line across his lips only made me sadder. There was no way he could cheer me up or make me laugh like my soul buddy could.

I managed to somehow make up a bunch of excuses for not socializing or exploring the island. Dr. Walker believed my little spiel about being homesick. But it was partially true. I did miss home. My room. My horror movies. Even my mom.

Staying in my room wasn't too hard. Most of the hours in the day were spent binging on *Netflix* shows and periodically stalking Sonny and Tristen's social media profiles. Well...maybe periodically wasn't the correct word. More like frequently. Or maybe an unhealthy amount of times. But oddly, neither of them had posted anything new since before I left. This made me a little uneasy, and thoughts of their relationship flourishing once again made everything else harder to deal with. I probably should have left my room to meet the others who were like me. It would have possibly made life better. But I'd expertly dodged any and all contact with the other "subjects." It wasn't that difficult to do. There didn't seem to be many of them ever around. The only time I was forced to speak to someone else was in the Z lab when I had to get blood drawn or answer really annoying psychological questions for Dr. Walker.

There were some more of those weird sleep studies done on me, and I'd wake up really groggy and tired and achy, but there would always be a tray of delicious boar waiting in the hallway outside my door. Number One made sure that the chefs from the mess hall delivered all of my meals. This was nice. Ever since I started eating the rare boar meat, I found myself losing consciousness during my meals. Almost like when I'd eaten Phoebe or bitten Sonny's arm. It was like I'd go into some kind of food coma, which made me very self-conscious. I had no idea what I looked like, but judging from the mess of raw chucks and bloody juice all over my face, I assumed I really did resemble a zombie.

The taste of the boar was a reminder of the most glorious, delectable, incredibly satisfying flavor that had ever graced my mouth. But I did not EVER want to repeat what I did back home again. I knew it was a poor choice of words considering the consequences and what I had lost, but it was seriously *that* good.

Eating human meat was not okay. I didn't care if I was a zombie—mythical abominations known to the world as flesh eaters and brain fanatics. I was starving probably ninety percent of the time and I might have needed to eat living things to stay "alive," but chomping down on a human would never be justifiable. I couldn't just tackle anything or anyone I saw down to the ground and eat them.

I sighed. That thought seemed kind of nice. But no! Never again! No humans!

It was Friday morning and I was relaxing in the bed with my headphones on, watching my room slowly illuminate from the sunrise. Getting sleep these days was impossible. My bed was ultra-comfy, but my mind raced and raced all night long. I found myself tossing and turning for most of the night, fighting all my urges to check messages and emails every twenty minutes. God! I knew I was obsessing way too much. But it seemed so impossible to me that he would just forget me. Just like that. Why hadn't he written? Or called?

I reached over to check my phone again, giving into the stupid impulses. It was seven in the morning. The sound of a door shutting provoked me to finally get out of bed. I poked my head out of my room to take a quick glance. A short girl in pigtails was walking toward the front doors to leave the hut. She looked like the same young girl I saw at the beach my first day here.

"Are you Grace?"

I turned in the opposite direction to find a girl wearing all black standing in the middle of the hallway.

"Yes."

"Hey, I'm Destiny. Nice to meet you."

I nodded and immediately felt intimidated. She was kind of... scary. Her long raven hair with blue streaks nearly touched her butt, and most of it was swept across her face, covering her features. Her shirt and skinny jeans were black and super tight, and I could see a bit of her pale stomach, belly ring glistening with every breath she took. Tall, black, lace-up boots hugged her legs, and she only had on one black fingerless glove. Her porcelain skin made her dark clothes seem even darker. Mysterious shadowy eyes stared back at me, almost haunting in a way. Maroon eyeshadow matched her lip color and the silver loop hanging from her bottom lip matched the one in her eyebrow. She was more Gothic than anyone I had ever seen in real life or on television. She looked like she could have been a member of the *Addams Family*. But she was still very pretty.

"Uh...hi." I held out my hand to shake hers, but she shrugged and looked down at the pile of books she held close to her chest.

She giggled. "Where have you been? I've been waiting to meet you. Well, me and like...everyone else."

"Why...er...why is that?"

"You're Patient Zero. Duh! Listen, I gotta go. I'm late for class. But, hey, let's hang out later. I know where you live now," she said with a smile and a wink. I returned a half smile and watched as she scurried down the hall. I quickly shut the door behind me to avoid meeting anyone else.

My computer dinged and a bolded headline popped up on my email page. I hurried over only to find that it was more junk.

"Damn it," I whispered.

A knock came from my door and I reached over to open it. It was Dr. Walker.

"Good Morning, Grace. I trust you're feeling well today." He stood in the doorway with a grin. It was kind of a surprise, really. Normally, I'd walk over to the Z lab with Number One whenever I had to get tests done. But for some reason, Dr. Walker was here. Waiting in my doorway. With a creepy grin.

"Good morning."

"I have a surprise for you."

A surprise? For me?

"Follow me."

Before I could grab my bag or my cellphone, Dr. Walker had his hand on my shoulder and moving me into the direction of the front door. He led me outside onto the porch. The sun was still rising, but it was pretty bright already. The flowers in the courtyard bloomed, showing off their brilliant hues of orange, pink, purple, and red. The palm trees stood tall and their leaves wafted softly in the breeze.

We walked to the center of the courtyard. The day after I'd gotten to the island, Dr. Walker and Number One had showed me around, and Dr. Walker explained what each of the huts were for. There was the Laguna hut, which was where the female "subjects" resided. The Venice hut was right next to ours, which was where the guys lived. The two-story hut-style building past the female and male huts was called El Matador, and it was where classes were held during the week. I asked him where the names came from, and he said that he chose those names because they were some of his favorite beaches in California. I raised my eyebrows at him and resisted the urge to show a displeasing frown at the thought of Dr. Walker frolicking in a Speedo on a Pacific Coast beach. He was a good-looking man, but he was starting to feel more like a weird uncle to me.

Then there was the Malibu hut, which was the common area. I hadn't been in there, but he said there were TVs and a pool table and video games. It seemed like a cool place to hang out.

The Newport hut, or mess hall, was where everyone gathered for breakfast, lunch, and dinner. I had asked him about the raw boar he served me the first night here. He explained that everyone else like me also ate *fresh* food. Some of it was frozen in order to preserve it, and then thawed before serving, but nothing was ever cooked. He said that he'd planned on transitioning me to raw meals but decided not to when my test came back "abnormal." He wanted to make sure I was getting what I needed.

I didn't argue.

Finally, there was the Z lab, which I learned was dedicated to his late son, Zack, who'd drowned. Just like the Z in Serum Z.

We walked over to El Matador and through the doors. Since I had decided to be a recluse and stick to the Laguna Hut and the

Z lab, this was my first time in El Matador. The inside didn't look much different than ours, only it was two stories. There was a long, wide hallway with wooden floors. The hallway was lined with doors to what I assumed to be classrooms. Straight ahead were stairs leading up to the second floor.

We strolled down the hall. The doors had rectangular windows, allowing me to get a peek inside of the only one that was lit. All I could see was a teacher sitting at a desk, but it reminded me of a classroom at Middleton High. We stopped at the last room, which had a sign on the window that read RESERVED. Dr. Walker unlocked the door and flicked the light on, and my eyes sprung open the moment we stepped inside.

A large white table was placed in the center of the room where white plaster sculptures—some of only a head, some of the head and torso—were lined up side by side, resembling an assembly line of unfinished mannequins. Shelves aligning one side of the wall were filled with paintbrushes and small paint canisters. I walked over to get a better view. There were containers piled high with colorful makeup and gels and glitter and random crafting items. The other side of the wall contained rows of nude-colored masks. I grazed my fingertips over the silicone material. The faces had no details—like a blank canvas. Empty molds of torsos and heads were scattered around the room, along with sewing machines and other machinery. I glanced at Dr. Walker, who was standing in the doorway with his hands in the pockets of his slacks, and a wide smile spread across his face.

"Is this—"

"An effects studio? Yes."

"You guys teach this here?" I asked, surprised that enough people would be interested for Dr. Walker to fund it.

"We do now."

I furrowed my brows in confusion.

"This is for you. Aren't you interested in becoming a professional makeup and special effects artist? Like for movies and things like that?"

How in the hell did he know? I had only made that decision the morning I left home. Tristen was the only person I told.

"I...I didn't know you knew about that."

He strode toward the table, reaching over to touch one of the sculptures. "Grace, when I told you that we would take care of you, I was serious. You are very special to me and to everyone else here."

But I couldn't understand why. Why was everyone so interested in me?

"When I first saw you years ago, sick and dying, you reminded me so much of my son." He walked to the single window on the far side of the wall and peered out. "You were so tiny. So sick. Helpless. The event that took place the day Zack died replayed in my mind, as if I were watching *him* in that hospital bed again." He turned to me. "Do you know that he would be in college right now?"

I shook my head. Dr. Walker creeped me out at times, but my heartstrings were slightly tugging for him at the moment. I thought of my mother and realized that she was in the same situation he was in at one point. She had to watch me die. I was pissed with her, but it wasn't for the decision she made to allow Dr. Walker to inject me with Serum Z. She was only doing what she could to save my life and I understood that.

I looked down at my hands.

"I didn't want Eve to go through what I had gone through. Losing my son was...the hardest thing I've ever had to endure. Knowing that I would never see him again. Knowing that I would never hear his voice or watch him play or hug him ever again. It changed my life and my feelings about what the meaning of life truly is." His voice cracked with obvious emotion.

"Is that why you made Serum Z?"

He walked closer to me. "I made Serum Z so that people can have a second chance."

"But you didn't know this would happen. That I would become what I am."

He gave me a crooked smile. "No, I didn't. But you are alive, Grace. You're here. And every subject in this facility is alive and was given that second chance."

I thought Patient Zero was a bad nickname. But referring to everyone else as subjects was definitely worse.

Dr. Walker continued, "Unfortunately, my team and I were unaware of the side effects. Being that you were the first patient, the first time we ever used Serum Z, we had no idea what would happen. After you were injected and revived and we found out what your side effects were, we continued our research. We thought there had to be a way to fix the complications. We have been working diligently to figure out ways to reduce the side effects or wipe them clean altogether. But we soon came to realize that, as with many medical experiments and research, there were just going to be pros and cons to this drug.

"You already know the cons. Unfortunately, we haven't found a way to reduce the side effects. But the pros? Grace, the pros to this drug are phenomenal." His eyes widened and he leaned in closer to me. "You have the capability to heal within minutes. You're stronger. Smarter. Better. And you are immortal. Immortality, Grace. It's the ultimate pro." His eyes were twinkling.

I knew I had all those things he mentioned. I did feel stronger when I ate. Healed quicker. And I was smarter with a belly full of raw meat. But the immortality "pro" is what got me. He brought it up back in the States, but I was too freaked out about everything else to completely understand. I knew what immortality meant: the ability to live forever. But was he being serious about living forever?

He must have read my mind because he said, "We discovered through our research that with the proper nutritional aid, our subjects would be given the wonderful gift of immortality. Of never dying again. You and everyone here, and possibly everyone in the world, could live forever. Dying would no longer be an option. No more pain. No more loss."

"Is that why I'm here?" I asked, not sure of where I was really going with that question. I knew I was here for treatment. But I thought that treatment would eventually lead me to become cured.

Dr. Walker put his arm around my shoulder, leading me toward the door.

"Grace, you're here so we can take care of you and give you the proper treatment for your condition. We only care about your well-being. The other subjects are very thrilled that you're here, too. You're Patient Zero. You're the reason why they are alive. They all want to thank you."

He pulled the door closed behind us and locked the effects studio.

"I don't know why they would thank me. I didn't *make* Serum Z," I pointed out.

"No, you didn't. But it worked. It did its job, which was to revive you and you proved that."

We headed back to the center of the courtyard. "I know that all of this, learning who you are, moving away from home...I know this is all a lot to take in. But there's also a lot of good that could come from it all. You and the other subjects here are one of a kind."

My breath hitched at the thought of Tristen telling me the same exact thing.

"You are all special. You have amazing capabilities now. You'll learn to love who you are eventually. Just give it a chance. For now, I would really like for you to come out of your shell. You'll start your classes next week. After all, it's important to finish your education. But I would also like for you to explore the grounds. Meet some of the other subjects and consider engaging in some of the activities we have to offer. There's a list on the bulletin board in the Malibu hut and anyone would be willing to join you."

I didn't say anything. Just nodded once. He looked down at his watch. "I have to get back to the Z lab. It's going to be a beautiful day. Why not go and enjoy the beach?" he suggested as he turned toward the Z lab.

I looked up at the blue, cloudless sky. Maybe I would go to the beach today.

But first...

"Dr. Walker!" I yelled behind him. He turned to me with raised eyebrows. "I was just wondering when Tristen would be able to visit. You said after my tests were done, he could come."

"Ah, yes. Don't worry. I haven't forgotten. Enjoy the rest of your day, Grace." And then he was gone.

I headed back to my room, feeling disappointed. The deal was that as soon as I was done with my testing, Dr. Walker would fly Tristen here. But it seemed like he might not have been serious about it. Or maybe I wasn't done with my testing. I could feel the uneasy fear forming in my chest at the thought. The mysterious soreness after I woke up was a bit unnerving, but it wasn't all that bad.

Honestly, though, I didn't even know why I was asking Dr. Walker. Tristen hadn't tried to contact me. He might not even want to come. And I realized that I could try to contact him myself, but I was the one who told him to move on. Get over me. Don't wait for my return. I essentially threw the ball in his court.

Fine! I made the decision, right there in the middle of the courtyard, to call Tristen.

My feet moved and suddenly I was jogging over to the Laguna hut to get to my phone. I could see Number One standing at the entrance. When I reached him, he opened the door for me.

"You're in a hurry," he pointed out. "You feeling okay?"

"Yup. I'm fine. I just...forgot something in my room."

"Are you hungry?"

I paused and studied him for a moment. He stood tautly in khaki slacks and a white collared shirt. His stern facial expression made him appear like he was about to scold me for stealing a cookie out of the cookie jar. But his ocean-blue eyes...they were soft. Something told me there was more to Number One than he was letting on.

"Are *you* hungry?" I asked. He didn't answer right away. Instead, he stared back at me. His forehead wrinkled, almost like he was trying to understand what I had just asked him. As if I had spoken another language.

"Oh my gosh!" a little voice behind me shrieked.

I spun around. The small red-haired girl that I had been seeing around came over. Carrying a velvety, purple pouch in her hands, the poor girl looked like she was about ready to topple over from the enormous backpack she was carrying. But she stood motionless. Her big greens eyes beamed back at me, matching the wide smile that pretty much took up her entire face. She couldn't be more than ten years old. Her sweet small voice was pretty adorable.

"Um...hi?" Yes, it was a question. She looked like she was going to pop! I didn't know how else to respond.

"You're Grace!" She set her pouch down on the bench next to her and wrapped her arms around me. I held my arms out, not sure what to make of any of it. She backed away slowly after a moment. "I'm sorry," she said with a giggle. "That was weird. I'm just really excited to finally meet you."

I forced a smile, and she shrugged away her embarrassment with a swipe of her hair.

"It's okay."

"I'm Madison. But everyone calls me Maddi."

"It's nice to meet you, Maddi."

She looked up at me without moving her head, just her eyes. "Your room is next to mine. I wanted to knock the other day, but I didn't know if you wanted to see anyone. Are you going to be living with us for a while?" Her s's slurred just a bit. I assumed this tiny lisp was due to the metal braces that clung to her teeth.

"Yeah. For a little bit," I answered. Her face lit up as she sucked in a breath of air. She was ecstatic but trying her best to contain it.

Then, a pain shot across my stomach and I winced, involuntarily wrapping my arms around myself. Number One came to my side immediately, noticing my slight stumble.

"Grace, are you okay?"

I closed my eyes. "Yes. I...I just need something to eat."

"Are you okay?" Maddi asked fearfully. I didn't want the little girl to worry, so I nodded. The pain came on strong. Number One knew this and had me walking toward the Newport hut in seconds.

Once inside, he gently sat me down in one of the booths near a window. I glanced around, trying to find one thing to focus on so the room could stop spinning. Booths lined the walls of the mess hall. In the center stood a long buffet table, with smaller bistro-style tables scattered around it. There was a bar with black stools along the back wall, all decked out as if it were a tiki bar on a beach in Hawaii. It was made out of bamboo with little white lights hanging above it, similar to ones you wrap around a Christmas tree. There was no one else around. Number One ran behind the bar and through a door that I guessed led to the kitchen. He was back within seconds with a tray of food.

"Here you go, Grace."

He set it down in front of me. Before I could even think, my fingers shoveled the cold pieces of uncooked boar into my mouth. There wasn't anything else on the tray, only large slices of cool, thick meat. I could have sworn one of the slices stared at me while it swam in its pink liquid. But I didn't really care. The smell was enough to force my hands to pick up a piece and bring it to my mouth. I chewed frantically, desperate to feel the chunks slide down my throat. I closed my eyes in satisfaction, feeling every bitter, juicy taste explode in my mouth.

Once I felt I had enough, I opened my eyes. I didn't even realize it, but I had eaten every last morsel.

"Do you feel better?" Number One asked before reaching over to grab the empty tray.

I nodded.

"Good. I'll be right back."

I grabbed a napkin from the napkin holder to wipe my hands and my mouth, as if that tiny display of proper etiquette could mask what I must have looked like eating. I didn't really remember much except the taste, but I imagined I looked like a rabid animal.

*God, that boar is so delicious!*

I sat in the red vinyl booth and glanced around the room. Newport hut was actually pretty nice. I wondered if they ever served anything else besides boar. There had to be other items on the menu—other animals they hunted and killed on this island.

"Ready?"

"Yeah."

As we walked back to the Laguna hut, I realized that my hunger pains were coming on more strongly now than before. Back home, there was a little time between the moment I got hungry and the moment I felt the urge to feed on something moving.

"I feel like I'm getting worse. Do you think I'm getting worse?" I asked Number One. Chances were, he'd tell me to ask Dr. Walker, but I had to ask. I was worried.

"That should be something you discuss with Dr. Walker."

Of course.

We reached the Laguna hut, and I was actually pretty happy to get to my room and to my phone. Now that I had a full belly and a clear mind, it was time to take the plunge. I had to call Tristen. I just had to know what was up with us before it drove me insane.

Number One took his stance near my door. I entered my room and noticed there was someone standing on the patio, facing the beach. It was a guy. A guy with dark shoulder-length hair. He was wearing jeans and a T-shirt, and I could just barely see the white and black of his *Chucks* peeking out underneath the cuff of his pants.

It couldn't be.

# THE VISITOR

TRISTEN TURNED IN MY direction and my heart sank. I stopped breathing. I stopped moving. How could this be? Memories of our first kiss at the Halloween party flooded my mind, and I suddenly couldn't wait to feel his lips on mine.

I remembered that my legs could move, so I inched my way closer to the sliding door. For some reason, I felt afraid. It almost didn't feel real. Like he was a figment of my imagination. Maybe my hunger was making me crazy.

As if he could feel someone's presence behind him, he turned around, and we locked eyes. We stared at one another through the glass. His lips expanded across his face, revealing those brilliantly white teeth of his. His wavy hair danced with the breeze from the beach, and I couldn't wait any longer to run my fingers through it. I slid the door open, anticipation coursing through my movements. I lunged toward his chest and he met me halfway. The clean scent of his cologne found its way into my nose. I closed my eyes, thanking God that I could hold him again. His arms wrapped around my entire body and he squeezed me in a tight embrace.

I buried my head into his firm pecs. The tears that were fighting their way out of my eyes from the moment he turned to look at me finally poured out, winning the battle I had been fighting all week long. He rested his head on mine, and I could feel his cool breath on my forehead. I sobbed softly into his shirt.

"Shh, it's okay," he whispered.

"I-I'm sorry. I just...I just didn't think I would see you again," I admitted.

He pulled me away from his chest and cradled my face in his palms. "What? Why?" He seemed confused about this.

I couldn't look at him. "I don't know. I thought it was over. I told you not to wait for me. And you didn't call me, so I thought that you and Sonny got back together." I was rambling.

He chuckled and pulled me close to him again, wrapping his arm around my head. "I'm not back with Sonny. I didn't call you because I was too busy begging my mom to let me come here. She would only let me come if I made sure to do my future class assignments ahead of time, that way I wouldn't be missing any schoolwork. I was working my ass off on getting things done. Grace, I started missing you the moment you left. The moment you stepped into that SUV. I know you told me to get over you, but there was no way I was letting you go that easily."

We hugged in the doorway between my bedroom and the patio for what seemed like forever before Tristen moved us over to the wicker bench. He sat me down and took a seat next to me. Wrapping an arm around my shoulder, he studied my face before wiping the remainder of my tears off my cheek.

"It's okay," he breathed softly.

"When did you get here?"

"This morning. Man, it took forever!"

I thought the same exact thing. Three days of travel was too long.

"When did you leave New Orleans? You must have left, like, right after I did."

"Pretty much. As soon as you drove away, I went home and begged my parents to let me come here. That same day, two guys who looked like the *Men in Black* came to my door and asked me if I wanted to go to Costa Rica. It was kind of weird, but whatever. I'm here now."

"And your parents actually let you come?" I asked curiously. I knew my mom would have never let me travel so far from home alone...if I wasn't a freakishly hungry zombot.

"My dad was all right with it. My mom? Not so much."

"Well, what did you say? You were going to see your zombie girlfriend on an island in the middle of nowhere?" I couldn't help the sarcasm. Really, what parent would be okay with their son leaving with two mysterious men to some place they had probably never heard of?

What's an even better question? Was I his girlfriend?

"It wasn't easy. There was a lot of back and forth between my parents talking to Dr. Walker and your mom."

"My mom?"

"Yeah. Dr. Walker wanted me to come here to support you. I guess he spoke to your mom and your mom called my mom. She explained to them how important it was for me to come see you and that you were sick. Between her and Dr. Walker, they're the reason I'm here now."

My mother? Really? That was pretty surprising. Back home, she didn't seem too fond of Tristen. But it wasn't personal—just that he was a boy. And it was surprising that Dr. Walker wanted him to come so soon. Maybe he truly was a decent man. Maybe my anxiety was exaggerated and there was nothing to fear from him and he was being real about everything. Maybe he did just really want to help me.

Tristen swiped a stray curl behind my ear. "I missed your hair, Shelley," he cooed.

I smiled and felt my ears heat up from blushing.

"My hair missed you, too, Miles."

"So, you going to show me around this place? From what I've seen so far, it's freaking amazing! I'm kinda jealous."

"No. There's nothing to be jealous about, really. I miss home already."

"Well, have you met anyone? And how was your testing?"

I sighed. "The testing was...okay. It didn't hurt much. I'll tell you all about it later." I didn't feel like explaining all of the medical crap I had to go through. "And I've only met a couple of people. Dr. Walker said there were over thirty patients here, but it doesn't seem that way."

"Well, you haven't been here long. I'm sure you'll meet them soon."

Sonny came to mind. "Do you happen to know how Sonny's doing?" I gazed down at my hands. I couldn't look him in the eye when I asked the question. I was afraid to know the answer. More afraid of how he felt about it. He'd had time to think about that night. To think about how I must have looked drenched in blood after having done what I did to Phoebe. And his former girlfriend. I worried that maybe he would soon realize that I truly was a monster.

Tristen didn't answer right away. He took a deep breath and placed his hand on mine. "Grace, she's okay. Some of the guys from the team called me and told me she was still at the hospital, but she's okay."

I closed my eyes and exhaled, completely relieved to hear that I wasn't on my way to becoming a serial killer. I didn't know if I could handle learning that I had killed Sonny, too. And even though Dr. Walker told me that she was okay, I would rather hear it from someone who actually knew her.

He cupped my face in his hand again, gently forcing me to turn my head up toward his. "I hope you know that I'm not mad at you about what you did. I'm really not. I'm worried about you. I want you to get better. And I want to help you get better."

I gazed into his hazel eyes, then down to his lips. He slowly leaned in closer to me and I leaned in closer to him. It felt like his lips would never reach mine. But when they finally did, the taste of cinnamon sent a tingling sensation from my lips to my ears.

Somewhere in the back of my mind, the still-rational part congratulated myself for having the foresight to pop gum into my mouth after every meal. Because even though I never thought I'd get to kiss Tristen again like this, here we were. And I was thankfully ready for it. It was probably better for him not to taste the raw, bloody meal that had just been sloshed around the inside of my mouth and between my teeth.

Tristen kissed me softly, lips closed at first, before slightly opening his mouth. His tongue barely touched mine, but it was enough to wake up my sleeping hormones. Before I knew it, we were in a full-on make-out movie moment. The world closed in on us, and every thought I had in my crazed mind gradually floated away. We wrapped our arms around each other. His fingers worked their way into my hair, gently grasping onto the back of my head and massaging.

I had questioned our relationship. While traveling to get to this island, I had thought hard about the time it took for me to feel so emotionally involved with him. From the outside, it seemed so fast. He jumped from Sonny to me after one night. But I had been watching Tristen every day for three years. I liked him since the moment he started sophomore year at Middleton High. He was my secret crush for years. And apparently, I was his, too. He informed me the night everything happened that he liked me since the day he saw me, too. But before we could do anything about it, he got caught in Sonny Westwood's perfect little web.

For some strange reason, it made sense to me. She was perfect and beautiful and rich. Her friends were perfect and beautiful and rich. It was easy to get caught up in that. Easy to fall into the notion that if you hung out with someone like that long enough, you'd be like them. It was easy to get lost in the idea of being perfect and beautiful and rich, just like her. He didn't admit to this. No one did. It was just something I'd picked up on over the years of knowing Sonny. And maybe it was something that I felt, too.

I wondered how I could feel this much for someone so soon, but how could this be wrong? This undeniable perception of everything-is-the-way-it-should-be overpowered any doubts that I had. There was this sense of comfort when I was around him—like we have been together for years. The thought of us moving too fast flew out the window. I felt like I *should* be in his arms.

Neither of us took a breath during what seemed like the longest kiss I think I would ever experience in my life. He kept his hands on my back and in my curls, but the kissing got more and more intense by the minute. It was the perfect union of two people who longed for one another. And maybe a little bit of a horny girl and a horny guy who were just really attracted to each other.

A soft tiny giggle floated through the air and into my ears, almost as if it were a distance away. I ignored it at first, not wanting to break the moment Tristen and I were having.

"Maddi, dear, it's not polite to stare." I heard someone whisper and suddenly realized that we may have an audience. I broke away from the perfect kiss and glanced over at the screened-in porch next to mine. The little red-haired girl was staring at Tristen and me with a grin from ear to ear, her braces reflecting the sunlight.

Tristen chuckled. "I guess we have an admirer."

"I'm so sorry about that. We didn't mean to pry. We were just going back inside." An elderly woman stood up slowly from the wicker bench. Her gray hair was tied up in a bun with a few loose strands flowing in the breeze. It suddenly hit me. I knew who she was.

I stood up and walked over to the screen. "Ma'am!" I called out to her before she could make it inside.

She turned to me and smiled. "Yes, dear?"

"I...um...I've heard about you. Dr. Walker told me about you."

"I'm guessing he told you that I was the really old lady." Her voice seemed unsteady, and it reminded me of what a stereotypical elderly woman would sound like in a cartoon.

I smiled. "He might have mentioned that you were older."

"Oh, please. I'm a hundred and fourteen years old. I'm ancient!"

Despite the gray hair and shaky voice, her appearance told a different story. She barely had any wrinkles. Her posture was near perfect. Her dark skin was clear and blemish-free, and she seemed to be in pretty good shape overall. She was actually quite pretty.

"I'm Grace."

She laughed softly. "Oh, dear, everyone here knows who you are. You are quite the celebrity. My name is Estelle. But who really cares about me? Who is that handsome young man behind you?" she asked, peering to get a look.

I looked back at Tristen, whose face just turned a lovely shade of pink.

"That's Tristen. My...uh..." I was stumped.

"I'm her boyfriend." He finished my sentence and stepped next to me.

It was my turn to blush.

"Nice to meet you, Tristen. Now, I'm going to leave you two lovebirds. This old lady has got to get some food."

"It was nice meeting you," Tristen and I responded simultaneously. We watched as she walked back into her room.

"Holy crap! She's a hundred and fourteen? How is she alive?"

"Don't you remember? Dr. Walker told us about her. He said the serum brought her back to life and she's been alive ever since."

"I do remember him saying something about being immortal before you left. Do you think that's really true? I mean, do you think we can actually live forever with that serum stuff?"

I shook my head. "I don't know. I don't even know if I would even want to live forever."

Tristen looked at me with bulging eyes. "What? Why not? Shit, if that were true, I'll go tell Dr. Walker to stick me with the needle now!" He grabbed my hand. "Grace, we could live together forever. Wouldn't you want that?"

"But would we be living? Technically, we'd be dead."

We stared at each other in silence. The reality of what I'd just said finally hit me. I was a walking and talking and living dead person. I was a fictional character in movies. It wasn't enough to either be alive or dead. I had to be both.

I still had so many questions about my condition—about what it meant to be a real-life zombie.

# THE ZOMBRIDS

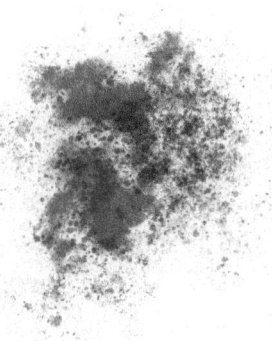

A KNOCK AT MY door brought me back from my thoughts. I kissed Tristen on the cheek before stepping inside my room and opening my door. Destiny, the Gothic chick I had met earlier, was standing on the other side.

"Hey, Grace. A few of us are going down to the beach. Want to join us?"

"Um, I kind of have company." I gestured at Tristen, who was now sitting on my bed.

"Oh. Well, bring him! Come on. It'll be fun!" she said.

"Grace, we should go. I'd like to meet everyone, too," Tristen said eagerly.

Damn. I really wanted to spend all my time with him. Alone. "Okay, let me grab my bag."

"Awesome!" Destiny smiled.

Tristen and I followed Destiny out of the Laguna hut. Number One was standing outside on the porch but didn't move when I walked past him.

"Aren't you coming with us?" I turned and asked.

"No. But I'll be able to see you if you need anything," he responded in his usual terse tone. The fact that he would be watching me should have been disturbing, but it kind of felt comforting. I didn't mind having someone watch over me, especially in a place that I really didn't know much about yet.

We walked around and behind the Laguna hut to the trail that led to the beach. There were three other people standing in a circle and talking. Maddi was dressed in a pink one-piece bathing suit and held her boogie board close to her. A girl with short black hair was busy tying Maddi's red locks into a ponytail. This was the same girl I had seen the first day. She was wearing really short, ripped jean shorts and a purple ruffled bathing suit top. She was very attractive. Tan and thin, but it was an I-workout-every-day kind of thin. She even had a four-pack and all.

A guy with spiky, sun-kissed hair kept his head down, looking at his phone. He was shirtless—also very tan. I tried not to stare, but his body was almost exactly like...Tristen's. He was thin but not too thin, with a muscular undertone. Except, he somehow seemed sexier. Maybe it was the skin-tight wet suit. It was only halfway on his body, the top part dangling around his waist, and he clutched a neon yellow surfboard close to his side.

I quickly glanced away and over to Tristen, who was staring off at the beach. I grabbed his hand and intertwined my fingers with his. He glanced at me and smiled.

"Hey, guys," Destiny greeted as we reached the other three.

"Hi, Grace!" Maddi flashed her braces at me. She was a happy little girl.

The short-haired brunette looked me over from head to toe before glancing at Tristen and introducing herself. "Hi, I'm Charlie."

Now that I was able to get a good look at her... Wow! She was gorgeous! Like an actress or something. Her straight, dark hair was cut to perfection. It was layered high in the back—a standard bob haircut. She had a little bit of bangs in the front, which framed her slim face exquisitely. She had high cheekbones and a rounded chin that led to a slender neck. She had dark arched eyebrows and her lips were a beautiful shade of pink. She looked exotic, as if she could be Brazilian or maybe even from another world. I stared into her eyes, taking in the icing on the cake: one green eye and one blue. How interestingly cool and sexy!

She was intimidating. And I wondered why the hell she just completely ignored me.

I smiled at her. "I'm Grace."

"Yeah, I know." She snorted. She couldn't have possibly given me any more attitude.

"See, I told you. Everyone's been waiting for you," the guy said in a foreign accent, still not looking up from his phone.

"Is everyone ready to get in the water? Come on, let's go!" Maddi said, skipping toward the beach.

"Maddi, be careful!" Charlie called after her. We all began walking toward the beach when suddenly, I realized how impolite I had been.

"Oh, I'm sorry. Everyone, this is Tristen. Tristen, this is Destiny, and that's Maddi," I said, pointing to the excited little red-head running to the ocean.

Destiny shook his hand. "Yo."

I learned fast that Destiny wasn't an ordinary girl. Besides all the Goth, she wasn't very feminine, either.

The foreign guy finally looked up from his phone. "Hello, mate. I'm Ian."

Mate? Okay, he was Australian. Maybe. And I realized after hearing his accent that this was the guy who'd greeted me and told me I looked like crap (in so many words) my first night on the island. Oh...and whoa! I couldn't see him all too well that night because of the lack of light and the shadows, but he was very cute! I didn't remember living in California, but I imagined he was what a typical California surfer dude looked like.

We reached the shore, and Maddi was already in the water splashing around with her boogie board. Charlie went straight into the insanely blue water to meet up with her. Ian set his phone and board down to slide into the top portion of his wet suit. Once he zipped up, he jogged out into the water with his board and paddled out farther into the ocean toward the waves crashing in the distance.

"There's a storm coming," Destiny informed us, taking a seat on a long log partially buried in the sand. There was another long log parallel to the one she sat on and a pile of charred wood in between, reminiscent of some sort of campsite. They must sit out here late at night and hang by the fire. I chuckled to myself at the thought, imagining zombies gathered around making s'mores and playing guitars.

Tristen and I took a seat on the opposite side of Destiny. We were both wearing jeans and T-shirts, not really dressed for the beach. But neither was Destiny.

"Why aren't you swimming?" I asked, waving at her full-on Gothic gear.

"Are you joking? No way! I like being pale."

"This is nice, huh?" Tristen whispered into my ear. I turned to him, our faces so close I could pucker up and lay one on him.

"Yeah, it is."

The warm breeze tussled my hair and the smell of salty air filled my lungs. It was afternoon now and the sun was at its highest in the sky. The beach was really beautiful. It was like one of those calendar photos of a tropical island. I glanced over at our compound, taking in how surrounded we were by the thick rainforest.

"So, how long have you two been together?" Destiny asked.

"Um...not very long," I answered, slightly embarrassed. It had literally been about twenty minutes since we declared ourselves in a relationship. "We've known each other for a little while, though."

"Cool. Tristen, you don't care that she's a Zombrid?"

"A what?" he asked, leaning in and twisting his head as if to try to hear her better.

Destiny laughed. "Sorry, you don't know the lingo yet." She pulled a cigarette and a lighter out of her black backpack and lit it.

"So, what is that?" I asked.

She inhaled and blew the smoke out with one harsh exhale before answering. "It's a zombie hybrid. Half human, half zombie."

Well, that was new. I had never even heard of that in any of my favorite zombie movies.

"Are all the patients here Zombrids?"

She took another drag before answering. "Yup. We're all Zombrids. Thanks to you, Grace."

I was suddenly uncomfortable.

"It wasn't her fault," Tristen shot back.

"Oh, no! I'm not blaming her or anything! Really, it's thanks to Grace that we're all here right now. Alive. Well, halfway alive."

"What happened to you? How did you get injected with the serum?" I felt like I was prying a little, but I was really curious.

"You mean...how did I die? You don't get injected unless you've already died."

I nodded. That made sense. It was a drug to revive a person. FYI, I never in a million years thought I would be asking someone how they died.

"Overdose," she answered plainly.

Tristen and I didn't respond. I'd never hung out with anyone who did drugs. There were people at school who smoked marijuana and did other things, but Phoebe and I didn't care to hang around them. Phoebe did smoke pot with one of her boy toys once. But she said it made her feel like she was talking in slow motion, so she never touched it again. Drinking was pretty much as far as we would go as rebellious teenagers.

My heart hurt at the thought of Phoebe.

Destiny continued, "My parents were deadbeats. My life sucked in Chicago. So, I got high. A lot." She seemed very open about her past and completely comfortable to share.

I glanced over at Maddi and Charlie playing in the water, then at Ian in the distance. He was sitting on his surfboard now, waiting to catch a good wave. "What about them?"

Destiny turned and watched them with me. "Maddi fell and hit her head during recess at school. I always said those monkey bars were dangerous. She's the youngest Zombrid here."

"How old is she?" Tristen asked.

"Nine. Charlie's twenty-six. She was a hairstylist in Florida. Suicide."

I shot Destiny a look. "Really?"

"Yeah. Something about her boyfriend screwing her over. She doesn't like to talk about it much. As a matter of fact, she doesn't care too much for you."

Great. Another Sonny.

"Why?" Tristen asked, pulling me in closer to his body.

Destiny retrieved another cigarette from her bag and lit it off the one that was already going. "If you're trying to commit suicide, you want to die, right? She feels like it's Grace's fault that she's not completely dead."

"That's ridiculous."

She shrugged her shoulders. "I know. But whatever. I wouldn't pay attention to her. Anyway, Ian died in a surfing accident. Go figure."

"Man, that sucks," Tristen stated.

"Where is he from?" I asked. The "mate" kind of gave it away, but I wanted to make sure.

"I know. His accent is so hot, right? He's from Australia."

I peered out at him again.

"Aren't you scared to be with her?" Destiny asked Tristen bluntly.

Tristen squeezed me before answering. "No, I'm not."

"Well, any of us could eat you if we wanted to. But we won't. Unless..." She paused to take a drag of her cigarette.

I waited patiently, but after the first second, I couldn't any longer. "Unless what?"

"Unless you can smell him."

"What do you mean, smell me?" Tristen asked.

"Jeez. No one has told you anything yet, huh? Dr. Walker is usually pretty good at explaining all of this. He's been kind of busy lately, though. Your arrival was a big deal."

Before she could answer, Maddi and Charlie came to join us on the log.

"Maddi, come. Let me put your hair back into a ponytail, sweetie," Charlie said, and Maddi hopped over and sat in the sand in front of her.

"Charlie, would you care to explain why we won't eat her boyfriend?"

"Why? Dr. Walker hasn't told his Golden Subject any of that yet?" she asked, sarcasm dripping from every word.

I could feel Tristen's eyes on me before he leaned into my ear. "Bitch." I nodded and smiled. He gripped me tighter around my waist and kissed my cheek.

"Fine, I'll explain," Destiny said, rolling her eyes. "There are certain triggers in our Zombrid brains that cause the need to feed."

"What kind of triggers?" Tristen asked. I was sure he'd benefit from this information. After all, he was a human surrounded by flesh-eating Zombrids. I'd be worried, too.

"Like if someone has an open wound. Or if we haven't eaten in a while."

"Or if you get really mad," Maddi added.

Holy crap! Phoebe and Sonny flashed through my mind. I had been furious when Sonny just wouldn't let go of my hair, my most favorite thing about myself. I was, by no means, conceited. My petite figure—small boobs and tiny butt—didn't make me feel like I was as gorgeous as Charlie. But if I knew anything for sure, it was that I had great hair. My long and loose chocolate-colored curls gave me confidence about myself. And Tristen loved it.

Phoebe had a little cut on her leg that I pointed out to her just before she went to bed that night. I must have smelled it in my sleep when I was in the next room with Tristen. That must have been the trigger.

"If you are angry and hungry, the need to feed is crazy strong. Or if you just haven't eaten in a long time." Destiny switched her attention to Tristen. "So, as long as you make sure you don't have a cut, you don't piss her off, and she's fed, then you're all good. And you two look pretty happy, so..."

Fluffy.

"But I...ate a cat. And he wasn't hurt." I didn't think I was mad at the little guy, either.

"You must have been really hungry. And animals are different. Most are smaller than us and we're stronger than they are. Our instincts are to use that to our advantage."

"Makes sense," Tristen muttered.

"But they don't taste as good," Charlie added, not looking up from playing with Maddi's hair. Obviously, she has had human before.

"We eat a lot," Maddi said, breaking up the ominous feeling in the air after Charlie's statement.

Charlie smiled and Destiny laughed. "That's an understatement."

"Aren't there supposed to be more Zombrids here?" For some reason, I felt like we were the only ones around.

Charlie and Destiny exchanged glances at each other in silence.

"What?" I asked. The air had suddenly shifted. Something was clearly wrong.

# THE PROTECTOR

DESTINY GLANCED DOWN AT her boots and Charlie focused harder on Maddi's hair. I couldn't stand the deafening and awkward silence any longer. "What happened?"

"There were probably around thirty of us," Destiny started. "But Dr. Walker sent them to live on another part of the island."

"Hey, Maddi. Want to go see if we can find some seashells for your collection?" Charlie asked as she stood up from the log. She pulled a small plum-colored velour pouch from her back pocket and handed it to Maddi.

"Yes. Grace, you wanna come see my seashell collection later?" Maddi asked eagerly.

"Sure," I answered. I didn't mean to sound like I wasn't interested, but I had an uneasy feeling that Charlie was trying to get Maddi away from the conversation that we were getting ready to have.

"Come on, Maddi."

Destiny watched Charlie and Maddi walk toward the water. Once they were a safe distance away, she continued, "Maddi doesn't know about East Cocos. We try to keep it from her so that she doesn't get scared. She's too young to know about it."

"What's East Cocos?" Tristen asked.

"It's on the east side of the island. It's another facility. It's where all the really sick Zombrids go," she said. She didn't look up at us. Instead, she kept her head down, giving off a sad vibe.

"Really sick? What's wrong with them?" I asked. How could we be any sicker than we already were?

She inhaled deeply. "I'm guessing you've been doing all the testing, right?"

I nodded.

"You've probably had it done every day for the past week because you're new. It'll slow down, but we usually get those tests done at least once every few weeks. It's so Dr. Walker can see how our progression is going. Check to make sure our Zombrid brains aren't getting worse. Anyway, some of the others got really sick all of a sudden. So he took them to the East Cocos facility to protect us. You know, in case whatever is wrong with them could spread to us."

"What do you think is wrong with them?"

"We don't know. He hasn't told us much about it."

"Were you able to see any of them?" Tristen was just as intrigued as I was.

Destiny pulled out another cigarette.

"Should you be smoking that much?" I was getting impatient and irritated with all of the breaks in conversation. I needed to know more. Now!

"I'm half dead! I don't really care. Besides, Dr. Walker says I'm good. Anyway, yes, I did see someone. My girlfriend. Abby looked..." Destiny stared off into the distance. "She was messed up."

"Hey, who's ready for some lunch?" Ian interrupted. Still dripping wet from the ocean, he leaned his board up against the log and unzipped his wet suit. He pulled down the top half, allowing it to dangle from his waist. Beads of water dripped from his wet hair to his face, down his neck and to his chest.

Okay. I was staring.

I turned away as soon as I realized what I was doing. Destiny quickly wiped her cheek with her thumb, as if to hide a fallen tear. "Yeah, I'm starved. Let's go eat."

"Charlie! Maddi! We're headed to Newport!" Ian yelled out. Charlie and Maddi began to make their way toward us with hands full of seashells. As we headed back to the huts, Ian slowed his pace until he was walking beside me.

"Destiny took it a little rough when Abby went away," he whispered. "It's probably best if we don't really talk about her."

"I'm sorry. I didn't know—"

"It's okay," he said.

Tristen grabbed my hand and squeezed. I glanced at him and smiled. This was a ton of information to digest. Remembering my mother's philosophy, I mentally took a step back to get a bigger picture.

I was a Zombrid: half human, half zombie. Dr. Walker had been testing all of us at least once every few weeks, which wasn't a bad thing. If I could get sicker than I already was, I would actually like Dr. Walker to give me a checkup from time to time to see if I was okay. But if I did get sick, then apparently, he would send me off to the East Cocos facility. What did they do there? I imagined a big, riveted steel door with the word QUARANTINE engraved into it. What exactly was wrong with them? How was their condition worse than the rest of us? Was their *need* too much to control? What about the triggers? I mean, I already knew what I was capable of. Was Tristen in danger just being near me?

Finding out a little more about everyone else was kind of cool. It actually felt nice having so much in common with these guys, especially when it was dying and having the incredible need to eat human flesh.

The thought created a hunger bubble in my belly. I winced.

"You okay?" Tristen asked. He must have felt my grip tighten around his hand.

"Yeah. I'm just a little hungry."

We walked to the courtyard of the compound. Number One stood alone, as usual. Only this time, he was standing near the Newport entrance. He must have known the feeding schedule.

"Mr. Miles, you'll have to come with me," he demanded.

"What? Why can't he come have lunch with us?"

"Unfortunately, visitors are not allowed to eat with the patients."

Well, that was crap. But I did like that he didn't call us "subjects."

"Why not?" I asked, challenging him.

"It's just standard procedure."

"So where should I eat?" Tristen sounded a little bummed.

"The second story of the El Matador hut offers a small cafe area for visitors and non-patients."

"That's stupid," I complained. "He traveled a long way to get here and we can't enjoy a meal together?"

Number One adjusted his stance. "I'm sorry, Grace. It's just the rules."

"Well, *you* came in there with me. And you aren't a Zombrid, are you? I mean, are you afraid that I'll eat him?" I probably should have just let it go. But it bugged me. I wanted to spend as much time with Tristen as I could.

"No. I am not a Zombrid."

Tristen turned to me. "Grace, it's okay. I'm not that hungry right now, anyway. I'll be waiting for you in your room."

"But—"

He brushed my cheek with the back of his hand. "Go eat." He said it in his soft, sexy voice and gave me a smoldering glare. I gave in almost immediately.

"Okay."

He kissed my forehead before we parted ways, and I watched as he walked to the Laguna hut. As soon as he entered, I snapped back at Number One and gave him the stink eye.

"What gives?"

"It's just the rules, Grace. Non-Zombrid guests eat on the second floor of El Matador."

"But he'll be alone. I mean, I'm not going to eat him. Why would I? I'd have food in front of me."

"Are you sure about that?" he asked. I stared at him a moment, trying to come up with some kind of answer. But the sad truth was that I didn't have one. I didn't know if I would eat Tristen.

I huffed and stomped my way into the mess hall. Great. Now I had this to worry about. Not that I didn't think about it before. Obviously, the possibility of eating Tristen was something I considered before I even moved here. I mean, I did eat my best friend.

My stomach yelled at me, so I decided to leave the chomping-on-Tristen thoughts behind me and focus on the food I *could* eat.

The mess hall wasn't the quiet, empty place I walked into before. Music blared from the jukebox in the corner of the large room. The television behind the bar had the news on the screen. Someone stood behind it, wiping down the counter. Everyone from the beach, with the addition of Estelle, had already sat down and started eating. Estelle sat with Charlie and Maddi. Destiny and Ian were at a table next to their booth.

I walked over to the buffet table and grabbed a plate. Slabs of meat filled a row of platters, and I chuckled at the fact that I actually thought about which piece to choose. They all looked the same—pink and raw and meaty. I felt a twinge of homesickness when I realized that my mother's cooking was no longer available to me. All of the different flavors and variety. It was all so visually appealing. More so than a hunk of cold, dead boar on a plate. She really did try so hard to keep me fed and happy.

I filled my dish with as much as I could. It was boring boar, but my hunger spasms didn't care.

As I walked over to the section where everyone was seated, I noticed that no one was speaking. They were hovered over their plates, shoveling the meat into their mouths in a constant motion. I walked over to Ian and Destiny and examined them closely. There was only the sound of their chewing, maybe a grunt here and there. Destiny's hair fell to the sides of her face while she hunched over her plate of food, and I couldn't see her facial expression. But Ian sat more upright. His eyes were closed as he chewed frantically on a large piece of meat. Red juice dribbled down the sides of his mouth and dripped onto his plate.

Good Lord! Was that what I looked like when I ate?

I flinched and stopped myself from lunging forward when I felt another hunger pain shoot across my stomach. I sat down at their table, and before I knew it, my eyes were closed and all I could think about was the boar. I might have missed the appearance of my mother's cooking, but the taste of this animal was a million times better.

Once I came to and out of my eating coma, I opened my eyes and realized I was alone at the table. The booth next to me was empty. No one was around. I walked outside to find Number One standing near the entrance.

"Where's Tristen?" I asked.

"He's in the Malibu hut." As soon as he said it, the faint noise of what sounded like an air hockey table and music came out of the hut. It only took a few steps and I was already inside.

It had the same Hawaiian decor as Newport. In one corner, there were two couches surrounding a large flat screen on the wall. Maddi and Charlie sat on one, watching what looked like a *Disney* movie. In the other corner was a little bar with wooden barstools. Glass bottles filled with a red liquid lined the edge.

Across the room, there were two doors with a sign on each that read CHICKS and DUDES. Three arcade-style machines were lined up against the wall across from the bathrooms. In the center of the space, there was a pool table and an air hockey table, which was where Tristen and Ian were playing.

Tristen looked up at me. "Hey, you."

"Hi."

"Wanna come play? You can have loser, which will be me because this guy is pretty damn good."

"No. It's okay. I'll just watch," I said, moving over to the wall. I glanced over at Charlie. She and Maddi were snuggled up on the couch, watching the movie *Brave*. I really liked that movie. Destiny came out of the bathroom, drying her hands with a paper towel as she walked over to me.

"How was your lunch?" she asked.

"It was okay," I answered. I was embarrassed to tell her the truth, which was that I loved it.

"Oh, don't give me that crap. You know it was great." She laughed. "You don't want to admit it yet. It's all good, though. I know when I first came here I was uncomfortable about the food, too."

"Did you come here right after you...died?"

"Yeah, I did. But that's because I had nowhere else to go. I was pretty much living on the streets. Dr. Walker kind of saved me, in more ways than one," she said, sentiment evident in her voice.

We turned to watch the game. Tristen concentrated hard on preventing the little plastic puck from entering his goal, which seemed to be going at an unusually rapid speed when Ian hit it. I watched Ian for a moment, who was now wearing a tank top and shorts. He seemed to be barely moving his arm when he hit the puck, but it was sliding across the table at a high velocity. I felt sorry for Tristen when I realized there was no chance in hell he was going to beat him. Ian had just eaten. His belly was full, he was strong, and his mind was focused.

"How long have you been here?" I asked Destiny.

"I'd say about four years." Her eyes moved over to Maddi and Charlie. "Maddi has been here about a year. Charlie has been here three years. And Ian...I'm not too sure about him. He was here before I got here."

"What about Estelle?"

"Do you know how old she is?" she asked, pie-eyed.

"Yeah. She's one hundred and fourteen."

"I know! Isn't that crazy? God, it's so cool knowing that we will never die."

A chill ran down my back. "You're okay with that?"

"Of course I am! Who doesn't want to be immortal? Anyway, I think Estelle has been here about ten years. Before this place was even Everlasting Paradise."

Ten years? That was a really long time.

Destiny smiled at me. "Hey...I chose a number and divided it by five. Then I subtracted one hundred and fifty-four from the result and got six. What was the number I chose?"

The numbers she just spewed floated around in my brain. Divided. Subtracted. Result. "Eight hundred," I answered in ten seconds flat.

"Pretty damn good! I ask all the newcomers a math problem. It's fun." She reached inside her pocket and pulled out a cigarette and a lighter. "You know, since we're all smart and stuff. I'm going to have a smoke. I'll be back."

I nodded and turned toward the game, pretending to watch it. In the meantime, my head was swirling with questions. I wouldn't say that I was smarter than anyone else. I mean, math did come easier to me than most people I knew, but it could to a non-Zombrid, too.

Also, if Dr. Walker started this place so long ago, then why didn't I come here sooner? Was it because Mom didn't want me to come?

"Grace?" Tristen said.

"Yeah?"

"You okay?"

I didn't want to tell Tristen what I was thinking "Yeah, I'm fine. Hey, you want to go someplace...away from everyone? Maybe back to my room?"

"Sure."

We said goodbye to the rest of the group before I took his hand and led him to my room in the Laguna hut. I glanced over at my computer, feeling an urge to email my mother to ask her why she didn't send me here years ago. But Tristen grabbed me by my waist and pulled me to the bed. I allowed myself to fall back into it, giggling on the way down. Yeah, yeah. I was being a girl. But who cared? The one and only person that I wanted to be around was here, and I was really happy about that.

He brushed my cheek with the back of his hand. "Are you feeling better now that you've eaten?"

"You worried I'm going to take a bite out of you?"

"Hmm...why does that sound more naughty than scary?" he asked, smiling deviously at me.

"You really aren't scared that I'll try to eat you in the middle of the night?" Number One's question of whether or not I was sure I wouldn't eat Tristen started burning a hole in my mind.

"I really don't think you would."

"Why is that? I ate Phoebe and hurt Sonny pretty badly. You're surrounded by Zombrids right now. Any one of us could eat you."

"Because you like me too much," he stated, reminding me of that matter-of-fact tone Phoebe used to give me. I looked away, trying my best not to ruin the moment by remembering Phoebe's demise.

"Hey, you okay?" he whispered.

"I'm fine." I gently pushed him away and stood up from the bed. "This is just still all so surreal. I'm a Zombrid. How did this happen?"

"So, you're a Zombrid. It just means you're different. It's not necessarily a terrible thing, Grace."

I shot him a look of disbelief. "How is it not? I ate my best friend! And I liked her...a lot!"

Tristen stood up from the bed and walked toward me. "Yeah, you did. But now you're here in this amazing place and getting the food and treatment that you need." He tucked his finger under my chin and gently forced me to look up at him. "The worst has happened. You don't think it bothers me? What happened the night before you left? I killed someone, Grace."

The look in his eyes was almost heartbreaking. This entire time my thoughts had been on a constant loop, reliving what I had done to Phoebe and Sonny. But I had forgotten that Tristen was there, too. And I had forgotten what he did to save me. Eric was getting ready to choke me to death before Tristen smashed his head in with a bat. The guilt over having killed someone must have been eating him up.

As if to have read my mind, Tristen continued, "I didn't mean to kill the guy. It just happened. I walked back into the room and he was choking you, and I just reacted. And it's horrible to think that I actually took someone's life. If it wasn't for Dr. Walker, I'd be in jail right now. Arrested for murder. I don't know how he did it, but he made it seem like it was a murder-suicide—like Eric killed Sonny, and then himself."

A sick feeling flooded my belly. I hadn't known that. I didn't want to know that. Somehow, Dr. Walker made Eric look like an awful person, when really, *I* was the awful one. How did Dr. Walker make that happen?

"I know it sounds crazy, but I feel super connected to you now. Like, we have both done this horrible thing. And the only reason we did it was because we were provoked to. You're sick and I was protecting you. And I'd protect you again if I had to."

"Would I have actually died, though? I mean, can I die again?"

Tristen squinted his eyes as if to be mentally analyzing the question. "I don't know. I don't know what would end your life, if it could end at all."

Could I ever actually die? Like...die, die?

# THE NEWBORN

I THOUGHT ABOUT *The Walking Dead* and *Zombieland* and all the movies that required a blow to the brain in order to truly kill a zombie.

"Do you think that my brain would have to be destroyed?"

"Well, I don't think you have to worry about anyone shooting you. Who would do that?"

"I don't know. But I don't want to live forever, Tristen," I admitted. Before he could respond, there was a knock at the door. I stepped away to open it.

Maddi was standing in the hallway. "Hi, Grace! Um...I was just wondering if you wanted to come see my seashell collection."

I turned to Tristen, who gave me an unspoken go-ahead with a nod and a smile.

"Okay. Sure," I said to Maddi.

Her face instantly lit up. She took my hand, and we practically ran down the hallway to her suite. I could smell the lavender right as she swung the door open. "Wow, Maddi! It smells really good in here."

"Thank you," she said as she walked over to a dresser along the wall. "It's my mom's favorite flower."

I glanced around her room, realizing that I was completely different at her age. Hers was clad in pinks and purples. Her bed was covered in dolls and stuffed animals, all enclosed in a canopy of rose-colored, translucent drapes. Her computer chair was pink, and her desk looked like a kiddie version of mine. It seemed to fit her height just right. The walls were violet, with pictures and cutouts of butterflies and flowers. It was actually quite cute. But when I was younger, I had comic books and horror movie posters all over my walls. I wouldn't say that I was a tomboy, but I definitely wasn't as girly as Maddi.

She stood at her dresser, clearly proud for me to finally see her seashell collection that covered every inch of it. And it really was a collection! There were probably about a hundred shells, all different sizes, shapes, and colors.

"Are these all from the beach?" I asked, leaning in to admire them.

"Yeah. I love seashells," she said with an air of innocence.

"How come you love them so much?"

She grabbed a purple velvet bag and retrieved a large, white shell with what looked like spikes protruding out the sides. She held it up to her ear and grinned. I smiled back, patiently waiting for what she was going to say.

She pulled it away and held it up to me. "Listen."

I brought it to my ear. There was a distant sound of hollowness.

"Do you hear it?"

I pressed it down harder against my ear, trying desperately to hear something because clearly she wanted me to. When I didn't hear anything in particular, I smiled so I wouldn't hurt her feelings.

She smiled back. "It's my mom. She's saying my name."

I pulled the seashell away from my ear and gawked at it. Maddi reached over to grab it with her tiny hand and gently placed it back on her dresser.

"Do you miss home?"

Her smile faded. "Yeah, I do. But it's okay. I like it here." She walked over to her bed and picked up a stuffed animal.

"Weren't you scared to come here all alone?" I asked. Surely, she was. She was a little girl who left everything she knew. And she was a Zombrid. That was scary all on its own.

She shrugged her shoulders. "At first, yeah. But I can eat all I want here. My tummy doesn't hurt anymore. And Dr. Walker said that when I get better, I can go home."

"Did your tummy hurt a lot at home?"

She nodded. "Except..." She looked down at her doll and began pulling at a loose thread that dangled from its button eye. It was hard to believe that she was nine years old. She seemed much younger than she was. And really tiny for her age. Sweet and small and just so fragile.

I knelt down beside her. "Except what?"

"It didn't hurt anymore after I ate her."

"Ate who?" My heart began to race. I was nervous about what I was going to hear next.

"Emma." The whisper of her small voice made the hair on the back of my neck stand up.

"Who is Emma?"

"My little sister. Mommy and Daddy brought her home from the hospital. And then it happened."

My stomach turned. Emma was a baby. A newborn.

A light knock came from the slightly opened door. "Maddi, dear? Are you ready to watch that movie before dinnertime?"

Maddi jumped up from her bed and ran over to Estelle, who was now standing in the doorway.

"Oh, I'm sorry. I didn't realize you had company."

"No," I said as I stood up. "It's okay. She was just showing me her seashell collection."

"Ah, yes. She loves her seashells," Estelle said, reaching down to pat Maddi on the head. "Maddi, why don't you go wait for me in Malibu?"

"Okay. Bye, Grace."

"Bye!" I waved, but she'd already left the room and was skipping down the hallway.

Estelle chuckled. "So full of energy, that one."

I smiled. "Yes, she is."

She walked into the room and sat on the edge of the bed. "She showed you her *special* seashells, huh?"

I nodded.

"She isn't crazy, you know. She's just a child who misses her parents. She is trying to hold on to something."

"I didn't think she was crazy." It wasn't even a passing thought in my mind.

Estelle continued, "Her parents didn't want her anymore after what she did. They were disgusted and embarrassed by it, they said. The nerve of some parents. I wouldn't have just thrown my child away. She's such a sweet little girl, and she was sick. They didn't even bother to try to understand why it happened."

"She said she's going home when she gets better."

"She's not. Her parents want nothing to do with her."

This made me sad.

"Do you have children?"

Estelle chuckled. She picked up the same doll Maddi was holding and hugged it. "Dear, I'm one hundred and fourteen years old. I have great-great grandchildren."

I took a seat next to her. "How did you end up here? I mean, how did you meet Dr. Walker?"

She sighed. "I wasn't ready to leave this earth. God blessed me with many years, but when I realized that my time could be at any moment, He sent Dr. Walker to me."

"So, Dr. Walker found you?" I was confused.

"Yes. It wasn't hard to find someone over one hundred years old. People don't normally live that long. I even did an interview for the newspaper! Anyway, he showed up at my doorstep one day and asked if I wanted to be part of an experiment he was doing. He said that I could possibly live forever. Of course, I agreed. What did I have to lose? My time was coming up." She tilted her head to the side and stared off in the distance. She was remembering. "When the time came, when my body was just too old and worn down and couldn't function on its own anymore, my heart began to give out."

"So you weren't..." I was never going to get used to asking someone if they died or not. "You didn't die?"

She turned back toward me. "Oh yes, dear. You must die first. But when I did, he brought me back to life. You know, I had lived my whole life believing that when I died, I'd see a white light. But I didn't. It was just darkness. Then he gave me the serum, and there was light again."

That was a concept I didn't even think about. I didn't remember dying. Too young, maybe? I wondered what would happen if you got injected before dying.

"So, you're okay with living forever?" I asked, curious to learn her take on it.

"Well...I was. But this world has changed so much. And I have seen so much. There comes a point when you're just ready to let it all go."

I knew it! Not everyone wants to live forever. This lady has been around for over one hundred years. She must have been tired. And from what she was telling me, it seemed like she was ready to die now.

Estelle stood up and began to walk toward the door. "Well, I should go. Maddi is waiting."

"Estelle? You were Dr. Walker's third patient. Do you know what happened to the second patient?"

"He died, dear," she said over her shoulder.

"Yes, but where is he?"

She turned to look at me once more. "No, sweetie. He was injected but didn't make it. You will have to ask Dr. Walker for more details. I'll see you at dinner."

I sat on the bed for a moment after she left, thinking about what could have happened to the second patient. Who was he? Why did he die? I mean, really die?

I headed over to my room, mentally taking note of all of my questions for Dr. Walker. I'd just have to ask. There would be no reason for him not to tell me.

Tristen was on my bed, looking at his phone. I shut the door behind me before throwing myself on my back next to him.

"How did it go?"

I stared up at the ceiling. "She thinks she can hear her mom calling her name through a seashell."

"That's sweet...and weird." Turning on his side, he rested his head on his hand for support. He buried his other hand in my mess of curls.

"She ate her newborn sister. That's why she's here."

"That's pretty rough."

I turned to face him. "Tristen, what if I eat you?"

"You're not going to, Grace. Why do you keep bringing that up?"

"Because! I'm a Zombrid! I eat people. It's what I do."

"No, it's what you did. And you ate one person," he pointed out.

"And an arm," I said under my breath. "How are you not upset about what I did to Sonny? I know you still care about her."

"I do. Of course, I do. But she made it really hard to. She's a mean girl, Grace. Selfish and vain. I tried to change her. I tried to point out her rude behavior. And sometimes she would apologize and change, and I'd have hope, but then she'd do something screwed up like talk behind her friend's backs or make fun of people." He raised his eyebrows at me, and I knew he was referring to my former nickname, Granny Panty.

"Why didn't you break up with her a long time ago?"

He shrugged. "I don't know. I should have. But it's over now. And I like you. A lot. And I think you're going to be fine. You have a freaking bodyguard! He won't let you eat anyone. You're getting the food you need here, so you're going to be okay," he reassured me.

"I need to find out what happened to the second patient," I said, staring back up at the ceiling. I was really talking to myself. For some reason, finding out what happened to the second patient and those other patients at the East Cocos facility would make me feel much better about being here. As much as I wanted to feel comfortable, I still had this nagging feeling in my stomach.

Or was I hungry?

Tristen turned my face toward his. His fingers ran through my long hair before he found the back of my head and gently pulled me closer to him. I relaxed my body, kissing his soft lips once he leaned in close enough. The sun was setting, and my room was quickly losing light. We were finally completely alone.

His hand found my hip and he nudged me even closer. Our mouths opened and moved against each other's, and this was the moment I realized how much I loved kissing.

A sting in my stomach caused my belly muscles to tighten.

No. Not hungry. Not now.

Our legs intertwined; our movements became in sync. I rested my hand on the back of his neck and pushed my body as close to his as I could. I felt him kick his shoes off the edge of the bed before he got up to pull off each one of my flip-flops, squeezing my feet when he was done. He looked up at me, bit his bottom lip, and grinned.

Another ache shot across my stomach, a little sharper than the one before. I gripped my comforter tight until it passed, making sure he didn't notice. I focused my attention on his sexy smirk. My heart began to feel like it was going to jump out of my throat. It was racing at the thought of this moment being THE moment. The moment I could give up my innocence card.

He crawled back onto the bed, grazing his fingertips all the way up from my ankle, to my leg, to my thigh, then to my hip as he gently rested on top of me. He kissed my neck, and I closed my eyes, feeling a tingle radiate through my chest. His teeth lightly brushed against my skin. I threw my head back, allowing him more room to do what he had to do. I bit my lip, but it wasn't for the euphoric sensation Tristen was sending through my body. The throbbing in my stomach had become constant.

His kisses flowed up to my chin, then my jaw, and back to my lips. I allowed my hands to roam free on his back until I found the edge of his shirt. I pulled it up and over his head without even thinking—only that it was getting in the way. His skin was so smooth, and I could feel all the muscles in his back. They were so firm.

A sudden burst of pain emitted from my lower abdomen and my fingernails dug into his skin. A moan escaped my throat from the pain that had become too unbearable to hide. Tristen must have found this sexy or something because he didn't stop kissing me. He let out a low groan, then found the edge of my shirt and began to pull it up.

This was where I had to stop him. "Tristen."

He stopped immediately and looked at me. "Are you okay?"

"Yes. I'm sorry. I just scratched you."

He smiled devilishly. "Um, Grace...I'm totally okay with that."

I sat up and moved away from him.

"What's wrong?"

Grabbing on to my stomach, I tried to concentrate on his face. The room started to spin, and bile began to rise up from deep within. I immediately put my hand over my mouth to somehow stop the gag that was forming in my throat. Suddenly, I could smell a familiar odor. I pulled my hand away and studied my fingernails before smelling them. A delicious scent entered my nostrils, and I started to shake when I realized what it was. I had just scratched Tristen's back with this hand.

"Grace, you're pale. What's wrong?" he asked, placing a hand on my cheek.

I turned my head away. I didn't want him to touch me. I wanted him to get away from me. But sweat began to bead on my scalp. I was getting hungrier by the minute. I needed food, but I couldn't talk. The hunger reached up into my mouth.

Tristen must have realized what was going on and got up to head for the door. A second later, Number One was picking me up from the bed and carrying me down the hall. I rested my head on his stiff chest. He smelled sharp and clean. Tristen followed close behind. No shoes, no shirt. A grocery store would not have allowed him inside.

The nighttime breeze found its way between Number One and me, and it felt really nice on my clammy skin. Number One kept a straight face. He was on a mission. His pace was steady and fast.

"Tristen, stay outside!"

"But, is she going to be okay?" Tristen asked with obvious concern.

"Yes. Just stay here!" Number One ordered.

I closed my eyes, trying hard to keep from seeing the world twist and turn.

"Is she okay?" There was another voice, but it wasn't Tristen's.

"No. She needs food." Number One set me down.

"Here, I've got her." It was Ian. I could tell by his accent.

I leaned against him and buried my face into his neck. I couldn't stop the violent shivers. I couldn't keep my teeth from chattering.

A hand touched my cheek. "Hey, hurry up and bring the food! She's fading out!"

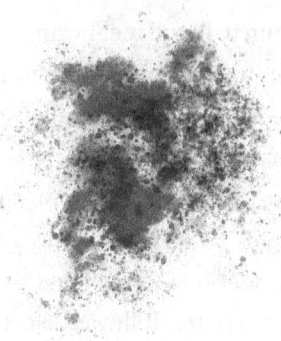

# THE PROGRESSION

MY EYES OPENED. THERE was a hand on mine. A hand that led to an arm, and an arm that led to Tristen sleeping in a chair. I glanced over at my other hand, which had a needle taped to it. A tube from the needle traveled to an IV bag that hung above my head. I was clearly in the Z lab.

I sat up slowly, trying not to wake Tristen. Quietly maneuvering myself out of the bed until my bare feet hit the cold floor, I took the white sheet and wrapped it around myself. I was naked underneath a gray hospital gown, which was tied in the back, but I could still feel the cold air on my butt. Even though there was something covering my body, it still made me feel very exposed.

Luckily, the IV stand had wheels. I walked over to Tristen, who was asleep upright in the chair. He looked so uncomfortable. I thought about waking him, but he was too passed out. Instead, I watched him for a moment. The tattoo on his arm peeked out from under the sleeve of his T-shirt. I never really got a good look at it before, so I lifted the sleeve to study the artwork. The intricately detailed bird rising up from a pool of fire was beautifully drawn, and the colors were vivid and bright. I remembered the night at Eric's apartment, when Tristen shared his story about the Phoenix and the love for his grandfather. I smiled at the fact that I knew exactly how important that tattoo was to him.

I took another sheet off my bed and covered Tristen with it before kissing his cheek. How did I get so lucky to find someone who would want a relationship with me after everything I had done? I was loaded with baggage.

I walked out of my room into an empty, quiet hallway. The lights were dim. It must have been really late at night. Dr. Walker came out of a room at the end of the hall. He seemed to be too focused on a folder he held in his hands to notice me. I started toward him, pulling my IV stand with me.

"Dr. Walker!"

He glanced up and smiled when he saw me.

"Grace, what are you doing out of bed? You should be asleep."

"What happened?"

"Come with me. We'll go to my office."

I followed him back into the direction he came from. Once inside his office, I sat down on his leather couch. He pulled his stethoscope from around his neck and put it into his ears. He sat close to me to listen to my heartbeat.

"How do you feel?"

"I feel fine. Why am I here?"

He pulled the stethoscope out of his ears and wrapped it back around his neck. "Well, you passed out."

"Why? Am I getting worse?"

"Yes and no."

Well, that wasn't vague at all. "What do you mean?"

"You were my first subject, which means that you've had this condition longer than any of the other subjects here. It would appear that your condition is progressing."

"What do you mean 'progressing'? Are you going to send me to East Cocos?" The word QUARANTINE came to mind.

"So, you heard about that. No, I'm not sending you over there. Those subjects are very sick."

"What happened to them?" I asked.

"There was an incident. A minor one. But we're taking good care of them and they should be healthy enough to come back to this part of the island soon. No need to worry. What happened to them won't happen to you."

An incident?

"So, what's going to happen to me?" A part of me didn't want to know the answer to this question. I knew I was getting worse. I could feel it. My appetite was not what it was back home. It was deeper now. The need was getting stronger.

"Let me begin by educating you on what's happening inside your body. As I've explained before, you're experiencing a need for something that you don't have. Your body is trying to replace the part of you that isn't alive. When you get hungry, your brain goes into survival mode. You don't get hungry like I do. You become starved immediately, almost to the point of feeling as though you haven't eaten in weeks. Your body begins to shut down. The same would happen to a person who was starved near death. Only, it would take longer for them to expire. This is why you feel terrible when you are just slightly hungry.

"However, because Serum Z is in your bloodstream, you'll never starve to *death*. Instead, survival mode will kick in. You'll begin to frantically search for what you need."

"So, basically, I could become a zombie who stumbles around in search of human flesh?" There was no way Dr. Walker could tell me this wasn't a scene from a zombie movie. I was a zombie. Period.

"If you're referring to what you see in the movies, sure. I will agree with you on that. You would pretty much act the same way they do. But, Grace, this is real life. And you know I don't like the term *zombie*."

"Would my skin start falling off? Like the zombies in the movies? You said I would act the same way they do. Would I look like them, too?" This was a pretty horrifying thought. I could just imagine my skin sloughing off my body, blood gushing out of every orifice. And my hair! If this was anything like how zombies were portrayed in movies, I would pretty much become bald! Maybe I had ambitions to make people look that way for TV, but I sure as hell didn't want that to happen to me in real life.

Dr. Walker hesitated for a moment before answering.

"Yes. Your body would not be capable of healing. The parts that required the nourishment to stay alive would no longer work, causing your body to deteriorate."

"So once I get what I need, I would go back to normal, right? All of those nonworking parts would start working again."

"Sadly, no. If you get to that point, then it's too late for your organs. And once you get into that frenzied state, your mind will no longer function the same as a normal human. All reasoning will be lost, and the only thing that'll make sense to you is to keep nourishing yourself with what you think you need. Unfortunately, we have yet to reverse this from happening." He sounded disappointed.

I looked down at my hands. "Well, what do we do? How do we stop this from happening?"

"You eat more. And you eat as soon as you feel hungry. It's as simple as that," he said plainly.

"That's it? Won't it just keep getting worse and worse? Won't I have to eat all day long?"

"As long as you get the right quality and quantity, you should be okay for now. The plan is to up your food intake. We're also going to play around with *what* you eat. Maybe serve you something other than boar. We have other sources of food on the island. We'll see what happens then. But that's why you're here, Grace. This is a research facility. We are researching. We're trying to find better ways of dealing with your condition. All of the subjects here will eventually get to the point where you are at now. They'll eventually require more and better sustenance to function at their full capacity. But because you were our first subject, and you've had Serum Z in your bloodstream for a longer period of time, you're experiencing it sooner than everyone else."

"What happened to the second patient? The one that was injected after me."

Dr. Walker got up from the couch and walked over to his desk. He took off his lab coat and placed it on the back of his computer chair.

"He died."

"Why? Didn't you inject him?"

"We did. But he was alive when we injected him. It was part of the research. We wanted to see what capabilities Serum Z had. We wanted to know if it could help someone who was only injured."

"And it didn't," I stated.

"No, it didn't. He died right after the injection. This was when we learned that a subject must be deceased in order for Serum Z to do what it was designed to do. Revive."

"What happened? Why was he injured?"

Dr. Walker leaned up against his desk and folded his arms. "Car accident."

I nodded once and looked away. There was nothing more I could say. I felt bad for the poor guy. He might have been able to live without the serum.

"Will I ever die?" Eric came to mind. If Tristen hadn't stopped him, could Eric have ended my life right then and there? Or would he have just continued choking me without any end results? I could almost see the confusion on Eric's face when he realized after ten minutes of squeezing my neck that I was still alive.

Dr. Walker cocked his head to the side and frowned. "You don't like the idea of being immortal."

I looked down at my hands again. His statement was true, and I felt guilty for feeling this way. Obviously, he was very proud of his discovery of eternal life. Now, here I was, getting fed and taken care of at his island resort-like hospital place, getting five-star treatment, and I wasn't completely on board with it. He probably felt offended.

"Immortality is not for everyone. It's something that should be earned. An offering that should be given to people who deserve it. A person who has done wrong in their life, things that cannot be forgiven, such as murder or acts of violence, should not be given a second opportunity to live. But a person like you or Charlie or Maddi, a person who deserves to have a future, should have the chance to live. You were all threatened to be taken out of this world much too young."

"But what about Estelle? She was already so much older."

"When I offered Estelle Serum Z, I was taking my chances. I wanted to find someone who was nearing the end. And it just so happened that she wasn't ready to go."

I wondered what he would say if he knew she was ready to die now.

He came to sit next to me again. "Living forever isn't about living forever, Grace. It means that there's an opportunity to do every single thing we ever wanted do in life—and then some—without the threat of having it all being suddenly taken away."

It was clear that Dr. Walker was trying to convince me.

"But what if that person doesn't want to live forever?" I challenged. "Is there a way to end it, or are we just stuck here?"

I didn't know why I was so against a never-ending life. I wasn't a very religious person. It wasn't like I even truly believed that there was a heaven up there for my soul to fly up to. I didn't know if there was a golden gate to enter. But it just didn't seem like it was the natural order of things. It didn't seem right. What could you do with hundreds and hundreds of years? You would have seen and done everything you possibly could before it just got too boring. You would eventually end up alone. Your friends and family would die, and you'd stay alive forever as long as you have Serum Z in your bloodstream.

He slid his glasses closer to his face. "A subject injected with Serum Z could live indefinitely, provided that the subject does not come into contact with flames. Decapitation would also permanently end a subject's life."

He didn't even blink when he said this.

"So, in other words, if I catch on fire or someone cuts my head off, then I'm done," I confirmed.

"Yes."

"I can get shot in the heart or choked, and I wouldn't die?" I could suddenly feel the grip of Eric's hands around my neck.

"Essentially, yes," Dr. Walker replied. "Your heart will stop from the bullet or you would stop breathing from strangulation, but after a few minutes, your heart will start beating and you will start breathing again. Serum Z will revive you."

"Why didn't you want me here sooner?" Not that I wanted to be here sooner. But I was still curious.

"Everlasting Paradise is open to whoever would like to live here. I had mentioned it to your mother several times, but she felt she could control your hunger herself. She thought that maybe you could live on eating the already deceased. But that wasn't the case."

I was glad that Dr. Walker was answering my questions so openly and honestly. There was just one more to ask.

"Will I ever have to eat human meat again? Like...*fresh* human meat?" I asked, hoping that his answer would be no. But when he took a breath in and moved his eyes away from mine, I knew what he would say.

"Well, Grace, this was something that I didn't plan to tell anyone just yet. But I trust that you can keep my little secret." He raised his brows as if waiting for me to agree to keep my mouth shut. I nodded. "We've found through our research that you may never need to eat human meat again. It seems that you and everyone else here are responding well to the raw animal diet. Your blood chemistries have shown some very promising results."

I pulled my lips in, trying my best to hide how glad this made me. Really, I was trying to fool myself. I didn't want to be so hopeful. But the thought of never having to eat human flesh again was exactly what I wanted. It meant that I *could* possibly live a normal life. And it was good. It was really, really good.

Dr. Walker patted my hand. "It's okay, Grace," he said with a chuckle. "You can be happy about it. I know how much you hated the idea of having to eat a human. We've just got to make sure that you eat often and enough of recently deceased animal remains to keep you out of that frenzied state. As long as you get what you need, there's no reason why you should ever be faced with the uncontrollable desire to attack a living human being again."

A yawn escaped my throat. I wanted to ask more questions, but my eyes were beginning to weigh down. The fact of the matter was this: I was a zombie. A monster in science fiction film. The boogeyman in a horror movie. The jerk chasing after you that just wouldn't die, no matter how many times you shoot him with a shotgun. I was freaking Jason from *Friday the 13th*! But it was really nice to know that Dr. Walker had found a solution to prevent me from actually *acting* like a zombie.

"You should really go get some rest. It's getting very late," Dr. Walker said as he moved over to the door to open it.

I stood up, thoughts of my immortal future reeling in my mind. I was about to walk out when I felt a slight tug behind me.

"Grace, don't forget your IV stand."

I turned and grabbed it. "Oh, I almost forgot," I said sleepily. "Thank you for getting Tristen here. It was a lot sooner than I thought it would be."

"You are quite welcome, Grace. I'm glad he's here, too."

I smiled and headed off to bed.

# THE LETTER

I YAWNED AND STRETCHED, raising my arms high above my head before opening my eyes. My weird dreams had ended when I came to the island, which was a good thing considering how morbid and real they felt just a couple of weeks ago. I had watched Tristen sleep for a bit last night before finally dozing off. Maybe that gave my mind some kind of peace.

Muffled sounds of people's voices echoed from the other side of the closed door to my room. I glanced over at the chair Tristen had been sleeping in, only to find that he wasn't there. Maybe he got hungry and went to find something to eat.

Speaking of something to eat...

As if on cue, a knock came from the door before a plumply-built nurse walked in, wheeling a tray of food.

"Good morning, Grace!" the nurse boomed. "How did you sleep?"

I sat up. "I slept okay. Do you know where Tristen went?"

"I've got some delicious breakfast for you. You're really going to love this," she said enthusiastically, wheeling the tray closer to me and hovering it just above my thighs. Did she even hear what I asked her?

"Thank you."

She uncovered the tray, and it was as if I was suddenly in some kind of trance. The plates were piled high with slabs of raw meat and sausage-looking links. There was also a bowl of what looked like tomato soup with noodles, the smell of which sent my senses into overdrive. It was, without a doubt, the same exact smell from the night I ended my beloved friend Phoebe's life. It was sweet and bitter, coppery and rich.

I couldn't wait a minute longer to tear into the irresistible cuisine that stared back at me. It was calling to me, whispering an order for me to take my first bite. And when I finally did, when the first tepid piece rested on my tongue, I drifted off into that faraway place again. That land where nothing else mattered, where every single thing in my life seemed like a million miles away from my reach, and I didn't care.

The fact that it was lukewarm did not bother me one bit. I felt the velvety texture in every chew, sliding down my throat before finding its home inside my ravenous stomach. The volume of the sounds around me slowly began to rise, allowing me to hear the drip of the IV splashing down in the bag, pages turning on the nurse's desk outside my room, and footsteps crunching on the dry grass in the courtyard outside.

My eyes were closed, but I could see tiny glowing flecks floating around as if it were being viewed through a microscope. My skin started to tingle with the mixture of the warmth from the light streaming in through the window and the coolness of the air flowing out of the vents of the Z lab. And before I knew it, I was reaching for food that wasn't there anymore.

I opened my eyes to Dr. Walker standing at the foot of my bed, reading my chart.

"How was your breakfast?" he asked without looking up.

I gently pushed the tray to the side and adjusted myself. "It was..." I couldn't quite find the words.

"Filling?" he finished.

"Yes."

"Good. We served you something different today. Something that your body really needed."

"What was it?" I asked, hesitant to know the answer. When I first had the boar, I thought it definitely came from a human. It tasted almost terrifyingly the same. But what I'd just eaten—it certainly wasn't boar. It was better. A million times better.

Could it have been human?

I stood firm on my decision to have a human-free diet. And even though I felt like there was something off about this place and Dr. Walker, I believed what he told me last night. Why would Dr. Walker lie about his research? He'd worked so long on it. Plus, where would he get fresh human from, anyway? Maybe what I'd just consumed was a different animal. A monkey or something. I wouldn't have wanted to eat a cute little *Curious George*, though. That thought kind of made me sad.

"Well, it's a special kind of animal indigenous to the island. It provides a lot of nutrients and proteins, exactly what your unique circumstances require," he explained. He walked over to my IV stand and squeezed the bag. He ran a hand down the line that led to the needle inside the top of my hand. "I think you are about ready to get back to Laguna."

I was relieved. The Z lab was not one of my favorite places. As a matter of fact, I would have liked to stay as far away as I could whenever it wasn't testing time. Besides, I wanted to get back to Tristen.

"Do you know where Tristen is?" I asked. He had to be waiting for me in my suite.

Dr. Walker didn't answer right away. He worked on getting the IV out of my hand. Once he was done, he stood next to my bed and stared at me a moment. I was beginning to feel like he was going to tell me something horrible—like I only had a day to live. I was against immortality, but I wasn't ready to die just yet, either.

"Grace," he began. I held my breath. "Unfortunately, Tristen had to leave."

"What? Why?" That didn't make any sense. How could he just pick up and leave? It wasn't like he lived on the next island over.

It took days to get back home, and he wouldn't just leave without telling me goodbye.

"It seems that his family no longer approves of his visit here. I had a lengthy conversation with his mother last night, which ended in our decision to get him on the next boat out as soon as we could."

There was sincerity in Dr. Walker's tone. His voice was soft and almost at a whisper. I stared down at my fidgeting fingers, trying to understand why his family would make him leave so suddenly. He was here for only a day. If they didn't want him here, why would they have let him come in the first place?

Dr. Walker pulled a folded piece of paper out of the pocket of his lab coat. "He wanted me to give you this."

I stared at it as he handed it to me, hesitant to take it from him. But that uncertainty only lasted a minute. I snatched the piece of paper out of his hands and opened it. I didn't care if Dr. Walker was standing beside me, watching.

*Grace,*

*I watched you sleep a little before I had to go. You looked so peaceful and I didn't want to wake you. My parents are making me leave, but I'll be back soon. I will text you when I get back home.*

*Tristen*

I didn't know what to say.

I felt Dr. Walker's warm hand on my shoulder. "I'm sorry, Grace. Maybe in the next few weeks, we can contact his family and ask if he could visit again."

I didn't say anything. I didn't know if I was pissed or hurt— pissed that he would leave me such an impersonal letter instead of waking me up to tell me goodbye, or hurt that he would leave me a letter instead of waking me up to tell me goodbye. It was all the same, and it all just didn't make a lick of sense.

I fought back the tears that were stinging my eyes.

"Your clothes are in the bag on the chair. I'll leave you to get dressed so that you can get out of here and back to your room. Nurse Irene will be in to go over your new food intake schedule. Now, it's important for you to follow this schedule," he said sternly.

I nodded.

"Your body is in need of more food. Your schedule will be changing to several meals a day. If you don't receive these meals, your body might go into shock again, and the consequences could be dire. We don't want you to even come close to that state of hunger."

Was that for my sake, or the sake of the non-Zombrids on the island?

I nodded again, and he checked my vitals before leaving the room. I got out of bed and headed toward the window. Scanning the courtyard thoroughly, I desperately hoped to spot a sexy, wavy-haired Tristen anywhere. Maybe I was dreaming. Maybe this was some kind of weird joke Tristen was playing. Maybe he'd jump ship and swim his way back to me because he didn't want to give into his family's demands.

I peered out into the early island light, but there was no Tristen. Anywhere. Only my fellow Zombrids sitting at a picnic table, laughing and chatting as if nothing was even wrong. Didn't they know that the first guy I ever cared about just left me?

There was a knock at my door and Nurse Irene walked in, holding a folder. "Okay, Grace. Let's get you back to your suite."

She went over all of the discharge paperwork with me. Apparently, my food intake schedule consisted of six meals a day, including at least two snacks. If for some reason I missed a meal, I was to report to Number One and he would make sure I got what I needed. If I began to feel any symptoms, such as increased fatigue, fainting, nose bleeds, ear bleeds, nausea, vomiting, diarrhea, or migraines, I had to report to the Z lab for immediate attention and treatment. My testing schedule would remain the same until further notice from Dr. Walker.

When she was finished with all of her medical jargon, I quickly got dressed so that I could get the hell out of there to check my emails and my phone. The refreshing warm breeze flowed through my curls as I stepped out into the courtyard. Physically, I felt like a million bucks! All five of my senses were heightened at maximum levels. My stomach was full and satisfied—the same exact way it felt after I did what I did to Phoebe.

It was still so hard to admit I'd eaten her.

I practically jogged across the green grass. The tears were still threatening to surge out of my eyes. I just couldn't believe that Tristen would leave a note instead of telling me goodbye face to face.

"Hey, Grace! Want to come hang out with us?" I heard Destiny's voice coming from my left, but I didn't stop. I shook my head harshly and continued on my way. I didn't have time to stop. I had to call Tristen.

Number One stood at the door as I approached my room. Before I could twist the knob to enter, he gently grabbed my arm.

"Grace, is everything okay?" he asked. He was clearly concerned.

I nodded, afraid to look up at him because if I did, I wouldn't be able to hold back the tears any longer. I stared down at the knob, waiting for him to get the hint and just let go. His heartfelt stare bore a hole in my face. He wasn't stupid. He knew something was wrong. And it bothered him.

He finally let go, and I instantaneously pushed open my door and shut it behind me. I lunged over to my computer, holding back the profanity that nearly escaped my throat when it decided to take its sweet-ass time to load up. And when it finally did, there was nothing.

Damn it!

Now, I was more pissed than anything. Where was my damned phone? I rummaged through my purse, throwing everything that was not my phone out all over the bed.

Got it!

I unlocked the screen. No missed calls. No messages. I dialed his number. Straight to voicemail. Taking a deep breath in and exhaling a big breath out, I plopped down on the edge of my bed, allowing my broken heart to bleed.

# THE ITALIAN

IT JUST DIDN'T ADD up. He was here for barely a day. He said that his mom was okay with it. That his mom talked to my mom and—

I interrupted my own thoughts and dialed my mother's number. I wasn't very happy about giving in to speaking with her, but I needed to know if she'd heard anything.

"Gracie?" I could hear the smile in her voice.

"Mom, have you heard anything from Tristen or his parents?" I wasn't beating around the bush. This wasn't the time to make small talk.

"Is everything okay, honey?"

"Yes. Just...have you heard anything from them?"

"Well, no. The last time I spoke to Mrs. Miles was the day Tristen left to be with you. Is he not there? What's going on?" She was concerned.

Shit!

"Nothing. He...he had to go. And I was just wondering if you'd spoken to his mom because apparently, she didn't want him here anymore."

"I don't know what to say, Gracie. Maybe she just changed her mind. Would you like me to call her and find out more information?" She was being super nice—maybe even overly nice. I could hear it in her tone. She missed me. But that didn't matter right now. And

I certainly wasn't ready to make amends with someone who lied to me my whole life.

But my heart stung a little. I missed her, too.

"No. No, don't worry about it. He just left this morning. I'm sure he'll call as soon as he can."

"Okay, honey. How are you feeling? Is everything okay? I'm sorry that he left, Gracie. When Mark explained that having Tristen there might help you ease into things, I worked really hard on convincing his parents to let him go. Being alone can feel...lonely. I was hurt and alone for a long time when your dad..."

She stopped. I thought maybe I'd lost her. "Mom?"

Mom cleared her throat. "Are you sure you don't want me to come see you? I can ask Mark and maybe he'll let me—"

"No. It's okay. I gotta go. I'll talk to you later."

I held the phone away from my ear, and before I disconnected, her sad voice said, "I love you, Gracie."

My chin began to tremble as I threw myself back onto the bed. What I didn't want her to know was that it would have been the perfect time for her to come visit. The honest truth was that I missed her. Dearly. But I didn't know how to handle missing her and the hurt she caused at the same time. How could those two emotions even fit together in the same category?

I didn't want to think about Mom. There was a gnawing feeling in the pit of my stomach, and it wasn't hunger. Something wasn't right about Tristen. Why did he leave? Was it something I did? We hadn't been a couple for long, but our relationship was headed into the right direction, I thought. While he was here, he showed no signs of being upset with me or having second thoughts about us. And what the hell was up with that letter? It was like breaking up with someone through text message. Who does that? Tristen didn't seem like the type of guy who would do such a cowardly thing. That alone left me more confused than anything.

And now that I thought about it, if I hadn't gotten stupidly hungry and started gawking at him as if he were my next meal, we might have consummated our flourishing relationship. Maybe he was upset that we didn't have sex. But, again, he just didn't seem like the jerky guy who broke up with girls because they wouldn't give it up. And, anyway, I wasn't going to eat him.

Who was I kidding? I could have totally eaten him!

Did I really think that with my uncontrollable urges, I was going to be able to have a normal love life with a non-Zombrid? Maybe he thought long and hard about it and decided to get as far away from me as he possibly could before he got eaten. Before I could kill him.

There was a knock on my door.

"Grace?"

I got off the bed and opened the door to Number One. "Yeah?"

"Are you okay?"

"Yeah. I just..." I didn't want to really tell him what was going on. Number One seemed to be the only person I could confide in at the moment, but talking about Tristen and my mom was the last thing I wanted to do. "Can we go somewhere?"

He stood up straight before answering. "Where would you like to go?"

"I don't care." I turned around to grab my bag before stepping into the hallway. "I just need to take a walk or something."

I had two options: curl up in my bed and cry myself to sleep or get out of my room. There were so many emotions going through me and I really didn't want to be left alone. But no matter what I did, I knew I would still be crying on the inside. There was nothing I could do about Tristen leaving, and that killed me.

We walked down the hall together, side by side.

"So, what do you do when you aren't watching my every move?"

He cleared his throat. "I either hang out in my hut or work out."

"Oh, you work out, huh? I thought maybe you were just born that way," I joked. I had no doubt in my mind that he spent most of his free time in the gym. I didn't know what he looked like underneath his perfectly tailored clothes, but you could clearly tell his muscles were screaming to get out of them.

"Where is your hut, anyway?" I asked curiously. The only huts I'd seen around here were the main ones.

"It's right on the beach. You didn't see it when you were out there yesterday?"

"No. I guess I missed it." Yesterday on the beach, I was getting a lot of information about my Zombrid ways, so I didn't pay attention to my surroundings. "I'd like to go exercise."

Number One brought his eyebrows together, almost as if he didn't quite understand what I said. We entered the courtyard and I glanced around anxiously. Destiny and the gang weren't around, but I wasn't looking for them. My heart pounded at the possibility of seeing Tristen.

Number One stopped to face me. "Are you sure? There are other things we could do. I could take you to one of the trails or to one of the diving sites."

"No, I want to exercise."

He glanced at me with skepticism behind his eyes before answering. "Okay. But first, we're going to stop in Newport to get some snacks to bring with us."

"Afraid I might get hungry and eat you?" It was meant to be a joke, but I was sure he had to think about that on a daily basis. He was surrounded by Zombrids all day long. And even though I was certain he could take care of himself with his Goliath-like features, he would be outnumbered.

But he'd be one lean piece of meat.

What the hell was I thinking? No, he wouldn't be lean meat! He would be bad meat. Bad!

I cleared my throat, hoping to wipe that morose thought out of my guilty mind. "So, let's go."

We headed over to Newport to retrieve a lunch bag full of snacks. I took a peek. There were a few small Tupperware containers filled with basically the same thing I had for breakfast this morning. The mouthwatering aroma reached my nostrils and I sucked it in with satisfaction. I wasn't hungry just yet, but I could feel my stomach threatening to growl at me soon.

We got to the trail leading to the beach. It was just past noon. The ocean seemed calm today, brushing up against the shore in even, serene rushes. There was something soothing about the sound of the water sliding up and down the wet sand. It reminded me of the lake near my house and the gentle smacking of the water on the steps of the lake's edge. It reminded me of that beautiful night with Tristen.

I lowered my eyes, trying hard not to think of him. But Number one must have noticed because he asked, "Do you want to talk about it?"

"You know?"

"Well, Dr. Walker mentioned that he had to leave."

"Did you see him leave?" I asked, desperately hoping that he did. I wanted to know what Tristen looked like as he boarded the boat. I wanted to know if he looked sad or upset or completely elated that he was finally getting away from me.

Number One frowned. "No, I didn't see him. He left in the middle of the night."

I didn't respond, and we walked silently for a moment. I wished so badly that he would have woken me up. Why didn't he wake me up?

"Do you have an exercise routine that you follow normally?" he asked. I suppose he was trying to lighten the situation.

"Yeah. I exercise all the time. Back home. In my room and stuff."

"You've never worked out before, have you?"

"Nope."

"It's okay. We'll just do some stretches and warm-ups today. Is this something you would like to do on a regular basis?"

I wasn't quite sure, but it may have seemed like Number One was a little bit excited about my interest in exercising. He was usually hard to read. He had an unyielding demeanor pretty much all the time. But I thought maybe, just maybe, there was a hint of keenness in his tone.

I shrugged my shoulders. "I don't know. Maybe."

"Well, we'll see if you even like it. Exercise takes determination and motivation. If you don't have those two things, you'll lose interest quick. You have to *want* to do it," he explained. His deep voice was almost intimidating. It didn't seem too far-fetched to believe that he might have been a drill sergeant at some point in his life.

"Got it." I wasn't completely sure if this was a one-time thing or not. At the moment, I just needed to take my mind off Tristen. I had never exercised before because I just never really felt like I needed to. Mom took yoga classes here and there, but she said it was a way to relieve stress. She didn't really do it to stay in shape. Exercising always seemed connected to losing weight, and I didn't feel like I needed to shed any pounds.

We walked for another minute and rounded a bend of trees. Right around the corner, a row of tiny, brightly colored huts came into view. There were five total, all aligned closely to one another, all A-framed with steps leading up to a porch. And they were truly tiny. I thought maybe it was the eye's perception from the distance, but as we trudged through the sand, closer and closer, they didn't get any bigger. It had to be one single room, the place where he slept. How the hell did he even fit in there?

But even with their small size, they were still super cute. Like little lifeguard houses on the beach. There was an outdoor gym nestled in the sand right next to the first hut, a thatch-covered roof sheltering it away from the weather. Very convenient. When he said he worked out, I assumed there was an actual gym somewhere around here. But I'd guess having his own private little gym area was nicer.

"Who else lives here?"

"This is where the other guards sleep. There's another row of living quarters on the other side of the beach, which is where some of the other staff live. I'm going to run inside and change. Do you want something to drink?"

"Sure."

"Okay. I'll be right out. You can just wait for me right over there," he said, pointing to the gym equipment.

I went and sat on the weight bench while Number One stepped inside of his sky-blue hut. The workout area also had an exercise bike, a treadmill, a stand full of dumbbells, and a few other machines that I didn't know the names for. One was that thing where you sit and lift the weights while moving your arms in toward your chest, then away. Kind of like a butterfly flapping its wings.

Number One was back out in no time, handing me a bottle filled with red liquid. I studied it. "What is this?"

"You haven't tried it yet?"

Now that he was finally wearing something other than a suit—a sleeveless shirt and slinky gym shorts—I was able to confirm my suspicions. He was the definition of fitness. His Herculean physique reminded of a *Marvel* superhero. Every muscle in his arm was beyond well-defined, so much so that I could visibly see and name each one if I wanted to. His shorts cut off just above his knees, but I could tell his thighs were as solid as his arms. And his calves were big enough for me to maybe draw a picture on them. Like an actual portrait. He was a beast!

"No. I haven't tried this yet."

"You should. The others like it a lot. I keep it around just in case someone needs one."

I twisted the cap and took a swig. The thick, scarlet fluid slid smoothly down my throat. As soon as my mind registered the taste, I knew instantly what it was. And before I could take it away from my mouth to protest, the bottle was empty.

"Do you like it?" he grunted as he swung a dumbbell in each hand up toward his chest. I was almost certain they weighed more than me.

I sucked my lips in. Guilt shrouded me. Not only did I love eating human and animal flesh, I apparently fancied blood, too. You could add vampire to my long list of credentials.

I ignored his question. "So, where should I start?"

He set the dumbbells back on the stand and walked over to the bike. "You can start on the bike. Loosen up your legs a bit. Stationary bike training is a great way to get a cardiovascular workout. It's a good way to start if you plan on working out on a regular basis."

I placed my bag in the sand and walked over to him. I couldn't remember the last time I rode a bike. This particular bike wasn't going anywhere, but it was kind of nice to be on one again. I sat down and held onto the handlebars, my feet on the pedals. Number One placed one hand on my chest near my heart and the other on my back and pushed.

"You've got to maintain good posture while you exercise. Keep your back straight and your abs tight," he informed me.

I did what I was told. "Yes, sir."

He left me to do my thing and moved over to the weight bench. He leaned back and lifted the bar up above his head, not flinching one bit as he maneuvered it up and down above his chest. I peered out into the ocean. Wow! I completely understood why he would want his gym equipment to be outside. He probably couldn't fit it in his Smurf hut, anyway. But it was absolutely stunning to watch the light from the sun reflect off the crystal-clear water that twinkled in the distance. The view, mixed with the warm breeze dancing through my hair, made me feel like I was filming one of those fitness shows that came on early in the morning. Number One definitely had a nice set-up here.

"What's your name?" I felt like an idiot having to ask him what his name was after all this time, but anything else had to be better than Number One.

He lifted the bar up and down about five more times before answering. His feelings might have been hurt. Jeez, I was a horrible person. This man was probably trained to stand in front of a bullet for me, and I didn't even know his name.

He sat up and reached for a white towel to wipe away the beads of sweat from his forehead. "Vito."

Good Lord! If this man wasn't Italian, then I didn't know what was! Scenes from the movies *Casino* and *The Godfather* flashed before my eyes. And the more I stared at him, the more I could see him cast in one of them as some kind of mobster.

"So...Italian?" I asked, just to be sure.

"Yes."

"Are you from Italy?"

"No, but I have family there. I'm from New York."

That was kind of surprising. I didn't hear the usual New York accent. I nodded once and looked away, trying to think of another question regarding his personal life before the subject was changed.

"How did you end up here?"

He walked over to the weight stand again and picked up a dumbbell, lifting it up over his head, pulling it up and down behind him.

"You want the full story?"

Um...yes please! Number One...er...Vito barely even spoke. To hear him utter more than two sentences at a time would be a treat.

"Sure," I mumbled, trying to mask my eagerness.

"I was in the Corps for four years. Served in Desert Storm. When I got out, I met my wife and we got married. Had a kid not long after. I joined the Academy and ran the street beat for a while. Met a group of guys who were into diving and decided to try it out. Diving near Cocos Island was a dream for all of us. We had talked about doing it for years until we finally did. And that's when I met Dr. Walker."

He didn't seem very enthusiastic about his story. I really doubted anyone asked him about his life. The only person I had ever seen him speak to, besides myself, was Dr. Walker. The questions were building and building inside me.

"You were a cop?"

"Yes."

"And you came here to dive, which was when you met Dr. Walker."

"Yes. He mentioned he needed security for his facility, so I took the offer." He moved over to the weight bench again.

"You just decided to pick up and leave America? What about your wife and kid?" There must have been a divorce because Cocos Island wasn't just an hour plane ride away. Even if there still was a wife in the picture, he must have to travel often to see his family.

Vito didn't answer right away and sped up his reps. I knew something was wrong. He lifted one more time, holding the bar high above him for a moment before setting it back on its rest. He sat up and leaned forward, wiping his forehead with the towel again. It actually looked like the wind got sucked right out of him.

And then, he finally answered. "They died."

Of course I had to be the one to drum up dark thoughts in someone. He clearly walked around every day with sad memories and the weight of a thousand tons on his shoulders. This explained so much of how Vito carried himself. He was in pain. Constantly.

I expected the conversation to end right then and there, but shockingly, he continued. "It was a car accident. Drunk driver ran them off the road."

My chest caved, and I fought the urge to go over and give him a hug. His sentences were so short, but there was so much meaning behind them. I tried to look him in the eyes, but his head hung low. This man lost his wife and his child in a single day. And even though he was so severe and serious the majority of the time, I knew that somewhere deep down inside him there was a simple, loving man.

"How old was your..." I trailed off. I knew asking this question might cross some emotional boundaries for him, but I wanted to know more about him now than ever before.

"My daughter. She was twelve. It was five years ago."

Holy crap! I was twelve five years ago! She would have been my age. Vito could have been my father.

He stood up and headed toward the treadmill. I kept pedaling my way to nowhere. I watched him start jogging with a perfect posture. His eyes focused intently on what was in front of him, but I knew he couldn't actually see anything. He was most likely remembering his life with his wife and his daughter.

I wanted to know his daughter's name. Maybe somehow I could reminisce about his daughter with him so he wouldn't feel pain. But I didn't ask. He had already revealed so much to me, and there was no doubt in my mind that it was a grueling task for a man like him to show his emotions.

So, we continued our workout together that day and the months that followed.

# 3 Months Later...

# THE BIRTHDAY

EVERY DAY THAT I woke up in my comfy bed, it took me a moment to remember exactly where I was. It was still almost unbelievable, even after three months of being here, that I decided to pick up and leave everything I knew. Everything that was home. Everything that was familiar and comfortable and easy.

Let me rephrase that. I wouldn't say that the days leading up to my departure were exactly easy. They were horrible, actually. And there wasn't a passing day that I didn't think about Phoebe and Eric and Sonny and my mother, even while getting acquainted with my fellow Zombrids and the food and Everlasting Paradise in general.

As for Tristen, I hadn't heard a single word—not a text message, an email, a phone call. Nothing.

I tried calling him, but it would either go straight to voicemail or ring until it did. I tried calling his parents to be sure that he, at the very least, made it back to the States safely. But they seemed to be avoiding me, too. I asked Mom to check up on Tristen for me. The only information she could get was that they had moved, and that was only because she went to their house and saw the *For Sale* sign. I still wasn't really on speaking terms with my mother, but we did communicate at least once a week. I was still upset with her. But I figured, out of respect, she should at least know that her daughter was doing okay. After all, she did help to get Tristen here to me, even if he left me high and dry.

Besides missing home, my life at the facility wasn't all that bad. Thanksgiving and Christmas came and went. It was weird spending the holidays away from Mom. It was weird even without Phoebe. We had always exchanged gifts on Christmas Eve because we were too excited to wait until Christmas morning. And Phoebe was the best gift giver. She always somehow knew exactly what to get me. I thought maybe she kept a notebook somewhere and jotted down ideas throughout the year.

But celebrating the holidays on the island wasn't all that bad. The Zombrids shared an enormous feast in the Newport hut and everyone even got me gifts. I felt super crappy for not thinking of getting anyone anything, but I had no idea they would go out of their way for me.

I started taking classes to finish up the rest of my senior year. The classes were taught by two different professors, both of whom had general knowledge in pretty much everything. According to V (I decided V suited him better than Vito), there were more professors at one point. But since the "incident" happened and most of the Zombrid population had to move to East Cocos, there was no use for that many at the moment.

Mr. Hernandez and Ms. Benson lived in the huts on the beach near V during the week. Other than seeing them in class and sometimes in the courtyard, they pretty much steered clear of the rest of us. Destiny mentioned that they traveled quite a bit to Costa Rica to volunteer and do other types of work. I believed they just didn't want to be around a bunch of starving Zombrids. I wasn't even completely sure if they knew *what* we were.

Apparently, there was going to be a graduation ceremony for those who finished school, which was only Destiny and myself. She had missed a ton of school on account of her drug addiction and homelessness. She only recently decided to even start classes. Maddi was still in grade school. Charlie had already graduated and earned some sort of hairstyling certificate in her past life. She was more or less the resident hairstylist. And a kind of surrogate mother to Maddi. I wasn't completely sure why, but we were still not on friendly terms. I just didn't get her aversion to me. And anyway, she was all about Maddi, which I'd guess was a nice thing. Maddi needed to have some kind of mother-figure in her life. She was still so young.

Ian finished his college classes about a year ago, but he still took some classes here and there. Probably for something to do. As a matter of fact, he and Destiny both decided to take advantage of my gift from Dr. Walker. Every Tuesday and Thursday, a professional makeup artist would come to teach us all about the world of movie makeup. It was beyond what I ever imagined I would be doing. Learning how to apply prosthetics and blending and making plaster molds was amazing! And the three of us had a blast doing it together.

I wanted so badly to tell Tristen all about the class. Evidently, it would seem that he didn't care anymore. Just all of the sudden. Out of the blue. And it bugged the crap out of me! Not knowing what the hell I did wrong or what his problem was ate me up inside more than my growing hunger.

Over the months, I decided that he left not only because his parents wanted him to, but because *he* wanted to. I had read his letter a million and one times, trying to somehow understand why he chose that particular method of communication to break up with me. I was sleeping in the bed right next to him. Why didn't he just wake me up!

Thankfully, between classes and hanging out at the beach and learning about my hut-mates and eating, there was a slight lessening of wondering what went wrong. But just a smidge. Nothing to write home about.

Destiny and Ian did help to relieve some of the stress regarding Tristen. They were both funny and fun to be around. Destiny was witty in a slightly creepy and Gothic kind of way, and Ian was just plain goofy. They were both naturally amusing and not afraid to tell it like it was. I liked that about them very much, but actually felt closer to Ian than I did Destiny. He was silly and laidback and just went with the flow of things. It seemed as though he didn't have a care or worry in the world. I might have actually started to like him.

I mean, he was smooth and sexy and had a smile that could melt your heart. You know, the one where the top lip kind of curled and you either wanted to pinch it, kiss it, or bite it. His accent was alluring and hot. He would certainly be on my list of guys that I would so date. But I wasn't looking for any kind of romance. Tristen was still heavily on my mind, and I missed him.

Destiny seemed to be the gossip queen in the group, and she mentioned to me that Charlie and Ian hooked up at some point. The way they carried on as friends didn't necessarily prove that to be true, but according to the Goth Princess, they were only friends with benefits. True or not, that encouraged me to stay away from flirting or doing anything even close to that with Ian. If we were speaking technically, I did steal Tristen away from Sonny. And believe it or not, I kind of felt guilty about it.

Charlie already hated me, so flirting with her ex-beau would only be motive for a physical altercation. Charlie didn't seem anything like Sonny. She was smart and tough and drop-dead gorgeous. And she could probably kick my ass. Sonny was more or less the typical blonde bombshell and socialite of our town. I could see Charlie as more of the sexy badass leader of an all-women's motorcycle gang, which is why I wouldn't want to piss her off. And two Zombrids fighting would probably get really ugly. Real fast. We might not bite off each other's arms but—

I don't know, would we try to eat our own kind?

My hunger was no longer an issue. There was no more passing out and/or awful pains. I kept true to my food intake schedule by dining on five meals and at least two snacks a day. It turned out that Estelle was on this schedule, too. I thanked God for this, because

I certainly worried about the others feeling like I got special treatment. Plus, it helped Estelle and me develop a nice friendship. We usually met up in Newport to have our meals together.

She was such a fascinating woman! After the usual silence that happened while we demolished our food, Estelle and I would sit and talk for hours every single day. Actually, she would talk, I would listen.

A person has not truly lived unless they've been alive for one hundred and fourteen years. I listened attentively every single time she narrated the story of her life.

She was born near the beginning of the 1900s and had seen everything from the Great Depression to the Age of Radios to war. She was there when Martin Luther King Jr. shared his dream and she was there when the first color film was released. She was involved in the Harlem Renaissance, performing in all-black plays as a singer and a dancer. She flew planes and drove boats—even rode elephants while on a safari in Africa.

She had literally been to the ends of the earth and back, traveling to almost every part of every continent. And somehow, she still had time in between to meet a dashing Navy man during Fleet Week, marry him, and have six children, all of which are grandparents themselves.

This was why I completely understood her desire to die. It justified the reasoning behind why I didn't agree with immortality. There would come a time when an immortal has done everything there was to do. Estelle's exact words were, "I'm tired. I'm ready to take a long, long nap."

I tried to not think about being immortal. Besides that and Tristen, there wasn't much to complain about at this moment in my life. I felt good and healthy. I'd made friends with some very interesting people. And Everlasting Paradise was indeed a paradise.

There was a knock at my door. I got up from my computer, grabbing my bottle of red liquid goodness. I did miss Mom's famous pomegranate juice (which turned out to contain human blood, too), but this was better. Drinking pure blood straight out of a bottle took some getting used to, except it didn't really take that long to get used to. It was sort of like an energy drink for us Zombrids. Ian called it Z Juice.

"You ready?" Ian asked.

"Yup."

Ian and I walked out into the courtyard to wait for everyone else at one of the picnic tables. It was Maddi's birthday, and we had decided to celebrate with presents and cake. There wasn't a mall or a store available where we could just go and buy whatever we wanted, but there was *Amazon* and they delivered to Everlasting Paradise. Dr. Walker must have made some kind of deal with the company because it was no easy feat getting to and from our island.

I learned that Dr. Walker had more money than he could ever count. Apparently, he was a doctor, bestselling author, philanthropist, and founder of a few charities. He was also already wealthy from the beginning, having come from a very successful family. He definitely was not afraid to spend his money, either. He made sure that every one of us had everything we would need on an island in the middle of nowhere. We had cellphone service, an Internet and cable provider, the best technological gadgets, and all of the essentials to make it feel like we weren't miles and miles away on a remote island.

We each had our own money, too. I had money that was put into my bank account by my mother every few weeks, but for the people who didn't have parents or family that could do that, Dr. Walker would give them a sort of allowance. Did they have to work for it? Nope. Being here was more than enough reason to earn an allowance, according to Dr. Walker.

Since we did have money, Estelle, Destiny, Ian, Charlie, and I decided to surprise Maddi with a glass display cabinet for her seashell collection. Not something someone would normally buy a girl turning ten years old, but we knew she would cherish it just as much as her shells. We also threw in some other gifts like clothes and toys to mix it up a bit.

"Hey, when is your birthday?" Ian asked while we waited for the rest of the gang to join us.

"It's June 10th. You?"

"January 29th."

"How old are you?" I asked curiously. I'd just realized that I didn't know how old he was. He had to be in his early twenties.

"How old do I look?"

I sighed. "Really? Estelle is over one hundred years old and I'd have never guessed that if I didn't know. I have no idea how old you are! You could be two hundred. I'm not even sure how this whole birthday thing works anymore."

Ian tried to contain his laughter but failed. "What do you mean? It works like any other birthday."

"Well, yeah. But do we age, or are we like...vampires? Will I always be seventeen?" It may have sounded like it wasn't a serious question, but it was. I really had no clue what the serum could have done to my aging process. Estelle turned when she was already an old lady, but she looked a whole lot younger than she was. Did it stop us from growing older? Did it reverse the aging process? I honestly didn't know if we could be compared to vampires or not. I didn't even know if vampires were real. Apparently, zombies existed in our world. So, why wouldn't vampires?

Ian turned toward me. "Vampires aren't real. Let's just get that out of the way first."

I was slightly disappointed.

"And no, you will not be seventeen forever. You'll still have birthdays. We grow older to a certain age, which is when we hit adulthood. After that, as long as we get the food we need, we'll look that way forever."

"So, Maddi won't look like she's ten forever?" I asked.

"No. She will get to her adult age and stay there. Estelle was already much older when she got the Z. But because she eats what she's supposed to, her body is in great shape and looks like it, too."

I suppose that made sense. Essentially, we were half dead. If we didn't get what our bodies needed, we would just...die. Deteriorate. Decompose.

"Do you understand now?"

"I think so. This is all still just so surreal. It's hard to keep up with everything sometimes," I admitted.

"I know. It's gets easier."

I really hoped it did.

# THE HUT-MATE

THE REST OF THE Zombrid crew came out to meet us at the picnic table. Maddi's braces twinkled when she spotted her pile of presents, but her eyes were set on the big one. It was wrapped, and I knew she was just dying to tear it open to find out what it was.

"Are we ready to sing the birthday song so Maddi can finally open her gifts? I think she might explode!" Ian said.

"Yup. Everyone's here. I'm dying for her to open our present. Well, I'm already dead, but you know what I mean." Destiny laughed at her own joke.

I glanced over at Laguna for a moment and saw V standing on the porch. He had his arms crossed and seemed to be staring straight ahead, but I wasn't completely sure because he was wearing dark sunglasses. I wondered if he was watching us and it made my heart hurt a little. He should be over here. He may have been my bodyguard, but he had also become my friend.

I motioned for him to come over, but he didn't budge. I jogged over.

"Hey. Come and join the party."

"No, thank you. I'll just stand here and watch."

"But why? It's not like they aren't your friends, too. You may not talk to them all the time, but you live here with them. Come on," I pleaded. "I'm sure Maddi wouldn't mind one more person at her party."

I grabbed his hand and pulled, surprising myself when I managed to get a few steps forward out of him. It was probably the Z Juice. Zombrids get pretty strong when they have what their bodies needed. I always kind of had a feeling but proved it to be right the other day when we were playing volleyball on the beach and I served the ball clear over everyone's head. It landed about ninety yards behind them in the sand. Ian was so impressed by how far it went that he had to measure. According to him, that was farther than most quarterbacks threw a football.

V resisted at first but quickly gave in and allowed me to link my arm with his. He walked with me like a gentleman. An image of V walking me down the aisle to give me away to my husband-to-be flashed in my mind. I gazed up at him right as he looked down at me, and there was a smile. A minute smile, but it was still a smile.

He was the closest thing to a father I've had in a long, long time.

"I make you do these things because I care, V."

"I know."

We got back to the table and sang to Maddi. After all the clapping, Estelle cut the birthday cake and handed out slices while Charlie prepared the presents for Maddi to unwrap. A piece of cake was handed to me, and I turned to hand it to V.

"Um...no, thank you. I'm fine."

It took me a moment to understand why V would refuse a slice of the decadent dessert. Then, I finally realized that it wasn't made with the normal ingredients regular people used.

"Oh God! I'm sorry. I totally forget sometimes that you aren't a Zombrid."

"It's okay."

I licked icing off my finger. "What do you think about us, anyway? I've never asked you that before." I spoke low and in his direction. I didn't want the group to listen in and put V in the spotlight.

"Nothing really. You all are just people with the same medical condition," he said.

"Yeah, but aren't you a little freaked out that we are Zombrids?"

He pursed his lips as if pondering the question.

"No. You're still human. You're still you, just with a medical condition. And I'm paid to watch over you, no matter what you are."

That probably would have hurt my feelings if it weren't for the fact that over the past few months, V and I had grown quite fond of each other. He did his job, which was to watch my every move to make sure I was safe and fed. And I made sure to make him feel included when the group did things like this.

I had learned that since my Zombrid blood was the oldest on the island, it was practically sacred. This was why V protected me. At first it was because I was new to the island and he was just making sure that I was getting used to Everlasting Paradise. But then, Dr. Walker had asked me if I wouldn't mind giving blood for the purpose of studying it. Apparently, he was using my DNA as a sort of footprint to further his research.

But V wasn't just my bodyguard. Our friendship had grown. I invited him for walks on the beach and to come help me with homework all the time. We exercised and talked about life. I even put him through long hours of venting about Tristen. It was probably torture for him, but he did give me some great advice.

"Grace," he had said, "you have too much to look forward to be hung up on one guy. If it was meant to be, it will be. But you should really focus on what you have now."

It was an easier-said-than-done type of advice, but I appreciated that he was even listening long enough to offer some guidance. He had a tough exterior, but he was a gentleman on the inside. He was an intelligent person who missed his family dearly. And I didn't care how much he pretended to only be interested in doing his job. Everyone needed someone.

I often tried to convince him to speak to Robin, the receptionist on the first floor of the Z lab. V was intimidating and closed off, but he was still an attractive man. And judging from Robin's reaction every time she laid eyes on him, I got the feeling that there was some kind of chemistry between the two of them. He never mentioned anything about being with other women after his wife passed, but it had been five years. I just knew he needed a companion—no one could go that long without someone.

"I think you like me more than you want to admit," I teased.

"Maybe. Or maybe you're just a pain in my ass." He didn't smile, but I knew it was a joke. One day, I would get him to show some teeth.

"Oh my gosh! I love it!" Maddi stood next to her gift, smiling as wide as her face would let her.

"You can display your seashells now. And it even has a lightbulb inside!" Charlie was just as excited as Maddi was.

Ian glared at Destiny. "You didn't order the one with two light bulbs?" he chided.

"You better be joking."

"That's it. Destiny will never be in charge of the gifts again," he announced, smiling.

Destiny slapped Ian on the back. "How about I chop off your balls and—"

"Okay!" I interrupted, attempting to stop Destiny's vulgar language at a child's birthday party. "Why don't we watch Maddi open the rest of her presents?"

After Maddi viciously tore open her other gifts, V and Ian helped carry the display case back to Maddi's room. Charlie followed and stayed with Maddi to help her get all her seashells in place. Estelle went back to her room to relax.

Ian and V came back, and the four of us sat at the picnic table to pick off the rest of the birthday cake. Well, except V.

"Hey, mate. Do you want some cake?" Ian asked V.

"No, thank you."

"He isn't a Zombrid, dumbass!" Destiny jeered.

"Hey, you never know. Maybe he *likes* eating raw meat and guts."

"Um...no. Regular people would get really sick," I pointed out. They all nodded in agreement.

"But it's so good!" Destiny cried out.

"Oh please. You haven't even had the real thing," Ian scoffed with a mouthful of cake.

I looked over at Destiny in disbelief. "Destiny, you've never eaten human meat before?"

Okay, I still couldn't get used to saying anything with the words *eat* and *human* in the same sentence. And the fact that Destiny had never eaten human meat before was kind of surprising. I assumed that every Zombrid here did at one point. I would have guessed that maybe that was the reason why most of us were here. Our uncontrollable urges caused us to do something we shouldn't have done—like eat a human. And Dr. Walker sort of...saved us. But now that I thought about it, Destiny and Estelle were brought to the island immediately after they turned.

"No," she said as if to regret it. "Remember, I came here right when I was revived. So I've been eating boar and animal carcass ever since."

"What about you, Patient Zero? Have you had your taste yet?" Ian asked with a devilish grin.

My heart began to race. It had been months since I spoke out loud about what I'd done. I didn't even know if V knew the whole story, and I was kind of embarrassed to reveal it to him. I felt it would disappoint him, which was something I was terrified of doing for some reason.

I shrugged my shoulders as if it were no big deal. "Yeah, I have."

"Well, what happened?" Destiny asked. Of course, the Gossip Queen wanted to know.

I looked down at my hands. "I...I got into a fight with someone and bit her arm." I shoved a piece of cake into my mouth immediately after I said it.

"That's not so bad! She's still alive, right?"

"Yes. She's still alive. But then I...ate my best friend later that night."

I glanced over at V and his eyes met mine. I couldn't quite make out what I saw behind them, but for some reason, it felt like there was a magnet pulling me toward him. I fought the urge to run over into his arms. It was weird, but I wanted him to comfort me.

"Holy hell! You killed your BFF?" Destiny blurted out. "Don't they make crime shows about that?"

"Never mind the best-friend part. You got two meals in one night! That takes skill," Ian said, seemingly impressed. His comment pissed me off, though. It definitely wasn't a skill.

Destiny must have read my expression because she smacked him on the arm, knocking onto the ground the spoonful of cake that he was getting ready to put into his mouth.

"What? I'm not making a joke! It's tough to get a decent meal out in the real world when you are starving the way we always are. Grace, no offense. Really. I know it must have been hard for you," he said apologetically.

I didn't respond.

"What about you? Have *you* had a taste?" Destiny asked Ian, trying to match his rudeness.

"Yes. I have."

There was silence.

"Well?" she said, nearly shouting.

Ian opened his mouth but instead of spilling the beans about his first taste of human flesh, he looked up above my head and narrowed his eyes.

"Uh, oh. We've got fresh meat."

Destiny and V both gazed up. I turned around to look up at the balcony of the main building. It was where I had my first view of the Everlasting Paradise compound upon arrival.

It was afternoon, and the sun was right above us. Its rays of light beamed down directly into my eyes, which made it hard to see clearly. All I could see was Dr. Walker, Number Two, and a girl with bright hair standing near the railing of the balcony. They were facing each other and talking.

I held a hand over my eyes as if to give off a salute, trying to block some of the sun to get a better view. But before I could focus, they moved away.

"Where'd they go?"

"They're coming down the stairs now. Dr. Walker is probably giving her a tour."

I caught glimpses as they descended down the spiral stairs carved out of the cliff. Dr. Walker was first, followed by the girl who was wearing strappy heels and a really short jean skirt. Her long, tanned legs climbed down the steps effortlessly, and I instantly grew jealous of how gracefully she walked. Like a supermodel owning the catwalk.

As they stepped into the courtyard, I now had a better view of her wavy blonde hair. It reached the middle of her back and looked as though she had just left the beauty salon. A long, pink sweater draped her shoulders, hiding her arms underneath. Huge black sunglasses nearly covered her entire face. All I could see were her pouty, hot-pink lips.

Was this chick a movie star?

"Who does she think she is?" Destiny muttered.

"I don't know, but she is pretty hot," Ian remarked.

As they walked closer, Dr. Walker began his tour and pointed to the different huts. He then glanced over at us and mouthed something to the girl. My heart started racing, and I could feel the anxiety start to creep up from my toes to my throat.

As Dr. Walker and the girl strolled over to us, my breathing changed into short, quick pants.

There was no way.

"And these are some of your fellow hut-mates."

"Hi." I heard Destiny behind me.

"Hello." Ian followed.

Then V. "Miss."

Dr. Walker looked at me, expecting a greeting for our new hut-mate. But the words couldn't form in my mouth. The girl smiled wide and pulled off her enormous sunglasses.

"Hello, Grace. Did you miss me?"

# THE KILLER

I TRIED TO SAY something. Anything.

"Grace, you remember Sonny Westwood?" Dr. Walker asked. His voice was calm. *He* was calm. How could he be calm? This had to be a joke. A sick, cruel joke.

"Of course she remembers me, Mark. I'm unforgettable."

"I...I have to go." I turned on my heels and bolted.

"Grace!" I heard V call my name, but I didn't care. I had to get as far away as I could. Was I being a coward? Yes! But what the hell was I supposed to do? You know how they say your past eventually catches up to you? Well, it did. And sooner than I thought it ever would.

I ran past the Laguna hut. I really didn't feel like sitting in my room. That was basically an open invitation for someone to come knocking at my door to make sure I was okay. And I was far from okay. How could Dr. Walker do this? She hated me. I hated her, too. I hated her because she hated *me* so much. And I didn't even know why she hated me!

She hated me now because I bit her and took Tristen away from her, which ended up being a waste of everyone's time. We didn't even stay together. But why did she hate me before that? We had known each other for a long time, since grade school, but we never got along. I didn't even think we ever tried to get along. It was a hate/hate relationship for as long as I could remember.

I ran down the sandy trail to the beach, stopping right before I reached the watery shore. I let my breath catch up as I glanced around, realizing that this was just another place someone could come looking for me. Searching for some kind of hiding spot, the forest next to the retreat caught my eye. There was a trail leading into a wall of green foliage. When I reached the entrance to the rainforest, I followed the dirt trail. This was actually the first time I'd ventured outside of Everlasting Paradise and the huts. Some of the others went on hiking trips, but those were the days I decided to stay behind to hang out with V.

It was a really humid day and the smell of rain was in the air. I could feel the warmth radiating off the plants and trees that were on either side of the narrow footpath. The ferns towered over me. I had never seen leaves so big. I could probably curl up inside of one and use it as a blanket.

If I was claustrophobic, I'd probably be having an anxiety attack by now. The jungle had become very dense, and it was nearly impossible to see anything through the trees. I slowed down when I reached a weird-looking bridge. There were white balls hanging down, sort of like volleyballs suspended from wires. It was made out of metal, but it still didn't look very sturdy. Thankfully, the bridge didn't cross a two-hundred-foot cliff over water or anything. It was a cross-bridge for a narrow, shallow river. Its architectural shape reminded me of the Golden Gate Bridge. A metal plaque was welded to the frame and read GENIUS RIVER BRIDGE, MADE WITH MARINE DEBRIS.

I didn't know what that was about, but I stepped onto it and started walking across, grasping tightly to the railing when the wooden planks under my flip-flops began to shake. Upon closer inspection of the white volleyball things, I realized that they were actually buoys. They clanked together with every step I took while the river water rushed below me. It wasn't a long bridge at all, and after a few more long strides, I was on the other side.

I ventured deeper into the jungle, actually kind of enjoying the scenery. The trees stood tall, and soon I could smell the aroma of blooming flora all around me. There was a faint sound of raindrops landing on the banana leaves to my right, and then more on my left. And before I could even think about how much it was going to suck getting caught in a tropical shower, the rain poured down. I was instantly drenched. I reached a resting area with a lone wooden bench and plopped down, giving in to the water that landed heavily on my skin.

How could Sonny be here? Or better yet, *why* would she be here? And if she was here, then she knew what this place was...and what I was. To be honest, she had to be an idiot if she didn't have some kind of clue already. I bit and ate her flesh right in front of her face. She had to know that something wasn't right.

"Grace?"

I looked up to find Ian standing in front of me.

"What are you doing here?" I yelled over the rain. The sound of it hitting the plants and trees made it difficult to hear and it drowned out my voice.

"Are you okay? Everyone is worried!" Ian yelled back.

I stood up. "You didn't have to follow me! I'm fine!" I turned to continue down the trail, but Ian grabbed my wrist.

"Wait!"

"What? Why?"

He didn't say anything. I stared at him, watching the drops of rain slide down from his hair to his eyebrows, finding their way around and down to his nose and to his mouth. His white T-shirt was soaked and stuck to his pecs. I looked away when I saw that his nipples were visible.

Then, as quickly as it started, the rain just stopped.

I hastily pulled my wrist away from his grip. "Go back, Ian. I just wanna be alone for a bit."

"Why did you freak out? Who is that girl?" he pressed.

I started to walk again, hearing his footsteps slosh behind me in the muddy trail. I sighed loudly to make sure he could hear.

"Is she from your hometown? Is she the girl you ate? Your best friend?"

I came to a halt and spun around. "What? No! How could she be? I killed my best friend!" I quickly turned away from him when the tears threatened to fall. I didn't want to start crying in front of him. I didn't want to start crying at all.

"Well, I don't know. Maybe she didn't die. Maybe you didn't kill her."

"Ian! Stop it! Please! I don't want to talk about Phoebe. I killed her, okay? I killed her!"

I saw the exposed root coming out of the ground, but it was too late to step over it. I tripped and fell down, landing hard on my knees.

That was it. That was enough for an official breakdown. Thoughts of Sonny, Tristen, Phoebe, and being away from home all whirled around my head, and there was no longer stopping the tears. They came rushing out of me, and before I knew it, I was sobbing uncontrollably.

Ian lightly shoved my shoulder. "Grace, don't cry. You're acting like a wimp! I know it's tough, but you have to get over it."

"No, you don't!" I stood up, shoved him back, and turned to start walking again. "You have no idea what it's like to kill someone you love!" I yelled into the air. How dare he call me a wimp?

When I didn't hear his footsteps again, I turned around. I immediately threw my hand over my mouth to stop the sound of my laughter. He was sitting in a puddle of mud, completely covered from the waist down.

"Oh my God! I'm so sorry!" I said with genuine sympathy. I didn't mean to push him so hard.

He cocked his head to the side and frowned. I paused, guilt-stricken by the fact that I wanted to die laughing. But he grabbed at his ankle and grimaced.

My cackles immediately stopped. "Oh my God. Are you hurt? Did I hurt you?"

His fake pain didn't last long because not a second later, he started laughing hysterically. I pushed his shoulder and he splashed me with puddle water. I bellowed out the deepest, loudest laugh that had ever come out of me. Our laughs grew and grew, to the point where we were clutching onto our stomachs and gasping for air.

Finally, he held out his hand as if to ask me to help him up out of the puddle. I reached out, and like a naive sucker, offered my hand to him. He pulled with one strong tug and I landed on top of him, causing us both to splash mud everywhere.

I giggled all the way down, trying to remember the last time I had this much fun. I rested my head on his chest, allowing it to bobble up and down against his hysterics. When our laughs finally settled down and we tried to catch our breaths, I leaned back. He had his head lifted above the muck and mine hovered right over his. We were face to face and staring into each other's eyes.

And without another thought, I leaned forward and kissed him.

I didn't know what I was thinking. But at that moment, I was a girl and he was a guy and we were covered in mud. And it just felt... right.

He kissed me back without hesitation, wrapping his arms around my waist. Our mouths parted and his tongue found mine. The kiss was heavy from the moment it started. Our bodies made swift movements, and soon it felt as though there was a tension between us that just needed to be broken. I sat up and straddled his body, pulling him up with me. His hands moved to my butt and squeezed, causing a sensation in me that I had never felt before. I felt hungry, but not for food. There was a voracious feeling in the pit of my stomach. I wanted all of him, right then and there.

He stood up, picking me up with him and maneuvering my legs around his waist. We didn't break away from the kiss. As a matter of fact, the sense of urgency grew, and before I knew it, he had thrown me down on the ground, away from the puddle. The sound of birds chirping and insects buzzing surrounded us as he kissed me with ravenous passion. I found the edge of his wet T-shirt and reached inside. But before I could scratch my nails down his back, he took my wrists and slammed my arms down on either side of me. He bent down and nuzzled his face into the nape of my neck, alternating between kissing and biting my skin. I didn't turn my head. Instead, I fought against him. For some strange reason, it made me feel sexier, and that hungry feeling I had turned into an essential desire that had to be satisfied.

Ian finally let go of my wrists and sat up to pull his T-shirt off. I watched the muscles in his chest and arms flex with every movement. He threw the shirt to the side, and before I could think, he had mine pulled up and over my head. The color of his eyes changed, and he suddenly had a dark, mischievous expression on his face. He came down on me again, this time heading straight for the part of my breasts that wasn't covered by my bra. Thank God I wore the black lacy one Phoebe forced me to buy at *Victoria's Secret*. I could almost hear her saying, "G, you need this! Always be prepared because you never know when some hot guy is gonna rip your shirt off!"

I moaned. The contact between his lips and that area of my body sent tingles through every nerve. It was unbelievable, really. A few months ago, the only person that I wanted near my body was Tristen. Unfortunately, he didn't get that far with me. But if he did, he would have been so gentle. So sweet.

Now, here I was with Ian, the Australian opposite of Tristen. Ian was tough and rough and biting me a little too hard.

"Ian," I breathed.

He wasn't Tristen. I wanted Tristen and Ian wasn't him. Did I even like Ian?

"Wait," I mumbled.

I thought I made a deal with myself that Ian was off limits. If Charlie found out about this, I was sure she would try to drown me in the ocean.

"Ian..."

Sure, Ian was hotter than hot. He was sexy and seductive, and you had to be an idiot if you weren't aroused by him in some kind of way. But I wasn't ready for this. Ian was clearly very experienced at this and I wasn't at all. I wasn't ready to give myself to someone this way.

"Ian, stop!"

"What's wrong?" he asked, but he was still making out with my chest.

I grabbed a chunk of his hair and pulled his head away. "I don't want to do this."

He sat up. "You sure?"

"Um...yes. I'm sure."

"Okay. You say no, then it's no," he said nonchalantly, almost as if it wasn't the first time this had ever happened.

He bent over to grab his T-shirt. I covered up my almost naked breasts with one arm and picked up my own T-shirt. I turned around to put it on, suddenly feeling self-conscious.

"Grace, don't be silly. You have nothing to be embarrassed about. You are hot!"

"Well, thank you. But—" I was fidgeting from his comment and couldn't find the hole in my shirt to fit my head through. He came over to help me.

"But what? Grace, you don't give yourself enough credit. You are tougher and hotter than you think."

"Well, I don't feel like it," I admitted.

We started to head back toward the beach. "Why not? What does any other girl have that you don't? I'm not going to run down a list of things to help boost your ego or make you more confident. You already know what they are. You just have to believe it. Besides, you're a Zombrid! That makes you a badass in and of itself."

"Why do you think being a Zombrid is so awesome? I've killed someone. Someone who didn't deserve to die," I said, hearing the remorse in every one of my own words. I truly hated that I killed someone, let alone my best friend.

He stopped and turned toward me. "You said earlier that I didn't know what it felt like to kill someone I loved. Well, you are sadly mistaken. I do know how it feels."

I instantly felt ashamed. How could I have been so inconsiderate? I didn't even think twice about what he had been through. He wasn't able to respond to the question earlier about whether or not he'd eaten someone.

I stood still and quiet, waiting for him to finally share his story.

"I ate my girlfriend, whom I loved very much, mind you. And she tasted so good that I decided to hunt. Every other night, I would sneak out of my flat to find fresh meat. I got nicked only because my roommate found out and told the police. Everyone thought there was a serial killer on the loose."

I swallowed hard, not sure of how I should feel about what I'd just heard.

"So, you were the serial killer? How many people did you eat?"

He stepped forward and began walking again. "Seven or eight. I can't remember. Those couple of weeks feel like a blur now."

I couldn't believe it! My virginal card almost got punched by a serial killer! I didn't know whether to be afraid and run for my life, or to just play it cool and listen to the rest of his story.

But it turned out I didn't have a choice, because he continued, "I know what you're thinking. I'm a horrible person. But those people that I ate were either criminals or deadbeat assholes."

"But who were you to judge whether or not they deserved to die? Ian, does the rest of the group know this?"

"Nah. Just Charlie. And Dr. Walker, of course. But why do you think I ended up here? I was on a rampage. I was pissed about what I had done to the love of my life. I was going to marry Erica. And

I had to take my anger out on something. Someone. But then Dr. Walker came and changed my life."

His accent made it so difficult for me to read him. I didn't know if he was remorseful or not. His personality was so easygoing. Did he even care about what he did?

"How did he change you?" I asked, truly curious to learn how Dr. Walker managed to affect someone who was obviously so far gone.

"He taught me how to control my cravings and my anger. He taught me how to get past that dark time in my life. He basically told me to pull my head in and quit being a twit."

"You can do that? Control your hunger?"

"From eating humans, sure. It takes a lot of willpower and focus, but it can be done. Dr. Walker didn't necessarily show me how to. It was using my own techniques, but he certainly kept me motivated. We were actually working on starting a class to show the other Zombrids how to control their cravings for humans, but that's when the lot of them got sick and were sent off to East Cocos."

I wanted to take those classes. Right now.

"Will you teach me?" I asked eagerly.

"Yeah, sure. I can do that. We'll set something up."

This made me happy. The fact that we didn't have to have a human-infused diet made me happy. And now this? Also, I'd like to point out that the more and more I heard about Dr. Walker and his interest in helping us Zombrids live our best—and non-murderous—lives, the more and more I realized that he could really be an all-around decent person. I'd always had my doubts about him. There was always a lingering question in the back of my mind, but it seemed everyone here thought differently. They appreciated all that he had done for them and praised him in positive ways.

"So, if you were to go back out into the world, you won't kill again?"

"Well, I wouldn't say that," he said with a wicked smile.

We finally reached the beach. The dread was coming back as I thought of my reunion with Sonny. It was bound to happen. There was no escaping it. But before I could face that music, I had to ask Ian one last thing.

"Ian, why did you stop?"

"Stop what? Killing people?"

"No. I mean, why did you just stop trying to...be with me?"

"Oh, you mean have sex with you? You said no. No means no, Grace. Any decent man would agree."

He might have been a serial murderer, but at least he was respectful of women. But he wasn't getting me.

"No. Why didn't you even question it? You acted like you didn't really care." He might have hurt my feelings a little.

He chuckled and stopped to look me in the eyes. "Grace, trust me. There was nothing I wanted more than to have intercourse with you. But I'm not stupid. You aren't over your ex. You aren't over a lot of things. And you were looking for instant gratification. I was willing to oblige, but the second you stop it, it stops." He was so sure about what he was saying. This might not have been the first he had to give this speech, but it was genuinely convincing.

I nodded. "Well, I appreciate that."

"No problem. I'm not looking for any kind of relationship, anyway."

"Well, neither am I," I shot back.

He laughed under his breath. "Okay."

Ian took a step forward, but I didn't move. "What is that supposed to mean?"

"It means, okay."

"No. You think that if I sleep with you, then I'm going to fall for you. You think I'm *that* girl, don't you?"

"I didn't say any of that. Those are your words, love," he insisted.

I started to walk again. "Oh, please. Do you think you're God's gift or something?" His little remark irritated me. Did I give off the clingy, obsessive vibe?

"Again. Your words."

I shoved his shoulder. "Whatever. I heard you love Charlie, anyway," I taunted. I didn't necessarily hear that he loved her, but he deserved a good teasing.

"Oh, no. No love there—emotionally speaking. She and I just have sort of an arrangement. She needs...special attention sometimes."

"You are such a pig."

"Am not! I just like to have fun. Something you should consider doing," he said while pointing a finger in my face.

I grabbed his finger and twisted.

"Ouch!"

"You need to shut up!"

We approached the porch of Laguna hut. V was standing near the door. I raised my eyebrows at him and gave a slight smile. He acknowledged and nodded. It was a kind of code we had between each other, which indicated that I was okay.

"Speaking of shutting up, what's with that new chick? You know her, right?"

I groaned. "Yes, I know her. She was my first taste."

"Oh, yeah. The fight. And then the arm thing. Got it. Good luck with that."

I rolled my eyes. "Thanks."

"See you later, Grace. Thanks for...everything," he said, giving me a conniving wink.

"Goodbye, Ian."

I walked up the steps to the porch and caught V eying me. "What?"

"What did he mean by that?"

"By what? Nothing. He's an idiot." I shrugged.

"He didn't...do anything to you, right?" he asked dubiously.

Where was he getting at?

"No!" I looked away, but I could feel his eyes burning a hole in my face. "We might have kissed. But that was it." It wasn't the whole truth. There was touching involved, but he didn't have to know that.

V didn't say anything. Instead, he gave me a disappointed glare.

"What? What's the big deal?" I asked.

"Nothing. He's just not the type to date or stay faithful in a relationship."

"Why does everyone think I'm obsessed with relationships?" I snapped. Did I look like *that* kind of girl?

He straightened his posture. "I just don't want you to get hurt."

"Well, I can't get any more hurt than I already am." I stomped off to my room. I instantly felt guilty for snapping at V. But he was dealing with a teenage Zombrid with a lot on her plate. He had to understand. Or at least act like it.

I passed Estelle's suite, then Maddi's, quietly celebrating that their doors were closed. Destiny and Charlie's suites were past my room, so I couldn't see if their doors were closed. I walked lightly down the hall, trying not to make too much noise on the hardwood floors. I was avoiding having any contact with anyone. I just really wanted to get back to my room, shower, check my emails and messages, and maybe take a nap. I didn't know when I was going to run into Sonny, so I needed to make sure I was mentally prepared for her snide remarks and mean comebacks. My nerves were still shaken up just by seeing her. And even though Ian and I had a little tryst that went nowhere, it was still pretty crazy. I almost lost my virginity. I almost had sex! And to a serial killer! I needed to regain control of my obviously befuddled brain.

I opened my door and Sonny Westwood turned away from my computer.

"Oh, Grace!" she shrieked, clutching onto her chest. "You scared me!"

Of course she'd be in my room waiting for me. I should have known better.

# THE TEARS

I MARCHED OVER TO my computer and shut off the monitor. She had been looking at my emails.

"Sonny, why are you here?"

"You ran away like a bat outta hell earlier, so we didn't have time to catch up. I thought I'd come to your suite and wait for you." She examined my muddy body from head to toe, scrounging her nose and wrinkling her forehead as if she'd just smelled something bad. "Wow, you really don't care about your appearance, do you?"

I ignored her jab at the state of my clothes. "No. I mean, why are you *here*? At Everlasting Paradise?" My fuse was already burning low.

She stood up from the chair and wandered over to my bed, glancing around my room with a distasteful scowl before taking a seat on the edge. I watched her closely, still not trusting her intentions. I never could. She just seemed like a girl who could snap at you at any moment, and I didn't put killing someone past her. But she wouldn't kill in the obvious way, like by using a gun or a knife. She was the type who would slip poison into a drink. A silent killer.

I analyzed her body language and expressions as she crossed her perfectly tanned legs. Her heels were six inches high. Her denim skirt was so short that one wrong move would show off her hoo-haa. Her low-cut shirt showed off her cleavage. The only modest article of clothing she wore was the sweater that was still draped over her shoulders.

"Do you want me to start from the beginning, when you stole my boyfriend and bit my arm before you ate it?"

Okay, I guess I deserved her sarcasm.

"After that," I said through gritted teeth.

"Well, after you bit me, I went to the hospital. That was all I could remember before I woke up a couple of days later. Apparently, I lost a ton of blood, thanks to you. So I was unconscious for most of the time. When I woke up, the doctor was standing over my bed. And that's when he told me the news."

I was confused. She must have read it on my face because she chuckled.

"Oh, what, did Tristen not tell you?"

"Tell me what?" The worried butterflies in my stomach began to fly in all directions.

She unbuttoned the top part of her sweater with one hand and let it slide down her shoulders and onto the bed. All of the air expelled out of my lungs in a single breath. My jaw dropped, and I was sure my heart stopped for a moment.

She looked down and cupped what was left of her arm. It was bandaged from just under her elbow up to near her shoulder. Below that, there was nothing. There was no forearm. No hand. Nothing. Just empty space.

"Sonny," I managed to breathe out. I wanted to cry.

She smiled. "Hey, it could have been worse. I could have ended up like your bestie and her boyfriend, right?"

"I...I'm so sorry."

Suddenly, she was serious. "Look, what's done is done. I didn't come here for apologies from you."

"But...why? What happened? I mean, I didn't think that I'd hurt you so badly." And that was the truth. I knew I'd bitten a portion off, but I had no idea it was all of her arm. But it made sense—I tend to lose track of time and what's going into my mouth when I was in that mode.

"Apparently, you bit off so much that the doctors had no choice but to amputate. It was too mangled to save. I've had all kinds of surgeries since then."

I wanted to touch it. I wanted to nurture her and beg for her mercy.

"Oh God! Don't do that! Don't give me that sorry look. Yeah, I wanted to kill you at first. I wanted to ask Daddy to hire a hit man to come find your ass and bury you alive. But I've had a few months to get over my anger. Besides, frowning causes wrinkles." She caressed her cheek with the back of her hand. "Like I said, it's done. But I have to say...brava, Grace. You were able to steal my boyfriend and render me imperfect. I'll give you credit for that. Your revenge plot was one to be admired."

"You think I did this to you on purpose?" I snapped, feeling defensive, as if she should know I'd never do that to her. I wasn't like her. Sonny made my life hell, but I would have never devised some diabolical revenge on her—especially something this horrible and cruel.

"Oh, you didn't? I thought maybe after all the years of making fun of you, you finally found the balls to stick up for yourself. That's kind of disappointing."

So, did this mean that she was going to seek revenge on *me* now?

"How did you even end up here?" I asked, still puzzled by how it could have happened.

She stood up and strutted over to the sliding glass door. Her half-arm dangled, and although there was a part of her literally missing now, she still somehow looked like the Perfect Sonny I left back in New Orleans.

"After finding out that I no longer had my arm, I was mortified. I mean, how the hell was I supposed to be me without it? How was

I supposed to get dressed and drive and shop? I know there are people out there who function without body parts, but come on! I'm not one of those people," she said with disdain. "Then, one day, Dr. Walker showed up in my hospital room. He told me who he was and said that he could fix my arm for me if I really wanted it. He said that he was an experimental doctor and blah, blah, blah. But the only way to fix it was by injecting me with a serum."

What?

"Wait!" I stood up. "He gave you the serum? But how? You have to be—"

"Dead. I know." She laughed. "Do you think I'm stupid or something? He told me everything. Everything about this island and what you and your little Zombrid friends are."

"But you didn't die. And he couldn't give it to you if you were alive because it would kill you." None of it made sense. Dr. Walker specifically told me that the second patient died from the injection because he wasn't dead. So how...unless...

It was like a lightbulb lit up above my head and Sonny could see it.

"Ding, ding, ding. You got it!" Her eyes widened and whispered, "I died."

I was more confused now than I had ever been in my life. I shook my head, not understanding where she was getting at.

"I wasn't dead initially, but when Dr. Walker said he could help me and explained that the serum can only work on a dead person, that's when I decided to die," she said, shrugging her shoulders as if it were no big deal.

"Do you realize what this means? This means that you're a zombie, Sonny. This means that you'll have to eat raw things and be hungry all the time. You don't want to be that way," I warned her.

She smacked her lips. "Please. You don't know what I want, Grace. Besides, I can't have one arm for the rest of my life. Dr. Walker is going to attach a new arm, and because we have superhuman healing abilities or whatever, it's going to be like nothing even happened."

"How do you know?"

"Because he showed me. It's happened before to one of his subjects."

I briefly wondered who. Was it someone in our group?

She sighed as if bored. "Anyway, I'm a Zombrid now, too. I get to live forever and look this beautiful for a long time."

I rolled my eyes. "Sonny, this is not a gift. It's actually horrible."

"God, you're such a drag! I knew there was a reason why I never liked you."

I was pissed now.

I sat down in my computer chair. "You know, while we're on that subject, why do you hate me? What did I ever do to you? Besides what I did recently."

Sonny flipped her perfectly blown-out hair. "Oh, don't play dumb. It doesn't look good on you."

"What are you talking about?" I asked, seriously confused.

"Don't pretend like you don't remember what you did in fifth grade."

"Sonny, I have no idea what you're talking about." I quickly scoured my brain, sifting through my life as a fifth grader.

"Seriously? You don't remember choosing Phoebe over me to be on your team at recess when we were playing dodge ball?"

I flailed my arms out in disbelief. "What? I don't even remember being friends with you!"

"Yeah, because you and Phoebe were all popular and wouldn't even give anyone a chance to be your friend."

Sonny had to be joking. This was all just a sick prank that the other Zombrids were playing on me. It had to be. Me and Phoebe popular? We weren't popular. Sonny was popular!

I shook my head. "Sonny, I really don't remember that. Me and Phoebe were just...me and Phoebe. I didn't know you wanted to be our friend."

"Well..." She adjusted her skirt and attempted to pulled it down at the hem, as if she suddenly felt self-conscious and exposed. But it was far too short to cover anything. "You really hurt my feelings. I wanted to be, you know, cool and fun like you guys."

She was pouting. And she genuinely seemed hurt by the neglect. Hell must have frozen over. Or maybe Phoebe and I were so wrapped up in our own best-friend bubble that we didn't realize we were hurting people. I wondered how many other girls tried to be our friend, and it made me flinch with guilt. I didn't want to be the snobby jerk. And I knew for a fact that Phoebe didn't, either.

"I'm sorry, Sonny," I apologized. "We didn't mean to be... mean."

She waved her hand, dismissing my plea for forgiveness. "Whatever. Getting dissed only made me realize how much cooler I was than you. You two were so far out of my league, anyway. I mean, come on, you come from a broken family and neither of you were as wealthy as me. You're also kind of a nerd and your clothes are frumpy, at best. Is it really a surprise that we were never friends?"

I bit my bottom lip and cursed myself for almost falling for her fake-ass attempt at being a decent human being.

"How could you be so shallow? Even after everything that you've been through?"

"Yeah, and it was all your fault! Everything was fine before. I had Tristen and my girls and my arm! And then you came traipsing along and stole him from me!"

I stood up and moved closer to her. "I didn't steal him from you. He chose me! He was tired of you controlling him and treating him like shit!"

She moved closer to me, too. "I did not treat him like shit! I treated him like a king! He got everything he wanted from me!"

"Well, he didn't want anything from you anymore!"

We were now face to face. There were only inches of space between us. I was fuming with anger and could feel the fury radiating off her body. If Phoebe were here, she would have most definitely knocked Sonny's ass to the ground and started wailing.

But then, the most surprising and unbelievable thing happened.

Her eyes welled up, instantly turning bloodshot, and a single tear emerged from the corner of her eye. It rolled down her cheek, to the side of her nose, and then her mouth. Her bottom lip began to quiver. Sonny Westwood was crying.

I stepped away from her, not knowing what to do. This could be another ploy. She covered what she could of her face with one hand and sat back down on the edge of the bed.

"Sonny..."

"I thought that he loved me," she muttered between sobs. "I-I really thought that we would be together for a long time. At least until college."

My chest caved in with sadness as I watched Miss Perfectly Perfect breakdown right before my eyes. While I felt bad for her heartache, there was also a small sense of relief for the fact that it seemed she and Tristen weren't together. It was something I'd often thought about—that he broke up with me because he realized Sonny made him happier and left to be with her.

"And then he just decided to throw me away. Like nothing. Like I was a stranger. And now look at me. I'm missing an arm. A part of me is gone. Who would want to date me now? Huh?"

She looked up at me with the saddest puppy-dog eyes I'd ever seen. They were glistening with tears and her mascara was now running down her cheeks. I couldn't fight it anymore. Fake or not, she needed a friend. And even though I was far—very far—from ever being her friend, I had to at least pretend.

I walked over to where she sat and knelt down on the floor.

"But you're going to get a new arm, right? You'll be as good as new before you know it."

For some reason, it seemed that statement only made her cry harder. I took my chances and rested a hand on her bare knee. "He did love you."

She looked at me. "How do you know?" she asked through her sobs.

"Because he told me. He adored you in the beginning. But then things just got...complicated. He felt like things changed, but he didn't want to tell you because he didn't want to hurt you."

Okay, some of that wasn't exactly true. I wasn't one hundred percent sure that he truly adored her, but it was what she needed to hear. Her sobbing subsided and she wiped away the smudged mascara. I gave her a minute to collect herself before asking if she was okay.

She took a deep breath and sniffled. "I'm fine."

I got up and sat next to her on the bed.

"We aren't together anymore," I blurted out.

She shot me a look. "What? Why?"

I couldn't read if she was asking because she genuinely wanted to know, or if she was just being nosy. She might be silently throwing a party in her head.

"He came to visit me, but then left a note saying he couldn't stay. And he was gone. And I haven't talked to him since. That was months ago."

"A note? He didn't say goodbye in person? That's not Tristen. He wouldn't do that."

"Well, he did."

"Did you call him? Did you call Diane?" she asked with a sense of urgency in her tone. I assumed Diane was Tristen's mother, and a tiny twinge of jealousy burned my cheeks at the fact that Sonny called his mother by her first name. Obviously, she was comfortable enough with his family to do so.

"No. I mean, I did try calling his house, but no one answered. Have you seen him?"

She shook her head. "I haven't. I haven't heard a thing from him. And I haven't been to school since all this happened. I thought maybe you two were all happy together."

Sadly, she couldn't be more wrong. This concerned me. We all lived in the same vicinity of each other. Sonny did live in the richer part of town, but it wasn't far from where everyone else lived. Sonny might not have been at school, but her minions should have bumped into him at some point. Also, I'd hate to admit it, but Sonny probably knew Tristen better than me. If she said he wasn't the type of person to leave a breakup note, then she was probably right.

"Do you think he made it back okay?" She seemed to be thinking the same thing I was.

"I don't know."

She stood up. "Well, we need to find out for sure. I can call some of the girls back home to check up on things. They can talk to some of his buddies from the team."

"Okay."

"I'm going back to my suite to start calling," she said over her shoulder as she headed toward the door. She seemed to be fine after her little breakdown—like it didn't even happen. I had to be honest, it was kind of satisfying to have witnessed it with my own two eyes. I didn't mean that in a vengeful kind of way. It was just nice to see her function as a normal human and not like some stuck up I'm-so-perfect-and-no-one-can-touch-me bitch.

But now she wasn't human anymore. Maybe dying was actually a good thing for her.

Wait a second...

"Sonny! How did you die? You said that you didn't die initially from your arm wound, right? Then, how did it happen?"

She turned around. "Oh, don't worry. I didn't feel a thing. Dr. Walker injected me with something to kill me, and then he injected Serum Z."

Holy hell!

"He killed you?" I yelled, wishing a minute later that I hadn't. I didn't want anyone else to hear our conversation.

"How did you think I died, dummy? But trust me, it came with a price. My parents were all about the cause and their precious daughter getting a new arm. And now I have a share of Everlasting Paradise. Granted, it's a tiny share, but it still means I own you now. Oh, and that reminds me. I'm going to need you to show me the ropes. You know, like how to eat dead things and stuff. I'd imagine it's like learning how to de-shell a lobster. It seemed like it would be kind of gross at first, but now I'm just so hungry that I could probably eat a classroom full of kindergartners!" She laughed.

I was in such disbelief about the Dr. Walker-killing-her part that I let that last disturbing comment go.

"Have—" My throat was dry and made it difficult to speak. "Have you eaten someone? Like a human?"

"No. But I'm not opposed to it."

"Well, we don't need to eat humans. We can eat animals, as long as they're raw and fresh."

"Oh, okay. Then you need to teach me how to eat that," she demanded.

Was she serious?

"Sonny, it's just like eating anything else. I mean, you've eaten already. Wasn't it the same as just...eating?"

"Honestly, I didn't even remember eating. So, whatever. I'm sure you have things to show me around here. I'm going to call my people. Ciao!" She shut the door behind her.

This had to be hell. I had to be dead, completely dead, and this had to be some version of hell.

How did it come to this? Dr. Walker killed Sonny. But how could he do that? It wasn't ethical. And now Sonny had come back as a Zombrid, and for some reason, wanted me to be her mentor.

Screw hell. I was on another planet. In another life. Inside another universe.

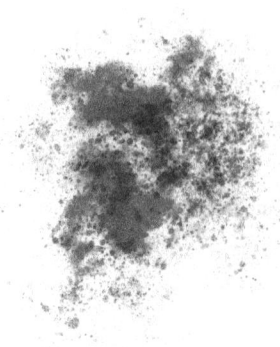

# THE COMPANY

HOW COULD DR. WALKER voluntarily kill someone for money? It was immoral...and illegal! The only plausible explanation I could manage to conjure up was that he was just using Sonny as an experiment for the arm transplantation. Other than that, it made no sense at all. He didn't need her money because he was already rich!

If she asked to be killed, was it okay? Was it okay to agree to something like that? Technically, she committed suicide. But she knew that she was going to be brought back to life, so was it necessarily committing suicide?

And Tristen. Where in the world, literally, was Tristen?

My head felt like it was going to explode. It was all too much to try to understand, especially when my stomach was yelling at me to feed it some food. One thing I had learned over the past few weeks: hunger and thinking just didn't go well together. At least not about something like this.

With a sigh, I glanced at the clock on my computer. It was time to have a pre-dinner snack. Abandoning my thoughts of Sonny's story and Tristen's disappearance—for the moment, anyway—I got up and made my way to Newport, trying to mentally relax on my walk over.

V was standing on the porch, right where I'd left him. At first, I walked past without acknowledging him. But then I realized that he'd been standing there for God only knew how long, so I turned back around. If I couldn't fix my love life, then I could at least try fixing V's.

"V, I want you to go to the Z lab and ask Robin out on a date," I demanded.

He didn't respond and just squinted his eyes at me.

"Take the night off. I'm fine. Nothing is going to happen to me. I'm tired of constantly feeling you watching me. I need a night off, too. I don't care what Dr. Walker says. I don't care if you're getting paid to be up my ass. I don't care if I'm special and need to be protected for medical and treatment reasons that could alter the future of the other Zombrids. I am ordering you to walk straight up to Robin's desk, smile, and take her back to your hut and do... whatever."

"Grace, I don't think—"

"No! I don't want to hear it," I said firmly, cutting him off. "I'm going to have a snack. Then have dinner. And then, I'm going back to my room and I'm not leaving for the rest of the night. Now go!" I didn't want to sound mean, but I felt it was the way I had to be with V. He spent all of his time watching my every move. There was no mistaking the huge crush that Robin had on him. Every time we entered the Z lab, her face would light up like the Christmas celebration in our local city park back home.

I wasn't completely sure if V had similar feelings for her. He was the hardest person in the world to read. But he was a man who was clearly in need of some kind of attention and affection from a woman. She was cute and sweet. At the very least, they could just become good friends.

I stared him down and waited for him to make a move. Finally, he gave in and made his way toward the Z lab, but not without a little speech of his own.

"Grace, if anything happens, you call me right away on my cellphone. I'm going to call the chef right now to make sure he has your food prepared and some backup just in case. If you decide to go anywhere else other than your room, let me know. Got it?"

I nodded. "Got it. Now go."

I noticed his tie was crooked.

"Oh, wait! Let me fix this." I adjusted it and patted his broad shoulder. "Good luck."

He smiled, showing no teeth (one day!), and started walking. I watched him as he marched on, resisting the urge to follow. I knew he was nervous. I could only imagine the butterflies in his stomach multiplying by the hundreds. He had to be mentally preparing himself for this huge step in his social life. He had to be thinking of the right things to say. It was what I did around Tristen in the beginning.

After making sure that he made it inside the Z lab, I carried on with my mission. I had to get to the mess hall to eat some grub.

Estelle sat at our usual booth. It looked like she had just finished eating and was now enjoying a warm glass of Z Juice. The chef met me at the bar with my special snack. I wondered what the workers of the facility thought of us Zombrids. Especially the chefs. Their jobs must have been easy. They really didn't have to cook any food. They basically hunted the animal, cut it up, and slapped it down on a plate.

I sat down across from Estelle with my bowl of mashed monkey brains smothered in a creamy, bloody sauce. It sounded pretty horrific and disgusting, but the taste was the complete opposite of that.

After blacking out from the deliciousness, I came back to reality and opened my eyes to Estelle. I was grateful that she was still there.

"How was your snack, dear?"

"It was good. Not enough. Still hungry," I answered honestly, wiping my mouth with a napkin.

She looked down at her watch. "It won't be long before dinner is served. Maddi enjoyed her day, didn't she?"

"Yes, she did. She was very happy with her presents. So, what are you getting into tonight?" I asked, curious to know if she would be doing something other than her usual relaxing and reading.

"I'm just going to relax and enjoy a book. I remember the days when I'd stay up at all hours of the night." She chuckled. "But those days are long gone, and this old lady would rather indulge in a good romance novel."

"You read romance? Do you have any favorites to recommend?" Romance wasn't exactly the section I would run to in a bookstore, but I didn't mind it.

"I read anything, really. But the dirty ones are my guilty pleasure," she whispered. I could feel the embarrassing rush of blood to my cheeks. Talking about sex was the last thing I expected to do with Estelle.

I giggled. "Estelle! You surprise me sometimes!"

"Honey, it's been a long time since I've had anything even close to it! I try to keep track of what's new and reminisce on those days by reading about it."

I felt sorry for her. She was a beautiful woman—even in her old age. It was heartbreaking to think no one has told her that in a long time.

She stood up and adjusted her long, embroidered sundress. "I'm off to my room before dinner starts. I'll see you here?"

"Yes, ma'am. Same as always."

She nodded and left the mess hall. I opted to stay in the Newport hut until dinner was ready. I sat at the booth alone and searched through my phone, checking emails and messages. I was pretty certain we were far beyond over, but I still checked every day. Tristen might realize how much he missed me one day.

Watching Sonny's concern earlier made me uneasy about the whole situation. I was worried when he first left, but after a few months, I got used to the idea that he had really decided to never speak to me again.

Okay. I didn't really get used to it. It still hurt. I guess I just grew to accept it. But it did seem so out of character. And even if Sonny hadn't been to school since all the drama happened, I honestly thought that she would have already known we weren't together. With as much popularity and awareness of other people's business as Sonny had—whether she found things out on her own or from her wannabe groupies—I thought she would have at least heard of his whereabouts.

Where could he be? I couldn't help but worry that something horrible had happened to him. There was no reason at all for him to go missing. He should have been back in the States. Mom did mention that Tristen's house was for sale. Maybe he met his family somewhere else. To wherever they moved to.

An hour passed when I reached level one hundred and twenty on *Candy Crush*. The chefs had just brought out dinner. I heard the door open and saw Charlie step inside. Our eyes met, but she turned away to the food at the buffet table. I watched her while I pretended to look at my phone.

She was such a beautiful woman, but she always looked so angry. It might have been whenever she was around me, because she didn't seem to look so pissed off when she was around Maddi and other people. I found it ridiculous that she hated me for reasons I couldn't help. I didn't get asked to be injected with Serum Z. And even then, it wasn't my fault it worked!

She filled her plate up as much as she could and walked over to a table on the complete opposite side of the room. I rolled my eyes at this. Could her hatred for me be that serious?

"You know, there is room over here if you want some company," I called out to her.

She didn't look up and placed her napkin on her lap.

"Okay. Whatever. Suit yourself. Just seems like a waste to sit by yourself when someone is offering."

Charlie stopped moving and took a deep breath in before standing up with her plate. She came over to my booth and took a seat across from me. I didn't move or say anything because, really, I was shocked. It was like watching a deer in the woods—they'll come closer and closer to you, only if you don't acknowledge that they are actually there.

I looked back down at my phone and let her float to that faraway land of deliciousness while she ate. I didn't want to stare. I felt like our eating time was kind of personal. Once she was finished, which was not even ten minutes later, she pushed her plate to the side and wiped her mouth. I assumed she would get up immediately to leave the table, but to my surprise, she stayed seated. I took this as my opportunity to finally confront her.

"Can I ask you something?"

She rolled her green and blue eyes. "How did I know this was going to happen?"

"What? I'm just asking you a simple question. What is your problem with me?"

She didn't say anything and began picking at her fingernails.

"Charlie, can we please be adults about this? I really have no idea why you dislike me so much."

She exhaled abrasively before answering. "Well, for one, I wouldn't be here right now if it weren't for you."

"How does that make any sense? I was five years old and dead when Dr. Walker injected me. I had no idea what was going on."

She looked up at me. "How old were you?"

Did I just strike a nerve? "I was five. Apparently, I was really sick, and no one could figure out what was wrong with me and I died. I didn't even know this until just a few months ago. So how could you be upset with me about something that was completely out of my hands?"

She exhaled again, but it wasn't out of anger or annoyance. Surrender, maybe?

"I didn't realize you were that young."

"I thought you guys knew all about me before I even came here," I said.

"We just knew that you were the first Zombrid. Dr. Walker's prize."

"The only reason why is because I just so happened to be his first patient. It could have been any one of you guys if it wasn't me. I mean, what if it was Maddi? Would you have hated her, too?"

Her eyes softened the moment I mentioned Maddi's name. She looked down at her nails again. "I could never be mad at her," she said in a low voice.

Her sourpuss expression faded, and she relaxed her shoulders. I thought she was beautiful before, but now it seemed that word just wasn't right. She was breathtaking. Why wouldn't Ian want something serious with this girl? I'd be honored to have her hanging on my arm if I were a guy.

"Then, please don't be mad at me. I don't know what happened to you, but I'm sorry if it was bad," I said sympathetically. I wanted her to know that I wasn't a terrible person.

She glanced up at me again. "No one knows, except Ian. And if you think that I'm just going to be all buddy-buddy with you and confide in you, then you're wrong."

This was annoying. "Fine, Charlie. I'm not asking you to be my best friend. All I'm asking for is a little respect. I'm tired of you treating me like I'm the reason for all the bad that has happened to you, which is impossible because I don't even know you. So, you know what? Just forget it."

I grabbed my phone and stood up. I had enough on my plate. And I already had to deal with one person that I didn't get along with too well. I didn't need any more drama.

Before I could leave the table, Charlie grabbed my arm. "Wait."

She didn't look at me. She shook her head slowly as if frustrated with herself about giving in. "Sit down."

# THE CIGARETTE

"I THOUGHT I HAD it all. I was young, just finished cosmetology school."

I couldn't believe Charlie was going to tell me her story. With the nasty attitude she had been giving me over the past three months, I thought she would never budge. I guess I should have tried harder before. I should have asked her what her problem was a long time ago. I just thought avoiding her would be best.

"I got my own apartment, had my own money, my own car, great friends. It was amazing! Then, I met Josh. I remember being at a bar with my friends, watching all the frat guys play beer pong. He wasn't playing. He was watching, too. Or at least I thought so. Whenever we talked about that night, he would tell me he had been watching me the whole time."

Tristen's face and the night before I left home came into mind, when he confessed that he liked me the moment he saw me.

"We started dating, and it wasn't long before I fell head over heels for him. He moved in with me. We talked about marriage and kids but decided that we were too young and that we'd wait. We had our whole lives together. I got a great job and he was working for his dad in construction. Everything was fine and perfect until—"

I was afraid of what she might say.

"Until I found out I was pregnant. When I told him the news, he didn't seem very happy about it. But I was."

I knew the ending to this story, just not the details. I knew that it wasn't going to end well, and my heart began aching.

She continued, "He asked me about getting an abortion, but there was no way I was going to do it. And the first time I heard her heartbeat, I knew I had to have her in my arms."

I smiled when a nostalgic grin appeared on her lips from this memory.

"Josh finally gave in and things got pretty normal. The months went by, and it seemed he was getting more and more excited about the baby. We moved into a bigger apartment and set up a nursery. My friends threw me a baby shower, and Josh and I picked out names. It was like a fairytale. We decided to name her Susanna, from one of my favorite movies."

That was a relatively mild name. I would have imagined Charlie naming her kid Willow or Ivy or something not so ordinary.

"Then, the day came. My water broke while I was cutting someone's hair." She chuckled. "It was embarrassing, but I was too excited to care. My co-workers rushed me to the ER and Josh met me there. The labor was nothing. I don't know if it was because I was so happy about finally being able to hold my baby girl that I just didn't even care about the pain. I pushed and pushed, cursing my body because I thought it was taking too long. I needed to see her right away.

"But on my last push, when she finally came out into the world, it got so quiet in the room. The nurses and the doctor didn't say anything, and I couldn't hear baby Susanna crying. I looked at Josh and asked what was wrong, because I just knew something was wrong. He was pale and didn't move. He just stood there. I asked the nurses and the doctor what was happening, but they were huddled in a corner with my baby. It took me almost getting out of the hospital bed before a nurse finally came to my side and told me to calm down. I watched them take the baby out of the room, and I started yelling. I just didn't know what was happening and no one would tell me."

My heart was breaking with every word that came out of her mouth. I wanted so badly for this story to have a different ending, but I prepared myself for the worst. She continued to look down at her hands, never looking up the entire time she shared her tragic tale. I knew those tears were getting ready to rush down.

"The doctor came back to the room after what felt like hours. But he didn't have Susanna. I asked him where she was, and he said she didn't make it. Her little heart stopped, and they couldn't bring her back. They asked me if I wanted to see her. I think it was the hardest decision I'd ever made in my life. I wanted to hold my baby girl, but I also didn't want to remember her that way."

She took a deep breath. "But Josh didn't want to see her, and he convinced me not to, either. We went home, and I sat in her nursery for days. I slept in there. I ate in there. I didn't want to leave. Weeks and months went by. I stopped going to work. I lost weight. I had no energy to do anything. I hated myself. I hated that I didn't hold her. I felt like I betrayed my daughter. Like I'd abandoned her."

She looked up at me, her eyes welling with tears. "And then one day, Josh came home and said that he was tired of it. That having Susanna was a bad idea from the beginning and that he was leaving me."

There was hatred hiding deep behind the tears that hadn't spilled over yet, but it was finally not directed toward me. The detestation she held for Josh was more apparent than any emotion I had ever seen someone have for another person.

"I let him go. I didn't fight him on it. I was too sad. But I wanted him to know how horrible he was for leaving me when I needed him most. I wanted him to feel guilty for what he'd done. And I just wanted to be with Susanna. So one night, I decided to do it. I cut my wrists and watched them bleed until I faded away."

You know those really sad *Lifetime* movies that play on Sundays? They're always about broken families or murders or babies switched at birth or something tragic like that. Yeah...this was worse. It almost felt uncomfortable—like there was so much sympathy and emotion running through me for Charlie that all I wanted to do was go to my room and curse myself for ever thinking I had it bad. But as much as I wanted her to stop, I also wanted her to continue. And she did.

"My neighbor was worried about me, so she came over and found me half dead. I was rushed to the hospital and died as soon as I got there. But, apparently, I was in the wrong place at the wrong time because Dr. Walker was there. He injected me with Serum Z without even asking." There was a noticeable anger toward Dr. Walker. I wondered if she treated him poorly because of this. I had never seen them interacting with each other before, so I wasn't sure.

"Does he know that you didn't want to be revived?"

"Yeah, he knows now. He knows I'm not happy about it. Anyway, I was injected and then released. I went back to my sad apartment and my lonely life. I threw out everything that reminded me of Susanna. Now, I kind of wish I didn't. But at the time, I was just so mad and sad."

"So how did you end up here?"

She grinned cunningly. "Well, I was a bad girl."

I was suddenly frightened by what was going to come out of her mouth next. I held my breath.

"Josh decided to contact me one day. I asked him to come over to talk and he did. At first, everything seemed fine. There wasn't any fighting. But then he apologized, and I just lost it. After everything, after convincing me not to see my own daughter before we buried her in the ground, he really thought that I would somehow forgive him. And then he said Susanna's name, and I just couldn't stop myself."

I was afraid to ask, but I did anyway. "What happened?"

She cocked her head to the side before answering. "I lost control. I was so mad that I couldn't even see straight. So I ate him." Those last three words floated out of her as if it were the most natural thing a person could say. "After what I did, I called Dr. Walker and asked him if I could come here. He had offered it to me before, but I had refused because I thought I wanted to go back to my normal life. But it was too hard. Being in a world without my baby was too painful. I wanted to get away from everything and everyone. Dr. Walker made Josh's death look like something it wasn't, and then he took me in. That's how I ended up here."

I didn't know how to respond to what Charlie just told me. First of all, I got way more of her story than I imagined I would. And second, I was even more afraid to piss her off now than ever before.

Ian and Destiny's voices came in through the door. Charlie straightened herself up and wiped the remainder of her tears off her face. She didn't say anything and stood up to meet Ian and Destiny. I didn't know what this meant for her and me, but I wasn't going to question it. I would just have to wait and see.

Maddi, Estelle, and Sonny came in shortly after. Once everyone had their plates full of bloody meat, we pulled two tables together and began our family feast. Except, this type of banquet didn't involve any friendly banter at the table. Before I went into my eating coma, I made sure to pay close attention to Sonny. I was curious to see how she was handling her new-found appreciation for raw meat.

I grabbed my plate, filled it up high, then purposely took my time to get back to the table. I wanted Sonny to start eating first so that I could examine the way her body functioned. How she moved. The way her fingers held on to her food. I wanted to see how much control she had once she started eating.

I sat down next to her at the table. A part of me expected— and wanted—to see her throw meat around and jump up and down on top of her meal like she was a wild animal. After all, she was a very new Zombrid. I wasn't completely sure if eating properly was something we could eventually learn to do. Our brains weren't capable of anything other than focusing on the blood and guts and meat. But if Ian said we can control our cravings to eat human flesh, then we might be able to control the act of eating.

I should have known better when it came to Sonny Westwood. She came from a ritzy, high-end background. Those types of people threw debutante parties and glided across ballrooms with their noses in the air and mink coats dragging on the floor. She sat with a perfect posture. Her legs were crossed, and her one elbow stayed off the table. She had her hair tied back in a neat bun, which wasn't a bad idea for us girls. The raw, warm, and slimy meat juice was not fun to wash out. But how did she even put her hair up with one hand?

She brought the meat up to her mouth and closed her eyes. She still looked like she had that vital desire to eat, just like the rest of us. But she did it with ease. With poise. And with only one hand. A pang of guilt shot through my body while I watched her use the only hand she had to feed her need. Being a one-armed Zombrid could not have been an easy task. With the raging hunger in her belly, it must have been difficult to satisfy it with only one way to scoop what she needed into her eager mouth. But, of course, she made it look like she'd been doing it for years. And it was sickening to watch her.

Once we were done gobbling up our raw cuisine, Estelle and Maddi got up to go watch a *Disney* movie in the Malibu hut. The rest of us stayed behind in the mess hall, including Charlie. I leaned over to whisper close to Sonny's ear while the rest of the group were engaged in their own conversation.

"So, did you find out anything about Tristen?"

"He moved. The girls said that they saw the moving truck outside his house a while back."

"But did they see *him*?"

"Nope. And they don't know where he moved to, either."

I wished I knew. I wouldn't go searching for him, but not knowing where he was bothered me. Sonny pulled out her phone and began thumbing through it.

"Looks like neither of us gets him," she stated under her breath. I pretended like I didn't hear that little comment. "So what do you guys normally do on a Friday night around here? Hey, does that bar have alcohol?" she asked, pointing at the bar.

"Unfortunately, it doesn't," Ian answered.

"Why not?"

"Because Dr. Walker says alcohol could interfere with treatments," Destiny explained.

"But don't you smoke?"

"Yeah, but he doesn't give a shit about that," she affirmed.

"That makes no sense!" Sonny exclaimed.

"Hey, I don't make the rules." Destiny pulled out a cigarette and held it up to Sonny. "Want one?"

"Um...not really." She caressed her cheek. "Wrinkles wouldn't look good on me."

"You don't have to worry about that anymore, doll. You're a Zombrid now," Ian reminded her.

She looked over at me. "Is that true?"

Why was she asking me for confirmation? "I don't know. I don't smoke, either."

"Well, maybe we should. Come on, Grace! Have one with me!" Sonny was excited—like we were old girlfriends trying to decide if we should ride a scary rollercoaster together.

"Grace, you want one?" Destiny asked.

"Please, The Golden Child isn't going to do it," Charlie chimed in, examining her nails.

I was confused by Sonny's sudden interest in my opinion, but Charlie's comment was even more baffling. I knew we weren't best friends just by the talk we had earlier, but I figured the revelation of her dark former life would put us past the unpleasant remarks.

I shot her a look and turned to Sonny, who also shot Charlie a look of distaste. Now this could be interesting. At Everlasting Paradise, Charlie was known as the girl with the bad attitude. Back home, Sonny was the queen of bad attitude. Two Zombrids with bad attitudes could be fast friends or worst enemies.

"I'm going outside to have a smoke. Whoever wants one can join me," Destiny announced and stood up from her chair.

"We'll all go with you," Ian said.

We followed Destiny out into the warm night air. I glanced over at the Z lab and wondered how V was doing. He wasn't around. I thought that could be a good sign.

Sonny took a cigarette and awkwardly held it between her fingers and her lips while Destiny flicked the lighter. She inhaled once, which was followed by a little cough. She inhaled again, this time longer and deeper.

"You like?" Destiny asked.

"Not really," she said, trying her hardest not to cough again. She turned to me and offered the lit cancer stick.

"I'm okay," I said. Smoking was just not my thing.

"Come on, Grace! Just do it. I mean, it won't kill you."

I rolled my eyes. I hated being in the spotlight. If inhaling rat poison into my lungs would stop Sonny from peer-pressuring me, then I would do it. I took the cigarette and wrapped my lips around the filter. It felt strange in my fingers, but I drew in a breath, anyway. I could feel the hot smoke fill my lungs. Gross! Definitely not for me. I frowned, coughed a few times in an attempt to get every last bit of unwanted toxic fume out of my lungs, and handed it back to Sonny. She frowned, too, and pushed my hand away. "No, thank you! No more for me."

"Give me that!" Destiny said, swiping it out of my hands. "Awesome. This just means I don't have to share my smokes with any of you weaklings."

Sonny pouted. "So let's do something."

"I'm up for nighttime skinny dipping, if you all are," Ian said nonchalantly, shrugging his shoulders. I wondered how many times he has offered that suggestion in his lifetime.

"Four girls at one time? Only in your dreams." Destiny snickered.

Sonny unraveled her neat bun and shook her hair out. "No way. I don't feel like getting my hair wet."

"We can go to the jungle." This time Ian had a slightly less sexual suggestion.

"Oh, yeah. Let's go to the jungle," Sonny shrieked excitedly.

"What would we do in there?" I asked. Something about walking through the jungle in complete darkness just didn't seem to interest me. There was no light out there. Our Zombrid eyes could adjust to the night and dark rooms, but what about the animals? Apparently, there was an endless supply of wild boar on this island. And who knew what else was out there. I might be half zombie and capable of taking down something larger than I was, but I really didn't want to put myself in that situation.

"We can hike," Charlie said with a snarky glare. She turned around and pulled Ian by the wrist. "Come on. I'm going to get my boots on before we go.

Sonny leaned into my ear. "What the hell is her problem?"

I wasn't about to tell Charlie's story. She said only Ian knew about her past, and it wasn't my place to disclose what she told me to anyone else. Besides, she still hated me. I didn't want to piss her off any more than usual.

"I have no idea. But just remember that everyone here has a story. So you shouldn't judge a book by its cover."

I hoped Sonny would just shut up about it. But that was unlikely.

# THE APOLOGY

WHILE WE WAITED FOR Ian and Charlie to get back from the hut, Destiny, Sonny, and I started walking toward the beach.

"She blames Grace for her not dying," Destiny said to Sonny.

"What? That's so stupid."

"More stupid than why you've hated me for so long?"

She narrowed her eyes at me. "Whatever. I live with you now. So you're just going to have to grow up and get over it."

Really? After all these years of making fun of me and bullying me and humiliating me, all because I didn't pick her to be on my dodge ball team, I was the one who needed to grow up?

"Besides, if anyone is going to be a bitch to you, it's going to be me."

I didn't know how to feel about that. Flattered?

Ian and Charlie met us on the beach, and we made our way to the entrance of the jungle trail. I thought about V again, remembering that I promised to stay in my room all night. Hopefully, if the date was going well, he would just let the night go on without worrying about me. But I knew better. He was probably going to come check up on me in the suite. I mentally swore to myself that I would be back in about an hour or two—with or without the crew.

There was a gentle breeze coming off the ocean water. The night sky was clear, and the stars were shining bright. The moon was our only light, but it was full tonight and lit up what it could of the dense jungle. Thankfully, we had the ability to adjust our eyes to darkness. If not, it would have been difficult to hike down the trail. Ian and Charlie guided the way. Destiny was in the middle, and Sonny and I followed close behind.

We walked for about fifteen minutes in silence. It was actually kind of nice—almost even therapeutic. I could hear Ian and Charlie speaking in low voices ahead of us. Destiny was quietly smoking another cigarette, and Sonny was fixated on her phone. It was nice to hear the soft sounds of insects buzzing around and frogs croaking in the distance. It was nature, and I loved the sound of nature.

"God! Why didn't you tell me to change my shoes, Grace?" Sonny whined. "My Jimmy Choos are getting ruined!"

That sound just ruined my night.

"Why do I have to tell you what to do?" I asked. Seriously, when the hell did I become Sonny's keeper?

"Because you're supposed to have my back."

"Oh, really? Since when?"

Sonny stopped walking and lifted her leg to daintily pull a large piece of muck off her heel. I didn't want to, but I stopped to wait for her.

"Why don't you just take your shoes off?" I asked.

She snapped her head up at me, as if I'd asked the most horrible question she'd ever been asked. "You're joking, right?"

"No. Take them off. It's just mud."

"Right. And ruin my fresh pedicure? I don't think so. I can't exactly do my own toes, you know. Which reminds me, I've got to get Margo out here. There's no way I'm going to live here without my beautician on hand."

An enormous part of me felt ashamed and guilty for Sonny not being able to do her own nails. I mean, she probably never did them herself anyway, but it sucked that she didn't have the option to—at least not until she gets the new arm. But I still rolled my eyes at her narcissistic remark. I worried that if I kept rolling my eyes around Sonny, they might get stuck that way.

"Fine. Then don't. Come on."

"You know, I don't like your attitude, Grace."

"Really?"

"Yes, really. You don't have to be mean to me."

"Just like you didn't have to be mean to me back home?" Two wrongs didn't make a right, but it was hard to be nice to her after all the flack she had given me in the past.

She threw her arms out in frustration. Or...her one arm. What was left of her other lay limp at her side.

"Okay! Fine! You want me to say I'm sorry? I'm sorry! There. Is that better?"

I couldn't help but wonder why the sudden change in her. Did becoming a Zombrid change her view of me? She actually cried today. And it wasn't because her Jimmy Choos got ruined. And now she was apologizing to me. Did she feel closer to me now that we were both zombies or something?

"I'm not asking for an apology, Sonny." And that was the truth. It just bugged me that after all this time, she could pretend like she didn't torture me for years.

We were silent for a moment, and then I said, "But since you're apologizing, I should, too. Again. I'm really, really sorry about your arm. And about Tristen."

For once, Sonny didn't talk back. She didn't counter with a jeering remark or a sarcastic chuckle. It looked like maybe she was thinking about it, but she didn't. Instead, she reached down to take off her overly expensive shoes. Her bare feet sunk into the moist soil and she shrunk about three inches.

"This actually feels kind of nice." She smiled, wiggling her toes in the mud.

"Told you. Now, come on," I demanded. "We're losing them." I could barely see Destiny. Sonny obeyed, and we finally caught up with the rest of the group.

"I really am sorry, Grace," Sonny said in a low voice.

"It's okay. If it wasn't for me, you wouldn't be here. And you would have your arm."

"Hey, shit happens. Besides, I'm getting a new one," she said in a hopeful tone. She gently rubbed her stump, pressing down on the bandages to make sure they were secure.

"Does it hurt?"

"A little. It's still kind of sore, but it's healing from the last surgery. Dr. Walker said that for a Zombrid, lost limbs take a little bit longer to heal than if it were broken. But it's still faster than if I were human."

I didn't say anything.

"You know what makes all of this better?"

"What?"

"The fact that you and Tristen aren't together anymore. Karma is a bitch."

I wanted to punch her nubby arm, but she was right. Karma *was* a bitch. I stole Tristen away from Sonny, and now we weren't together. But, honestly, there was a gratifying sensation in the pit of my stomach. Neither of us had him.

"Where are we walking to, Ian?" Destiny asked as she exhaled smoke out of her mouth.

"We're headed toward the falls," he called back.

"Um...no, we're not. This isn't the way to the waterfalls."

Ian and Charlie stopped moving forward. "What do you mean? I come this way all the time."

"Well, if you weren't yapping your mouth to Charlie, then you would have noticed that we missed the turn," Destiny informed him.

"So, where are we going then?" I asked. I grabbed my phone out of my back pocket and looked at the clock. I didn't have time to get lost. V was going to be pissed.

"Destiny, why didn't you say anything?" I couldn't tell if Charlie was upset or just giving her the usual attitude.

"Because I thought getting lost would be more fun." Destiny giggled.

Charlie huffed and folded her arms. Ian found it amusing and patted Destiny on the back. "Well done, mate."

"So, like, what does this mean? Are we really lost?" Sonny asked.

"Nah. We aren't really lost," Ian said. "This island isn't all that big. I've hiked pretty much all of it. Let's just keep walking. We'll figure it out."

"I can't, guys. I have to get back to my room." It wasn't like V was my dad or anything, but I just didn't want to worry him. And worrying was definitely something he did often when it came to me.

"Don't be so lame, Grace!" Sonny yelled before she smacked my arm.

"Hey! I'm not lame!" I yelled back, slapping her good arm. "Ouch!"

"Girls," Ian interrupted. "As much as I would like to see a cat fight, we should just get on already. I'll lead the way."

I exhaled violently, regretting the fact that I was going to give in. I grabbed my phone and sent a text to V.

**Grace Shelley:** *Hey, I just wanted to check in. I'm in Destiny's suite. I'm okay. She is having some girl problems. So don't bother us! Hope your date is going well;)*

Not even a minute later...

**V:** *I will be in the hallway in thirty minutes if you need me.*

Damn. I was going to have to sneak into my room later.

**Grace Shelley:** *Okay. I'll see you later. Oh, and I want to know everything about your date!*

**V:** *Fine.*

Ha! He hated talking about himself.

"Who ya texting?" Sonny asked innocently, trying to spy over my shoulder.

I blacked out my phone and put it back in my pocket. "No one."

"Uh-huh. You got a thing for your bodyguard guy, don't you?"

"What? No! He's...old!" Gross! V could be my dad! The thought of that made me sick to my stomach. Or was I hungry? I grabbed a snack out of my bag.

"That looks good." Sonny reached into my Ziploc baggie. I rolled my eyes.

We walked and walked for another twenty minutes before finally reaching something other than jungle.

"What is that?" Destiny asked.

"Oh, shit," Ian mumbled.

"Oh, shit what?" I asked, skeptical. But Ian didn't answer. He just glanced into my eyes, then shifted his gaze to Destiny.

A chain-link fence stood tall in front of us. Above it was barbed wire, like the ones surrounding a prison. I got up closer and touched it with my fingertips. It was old and rusted, certainly not up to par with the rest of the compound. I could see that a few feet behind the fence there was a concrete building, just like the Z lab.

"What is this place?" Sonny asked.

I turned to the group. "Is this East Cocos?"

# THE CELLS

I REALIZED THAT IAN knew exactly what this place was and didn't want Destiny to get upset about it. "Destiny, we can leave now, if you want," Ian said, resting a hand on her back.

"No! If this is East Cocos, we should check it out."

"Do you think that's a good idea?" Charlie asked. "It might not be best to see her."

It was nice to see these three band together. I had become close to Ian and Destiny, but the three of them have been friends for a while before I showed up. There was a sense of camaraderie between them. A sense that they watched over and genuinely cared for each other. Charlie and Ian were attempting to guard Destiny from what she might see. Abby, Destiny's girlfriend, was a part of the "incident" that got numerous Zombrids hauled off to East Cocos a few months ago. I didn't know much about Abby, not since the time Destiny mentioned her whereabouts that one day on the beach with Tristen. And when Ian told me that Destiny didn't like to talk about it, I never brought it up. But I did hear that they were completely in love.

"Have none of you guys seen this place before? Haven't you all lived here a while?" Sonny asked.

"I have, but I've never been inside. It's not along the trail, so it's easy to miss. And none of us even knew about it until recently when Dr. Walker told us he sent the sick Zombrids here," Ian explained.

Destiny began power-walking along the fence.

"Destiny, where are you going?" Charlie called after her and followed. Ian trailed behind.

"Should we go after them?" Sonny asked. I didn't answer. I contemplated really hard on whether or not we should follow. But when Sonny began to walk ahead, I realized I would be an idiot not to. The rainforest wasn't necessarily scary, but I sure as hell didn't want to be left alone in it.

We walked the length of the fence until a bright red light came into view. The fence curved left, and we followed it to find Destiny standing at the gate. Her fingers poked through the links, and I could tell she was holding on tight. She was staring at a large riveted steel door. The red light lit up the black letters that read EAST COCOS.

I was right about the door! Wrong about the QUARANTINE.

"She's there," Destiny whispered.

Charlie grabbed her shoulder gently. "Des, we can't go in there. I'm sure she's okay."

Destiny took hold of the hefty padlock that made entry into the place look impossible. She started shaking it, clearly wishing it would just fall off.

"Destiny! Stop it! We can't get in!" Ian yelled at her.

"What is wrong with her? And what is this place?" Sonny asked in my direction, low enough for only me to hear.

I answered back in a small voice. "There are some really sick Zombrids in there, and her girlfriend is one of them."

"What? Well, we have to get in!"

Ian gave Sonny a disapproving glare. "No, we don't. If those Zombrids are sick and contagious, I don't want to go near them."

Destiny began sobbing. "I have to see her! I have to see her, Ian! I can feel her. We are so close."

"We can't get in. There's a lock on the gate."

"Oh, move out of my way!" Sonny pushed Ian and Destiny away from the gate with her one arm. She analyzed the lock, then reached up and pulled something out of her hair.

"Grace, come hold this for me."

I obeyed, not because she told me to, but because I was curious to see how she planned to get this lock off. I held the lock steady while she knelt down and tilted her head to get a better view. She stuck a bobby pin into the tiny keyhole and wiggled it around several times.

"Come on. Really? This is so cliché. Does she think she's a secret agent or something?" Ian asked sarcastically.

There was a clicking sound and Sonny pulled the lock open. "Nope. My daddy is the president of one of the largest security companies in the country."

Of course he was.

"So?" Charlie sassed.

"So, they have to test out all the products. Picking a lock was a breach that needed to be tested. This lock is so old, a toddler could have picked it." She put the pin back in her hair.

Destiny couldn't wait any longer. She pushed open the gate and ran to the steel door. From the looks of it, there didn't seem to be a handle or a lock or even a way to open it.

"Okay, 007. How do we get in here?" Ian chastised.

Sonny glanced around before pointing her finger at the wall. "There! That small camera. It looks like it could be a retinal scanner."

"How are we supposed to do that? It's probably programmed for Dr. Walker and his staff," Destiny said.

"Let me try." A deep voice came from behind us, and I knew immediately who it was.

"V, what are you doing here?"

He held up his cellphone. "I tracked your phone."

There were a million things going through my mind. Some of them were curse words. He had a tracker on my phone? Did he not trust me? As much as I wanted to be pissed off at him for violating me in that way, I was half-expecting it and half-happy that he did it. V's whole job was to protect me. I was very valuable in the Zombrid world. V's ability to track me down was a good thing. What if I forgot to eat or didn't eat enough? I didn't want to ever get into that horrible state of mind Dr. Walker told me about. I didn't want to lose all brain function and turn into a man-eating death machine. V could quite possibly keep me from murdering someone.

"Shit. You're going to tell Dr. Walker we're here, aren't you?" Ian asked.

"No. Just move over."

"He is such a cutie. If you don't want him, I'll take him," Sonny whispered. I narrowed my eyes at her.

V stood stiffly in front of the eye scanner thingy and closed one eye. We were all silent, waiting to see if he had the right eyes to open this massive, fortified door. A second later, a low buzz sounded from the metal and the door popped open.

"Wait." He towered in front of us. I suddenly felt like we were his tiny children. He was so tall and burly and authoritarian. "Destiny, I know you want to see Abby. We're only going in so you can see her. The rest of you, do not touch anything. Do not talk. Do not go off alone. We stay together."

"Haven't you been in here before?" I asked. He was one of Dr. Walker's employees. I was certain that he had been to East Cocos, or at least knew of what it was like in there. In our many conversations, I never once thought to ask him about it.

Me and my stupid obsessing over Tristen!

"No. I've never been inside. It wasn't ever part of my detail. Everyone, just follow me." He turned around and opened the door.

Destiny followed close behind V, with eagerness in every step she took. Charlie linked arms with Ian. I stared at Ian for a second. It was hard to believe that just this afternoon I could have lost all of what made me pure to him. There was no doubt in my mind that he and Charlie had a connection that he and I would never have. I've never been in a friends-with-benefits kind of relationship, but the vibe I got from them seemed like there could be more than just sex.

Sonny linked her arm with mine. I looked down at it then back up to her.

"What? I'm kind of scared," she said innocently. A part of me wanted to snatch my arm away. It reminded me too much of my dear friend Phoebe. But I didn't. And I didn't know why.

We walked through the entrance. V's pace was slow and steady. He was clearly assessing the space. It was late at night, but there could still be employees here.

It was dim, with only a few faint lights illuminating the area around us. I immediately noticed a soft beeping noise ahead, kind of like a monitor of some sort. Our footsteps sounded loud and hollow. I glanced down and realized we were on a grated walkway on the second floor of the building.

We moved in slow strides together until the narrow walkway led us to a large, open room. We fanned out. V cautiously approached the railing and glanced down. I followed to see what he was looking at.

We both peered down at the main floor underneath us. It was barely lit, but I was able to spot gurneys and medical equipment scattered around.

"There are stairs," Destiny pointed out. She started to hurry over but before she could reach them, V grabbed her arm.

"We have to stay together."

She looked up at him and nodded, her eyes stained with black tears from her mascara. She desperately wanted to see her girlfriend.

"Let's go," he demanded, loud enough for all of us to hear.

We followed him down the stairs to the first floor. A single, large light fixture hung down from the ceiling in the center of the space. The low pitch of the beeping grew louder but seemed to be coming from a different direction. Behind us, maybe? I turned around to follow it but stopped when I heard a gasp.

Charlie was standing out of the light and off to the side, staring at something. She covered her mouth with her hand, and she seemed completely terrified at what she was looking at. Ian and Destiny rushed over to her.

"Holy shit," Ian said in response to what was in front of him. Sonny pulled me toward them, but I was reluctant. Curiosity coursed through me, but I was afraid to see what they were looking at. It wasn't until we got closer to them that I saw what was lining the walls of the entire first floor. Bars—like a jail. They were jail cells.

I tried to peer inside the three that we passed as Sonny pulled me closer to everyone else, but there wasn't much to see. They were empty.

Then we reached the cell that everyone had been gaping at. I gasped, trying to hold back the horrified scream that was forming in my throat.

"What the..." Sonny started to say what I was thinking.

A naked man dangled from the ceiling inside the cell, swaying slowly from side to side. His body drooped limply, and his head leaned forward, long hair covering whatever it was around his neck that suspended him in midair. I stared harder and analyzed him, realizing that chunks of his arms were missing. The skin around the wounds appeared rigid, almost as if it was torn off him. My eyes traveled down to his hands, and I was only able to count four fingers on his left, two on his right hand. He was missing the other fingers. He was dirty and pale, and he only had one leg. The other leg was gone from his thigh down. It looked like it was ripped away from his body.

"What happened to him? Did he hang himself?" asked Ian.

"I don't know," V responded, but he seemed hypnotized by what his eyes were seeing.

"How could he reach up there? There's nothing he could have stood on," Sonny pointed out. And it was true. The cell was empty except for his body. Ian stepped closer to the bars and leaned in a little to get a better view.

"Whatever happened to him happened a while ago because he reeks," he said, covering his nose.

"V, what is this place?" I asked, not understanding what I was looking at. From how Dr. Walker explained it, I imagined East Cocos to be like the Z lab. Maybe just another place for treatment. But this place was rundown and dilapidated. It was dirty and scary. And apparently had people hanging by their necks!

"I heard it was a jail long ago, before Dr. Walker ever came here. But it looks like it still is," he said.

That sent chills through me. A jail? These sick Zombrids were being held captive?

"Where are all the other Zombrids?" I asked.

"I don't know," Ian said. "There were about twenty-something Zombrids that were sent here. But I don't see anyone."

"Well, should we help this guy down?" Charlie asked.

"No." V stepped closer to the bars. "He's been dead a long time and I don't think he hung himself."

"You think someone did this to him?"

"I think he may have been someone's meal," he answered.

A muffled groan echoed behind us. We all turned around at the same time to examine the row of darkened jail cells that lined the opposite wall. Destiny rushed over to the first cell and peered in. When she realized it was empty, she moved on to the next, then the next. Until finally, she stopped at the fourth one and choked out a loud cry.

"Abby!"

We all ran over to her and peered into the cell. We couldn't completely see Abby. She was huddled up in the dark far corner of the cell. All we could hear was the groaning, which seemed to be growing louder and longer.

"Abby, baby. It's me. It's Destiny. I'm here to get you out," she whispered softly as she held on tightly to the metal bars.

"Destiny, we can't get her out," Ian said.

"Abby. Please, let me see you. It's okay."

"Get back," V demanded.

Something didn't feel right. I glanced at Destiny, who looked like she was trying to will herself through the metal bars. She pressed her body against them, trying to get a better view of Abby. The moaning got louder and sounded more strained. It was getting longer, and I wondered how someone could make such a sound without having to catch their breath.

"Abby, I'm going to get you out of here. Just let me see your face," Destiny cried. She pleaded with her and spoke as sweet as she could through her tears. We all stood silently, waiting for Abby to make a move. Any move.

There was a rustling noise, and Destiny stopped talking. Then, out of nowhere, Abby slammed into the cell bars. We all jumped simultaneously at the sound of her body crashing into the metal. The dim light seemed to be enough to illuminate her face. She opened her mouth and snarled, showing gritty, decaying teeth. What little hair on her scalp barely moved as she cocked her head to the side and stared at us. She didn't blink, and the whites of her eyes were bloodshot...and empty.

Destiny was nineteen, so I assumed Abby was around the same age. But she didn't even look close to the same age. Her wrinkled skin seemed to be sliding off her. Her cheeks were sunken in and her bones protruded out. She looked like a skeleton.

In a quick, sharp movement, she turned her gaze to Destiny, who was still holding on tightly to the bars. They were inches away from each other, and Destiny seemed to be speechless at the ghastly sight of her girlfriend.

"Destiny, move back," V whispered, slowly stepping toward her. But she didn't move. Her shoulders started shaking uncontrollably, and even though her back was to me, I could tell she was silently sobbing.

Before V could reach her to pull her back, Abby slid her very unhealthy, skinny arm straight through the bar in one rapid motion. Destiny didn't have any time to dodge, and before we knew it, Abby had Destiny's long black-and-blue hair gripped firmly in her hand. Destiny shrieked and Abby moaned louder. She grabbed Abby's wrist in an attempt to make her release her grip, but Abby wouldn't budge. V jumped into action, also grabbing Abby's wrist, but he didn't seem to have any luck with it, either. That was when my disbelief set in. There was no way that this girl was stronger than V!

Destiny and V wrestled with Abby's arm for a few more moments until V let go abruptly and let out a pained howl. He immediately clasped a hand onto his arm. I ran over to him.

"What happened!"

"She bit me!" He removed his hand to reveal a gaping hole in his forearm in the shape of a mouth. The skin was torn away and blood gushed out of him like a fountain.

"Destiny!" someone yelled.

When I turned away from V's injury to look at what was happening, I wished that I hadn't. Destiny's body was shaking violently as she tried with all she had in her to fight against Abby's strength. Abby pulled Destiny's face closer and closer to the metal bars. She was baring her teeth like a rabid dog, pressing her face against the bars so hard that it looked as if it was going to squish right through them. The bars were actually indenting her skin, making her face look like it was memory foam.

"Ian and Charlie, grab hold of her and pull her away!" I yelled, tearing a piece of my T-shirt off to wrap around V's arm.

But before they could reach her, Abby pulled Destiny's head back and slammed it against the metal. A loud ping echoed before her body went limp. Abby made one last long moan, then pulled

Destiny's face between the bars as much as she could and sunk her teeth in. We all stood motionless, unable to speak or move while we watched Abby pull and chew the flesh away from Destiny's face. Her movements were fluid and fast, almost like we were watching this all happen in fast forward.

"Ian, come on! Let's pull her away! Now!" V demanded, gently pushing me aside and out of his way. He grabbed Abby's arm and twisted while Ian pulled Destiny by the waist. There was a cracking sound, and I knew V had to break Abby's arm in order to get her to let go. Ian held on to Destiny's dead weight and gently set her onto the ground. Sonny, Charlie, and I ran over to her side.

"Oh my God!" Charlie shrieked.

My hand inadvertently covered my mouth because I didn't know what else to do. It was a horrific sight. Her face was completely covered in blood. The skin on her forehead looked like it was cut with a serrated knife, and the remaining rigid pieces flapped over her hairline and the rest of her face. The one eye she had left dangled off to the side from a single vein. Her right cheek was missing, exposing her teeth and cheekbone. Her breathing was shallow, and she took long, raspy breaths. This was due to the fact that she no longer had a nose. There was just a hole in her face.

"Oh my God! What do we do?" Charlie asked, clearly in a panic.

"We have to get her out of here," V said, bending down to assess her injuries.

"What about this medical stuff? Can't we, like...do something here? She's losing a lot of blood!" Sonny yelped.

"Are you a doctor, too?" Ian asked sarcastically.

"No, but we can try some—"

"Shh!" V interrupted.

We all shut up immediately and looked at him.

The feeling that we weren't alone washed over me, and it was confirmed when I heard the sound of voices and footsteps on the grated catwalk above us.

# LA CABEZA

"Y ENTONCES ME BESO!"

"¿Que! Hombre, ¡eres afortunado!"

Something about kissing and luck. I managed to learn a little bit of Spanish over the months, but not enough to make out what these two fast-talking guys were saying.

I mouthed *what do we do* to V. He glanced around before pointing over my shoulder. I turned to see that there was a door to another room. Ian, Sonny, and Charlie saw the door, too, and began walking slowly and quietly in that direction. V leaned over and picked Destiny up in one fell swoop. He winced. I knew for sure it wasn't because Destiny was too heavy. I glanced at his arm and saw that the piece of T-shirt I wrapped around it was already saturated in blood.

We scurried to the other room and closed the door softly. A bluish-white fluorescent light flickered above us. The room was not very big, and from what I could tell, it seemed to be some sort of surgical area. There were more gurneys, but with large light fixtures hanging over each one and metal push trays filled with surgical tools beside them. It didn't have that sterile feel—not like the Z lab.

And the gurneys. There were three total and two of them were...occupied. White sheets draped and outlined what I assumed to be bodies.

Sonny squeezed my arm. "Are those people?" she whispered.

The beeping that I'd heard earlier came from this room. A heart monitor machine thing was hooked up to one of the covered bodies and every few seconds, it beeped. At least one of these people was alive. Ian walked over to them and lifted the sheet, just enough for only his eyes. I was too afraid to know what was underneath it. I turned toward V, who was setting Destiny down on the third empty gurney.

Charlie ran to Destiny's side and began nurturing her.

"What now, mate?" Ian asked V in a low voice.

"We hope those guys don't come in here."

"What about Destiny? She isn't doing so well," Charlie informed us. I peered over to see for myself. It was hard to look at her. She no longer had a face. Even if she did live through this, how the hell were we supposed to fix her?

I glanced at V. "Are you okay?"

He nodded.

"Now he knows how I felt," Sonny said with a snort. I shot her a dirty look.

The voices outside the room seemed to be getting closer. V stepped near the door to get a better listen. After a second, he turned and motioned for us to make our way through a door that seemed to lead into another room.

"What about Destiny?" Ian asked.

"They'll probably just think she's supposed to be in here," V said.

We all moved quickly and silently, except Charlie. She was still at Destiny's side.

"Charlie," I hissed loudly. "Come on."

"I can't leave her." Tears trickled down her face. "What are they going to do to her?"

Charlie appeared to be shedding the tough-girl exterior and replacing it with genuine emotion as she huddled over Destiny's motionless body. I didn't even know she was that close to Destiny. The only time I had ever seen her showing any emotion was toward Maddi, which made total sense considering what happened in her former life. Her connection with Maddi went much deeper than just friendship. She saw Maddi as the daughter she almost had. And now she was sobbing over her friend, another person that she could potentially lose.

"I don't know what's going to happen to her, Charlie. But we have to hide," I answered back. A shadow appeared under the door. "Charlie, please," I begged.

Tears streamed down her face and fell in drops on Destiny's body. Charlie looked at me and simply shook her head. She didn't move a muscle. I drew my brows together, wondering what was going to happen when these two guys came in here. We didn't even know who they were.

The knob on the door turned. I spun around and slid through the crack of the door, shutting it quietly then pressing my ear up against it.

"Hey! ¿Que haces?" the man yelled in Spanish.

"Please, my friend! She's hurt!" Charlie explained. I could hear the crying in her voice.

"Miguel, ¡Ven aca!" He then changed his language to English, but with an accent that almost made it still sound Spanish. "You no be here!"

"Please, we have to tell Dr. Walker! She's hurt."

"What's happening?" Sonny asked behind me.

"Wait. Charlie is out there?" Ian asked, concern in his tone. I didn't respond, trying to focus on what was happening in the other room.

"Hand up! Hand up, now!" one of the guys yelled.

"She's in pain! We have to help her!"

The metal tray got pushed over and all of the surgical tools pinged against the floor. I held my breath.

"Stop it!" Charlie yelled.

Ian tried to push me away from the door. "What are they doing to Charlie?"

I pushed him back before he could reach for the doorknob to open it. "Ian, wait!"

"Miguel, ¡hacerlo!"

"Let me go!" Charlie yelled.

"¡Hacerlo!"

And then...BANG!

Was that a gunshot? Holy shit! That was a gunshot!

"What was that? Was that a gun?" Sonny asked in horror.

Ian tried to push past me again, but I held him back. "Stop it! We can't go out there."

I pushed my ear harder against the door, desperate to hear something from Charlie.

"Tenemos que cortar la cabeza."

Crap! Why was Spanish their first language? I combined the little I'd picked up here on the island with the one Spanish class I took sophomore year at Middleton and thought about that sentence in my head, repeating it out loud to better understand it. "Cortar. Corte. Cut."

Cabeza. You didn't have to know Spanish to understand what that meant. Most people did. Cabeza. Head.

Cut. Head. Cut head?

Dr. Walker's words flashed in my mind—*a subject injected with Serum Z could live indefinitely, provided that the subject does not come into contact with flames. Decapitation would also permanently end a subject's life.*

Decapitation.

I backed away from the door, trying to decide what to do. Should we go out there? Something just happened. Those guys shot someone. They were getting ready to cut the heads off two people! But if we could stop them, Charlie and Destiny might have a chance.

A gunshot wouldn't kill them, but it would take a few minutes for them to recover from the wound, which would be enough time to cut off some heads. Did we want to risk these guys doing the same to us? If we busted through this door, would they instantly shoot us and chop our heads off, too? And who were these guys? How could they be authorized to do such a thing? And where was Dr. Walker?

I started to panic. I needed V.

"Where's V?"

"We don't know. He was in pretty bad shape from the bite," Ian said.

"V," I called out as loud as I could without—hopefully—being overheard in the other room. There was no response. This room seemed to be a type of storage area for the surgery one we were just in. There were rows of tall shelves, all filled with medical supplies. I stalked down each aisle, checking to see if V was somewhere in between.

"Gracie, I'm scared." Sonny's voice was suddenly small. I chose to forget the fact that she just called me Gracie.

"Sonny, we have to find V. Just hang on a minute. He has to be in here."

Finally, in between the fourth and fifth storage shelf, I spotted V sitting on the floor. He was hunched over with his head down, grasping onto his arm. Blood was smeared on the floor in front of him.

"V? Are you okay," I asked, carefully moving toward him. I knew this seemed like a cheesy-horror-movie-cliché, but I was truly afraid. I had never seen V so vulnerable. Big, really muscular, brute boys don't cry over a bite on the arm.

"V?" I finally reached him and crouched down to his level. He was trembling. I still couldn't see the expression on his face, but I could tell by the way he was sweating and clutching on to his arm that he was in serious pain. His knuckles were white, the veins on the top of his hand clearly visible.

"We need to get you some help."

"Did you see her? Did you see Abby?" he asked hoarsely.

"Yes, I did." We all saw her.

"What was wrong with her? Why did she look like that?"

"She looked like death. I-I don't know."

"I have never seen anyone look that way. Why is she here? What happened to her and the others that were taken from the huts?" It seemed like he was asking himself these questions. I grabbed the upper portion of his arm and started to stand up.

"Come on. We need to get you out of here. We need to go see Dr. Walker."

He looked up, and I tried with everything in me to conceal the gasp that was rising in my throat. He was as white as a ghost. His eyes were glossed over and his lips were a light shade of blue. I could fill a cup with the amount of sweat dripping off his bald head.

"I didn't...I didn't know about this place, Grace. I didn't know it was like this."

My eyes stung with the threat of tears. He was trying to assure me that he wouldn't have lied to me. Had he known how "sick" Abby was and how uneasy this place felt, he would have investigated.

I tried to keep him steady as he stood up, but he swayed and staggered.

"Grace, I don't feel good," he said through chattering teeth. He looked like he was freezing. He seemed so small, and it didn't make sense. It was hard to believe such a manly man in a big, burly body would be so hurt by a bite on the arm.

He turned away and coughed. Blood splattered all over the boxes of latex gloves on the shelf. This was more than just a bite.

"Okay, come on. We have to go." I fought to help him keep his balance while we walked to meet up with Sonny and Ian.

"Grace, I don't hear Charlie or the guys anymore. Should we go back in there?" Sonny asked.

"No, we need to find another way out."

"Hey, mate. Are you okay?" Ian asked V.

V didn't answer.

"We need to get him to Dr. Walker. He's lost a lot of blood," I informed them.

"There's a door over there," Sonny said, pointing to the far corner of the room. Ian dashed over, and when he opened the door, a cloud rushed out and a blast of cold air clashed with my warm skin. We stepped in. It was some kind of cooler.

"It's freezing in here. What the hell is this place?" Sonny asked as she hugged herself.

"It's like a freezer," Ian declared.

A row of shelves filled with deep containers lined the wall in front of us. To our right were more shelves and another door. To our left was a plastic curtain-like divider.

"Come on, the door is this way," I called out, holding on with all my might to V's waist to keep him from falling down.

"What's over here?" Ian asked.

"Ian, we don't have time to explore. We have to—"

"Oh my God! Grace!" Sonny shrieked.

I turned toward her. "Sonny, keep it down! What's wrong?"

"You have to come. Now!"

I found a piece of the wall that was suitable for V to lean against and gently set him down before making my way to Sonny and Ian. They were standing and staring at something in front of them. I pushed the plastic curtain to the side and my jaw dropped open as I took in the horror that I was forced to see.

Do you know what a freezer in a butcher shop looks like? Normally, it's rows of animal carcass hanging on hooks. Most of the time it would be the torso or the legs of a dead skinned animal. All that was usually left was the red meat and bones.

And that was what I was looking at—rows of dead meat hanging on hooks. Only, they weren't animals. They were people. Actual people. Dead humans hanging upside down on meat hooks.

Their arms hung freely below their heads. Their feet were bound by rope. They were all naked, and I felt guilty for looking at them. But I couldn't help it. I had to look. They all appeared to have the same blue, almost transparent-like tint, and they were covered in ice crystals.

"They're all dead, Grace."

"Yes, Sonny. I know."

"Who are they?" Ian asked, walking closer to one of them. A man. He poked at the man's torso and the body swayed from side to side. I stepped closer to one, too. She was naked and all of her private parts were exposed. I knelt down and tilted my head to fix the upside-down effect. I focused on the woman's face, trying to determine if maybe I'd seen her before. But she didn't look familiar. She just looked like a sleeping, frozen stranger. There were no cuts or bruises on her body. No marks to indicate that she was murdered or killed in a horrific way. Her skin was pristine—like porcelain.

"Ian, these aren't the Zombrids who lived with you all, are they?" I asked. I didn't count them, but from the look of it, there seemed to be about fifteen bodies.

"No," he answered, walking farther back in between them. "I have never seen these people before."

"I don't understand. Were they killed? Are they like...our food?" Sonny asked, her voice high-pitched. She was frightened, I could tell. I have seen my fair share of carnage already. The sight of Phoebe's disemboweled body was awful and gruesome. I had hoped that I would never have to see that again, but I knew what a dead person looked like because of that. Thankfully, Eric's body was less traumatizing.

As for Ian, he apparently had been around more dead bodies than I ever wanted to be. He was pretty much a serial killer. It was why I didn't question his lack of emotion for Charlie or Destiny. He didn't seem as upset as I would be if a long-time friend died, and I'd think it was because he had a little psychopath in him. But Sonny was a newbie. She'd never eaten another human being before. This was the first time she'd truly seen a dead person.

Sonny's comment seeped slowly into my mind until it finally registered. Could these people be our food? Dr. Walker said we didn't have to eat human meat to stay normal. He said that we could live on raw and fresh recently deceased animal carcass. But...what if that wasn't true? Why else would these people be here? Hanging on meat hooks. Dead.

"Grace!" Ian yelled. I glanced in his direction through the sea of lifeless bodies. "Grace, you have to come see this!"

An enormous part of me fought to keep my feet planted right where they were. But the tiny part of curiosity was too overwhelming.

I maneuvered through the hanging people, trying my hardest not to touch them. As I made my way toward the back of the freezer, I noticed these bodies didn't seem as untouched as the first few. Pieces of their body parts were missing.

When I reached Ian, Sonny was standing next to him. Her hand covered her mouth and tears streamed down her face. My heart began to race at the sight of Sonny silently crying.

"What's wrong?"

There was another body hanging motionless. I analyzed the corpse from its feet down. It was naked like the rest of them, only it didn't seem as intact. Chunks of its right leg were missing. The cuts were clean, clearly done with some kind of surgical tool. There was no blood. Just holes.

My eyes followed its physique, and I was soon able to determine that the corpse was a man. His torso was also sliced up. His physique was muscular and fit, but his skin had been peeled back, revealing actual muscle. His neck had been cut open and a large portion of his head was gone. And then I looked at his face.

My knees buckled, and before I could stop them, they slammed into the freezing ground.

His face.

"Grace?" I felt a hand on my shoulder and heard Sonny's soft sobs in my right ear.

This couldn't be. There was no way.

"That son of a bitch," Ian muttered.

"Grace, how could he have done this?" Sonny asked. "How could Dr. Walker do this?"

"He must have kidnapped him, and then lied to Grace," Ian speculated.

This couldn't be him. He left! He left and went home! He wrote me a stupid note. How could this be him?

"But why would Dr. Walker have done that? Why would he kill any of these people?" Sonny asked, desperate for an answer.

This wasn't him. If it was him, he would have the tattoo. The Phoenix.

I leaned over to examine his arm. If it wasn't there, then this wasn't him. Just someone who looked like him. That's all.

"Grace?"

I closed my eyes and prayed. *Please, don't let this be him.*

And when I opened them, there it was. The Phoenix. The Phoenix on Tristen's arm.

# THE MONSTER

MY CHEST HEAVED. IT was him. It was Tristen Miles. Hanging from a meat hook. Dead.

I closed my eyes again and fought to catch my breath. Sonny wrapped her arm awkwardly around my side while her body started vibrating with silent cries. "Grace, it's h-him. It's our T-Tristen."

It was weird that she called him *our* Tristen, but I wasn't going to point it out. To be completely honest, she should probably feel more grief-stricken than me. She and Tristen were together for a while. But that didn't negate the fact that I cared deeply about him, too. My mourning didn't come from memories of Tristen and me together; it came from the prospect of what we could have been and the memories we could have created.

Tears threatened to rush out of me like a broken fire hydrant, but I held them back. I couldn't cry just yet.

I gently pulled away from Sonny. "We have to get the hell out of here."

"And go where? Dr. Walker is obviously evil. He's killing people!" Ian pointed out. I hurried back to V, who was now practically lying on the floor.

"We need to find a way off this damn island," I asserted.

"I can call my parents. Daddy can have a boat here in no time," Sonny offered.

"Ian, help me with V." We each grabbed an arm and lifted V onto his feet. "Sonny, it will take days for a boat to get here. We need a plane or a helicopter."

"Daddy has both!" She pulled out her cellphone. "Shit! No reception."

"We just need to get the hell out of this place first. If those guys catch us, we're dead," Ian reminded us.

We headed out another door and out of the cooler. I didn't pay much attention to our surroundings. My mind got left behind in the freezer with Tristen and the sounds of what might have been Destiny and Charlie's demise.

How could Tristen be dead? There was no doubt in my mind that Dr. Walker was behind all of this. He had to have done this to Tristen and those other dead bodies. He had to know about the two men fighting with Charlie. He lied to me. Tristen never left me on his own accord. And he probably didn't even write that note. It was his handwriting, but there were a million reasons how that could have been. Dr. Walker could have forced him to write it, or maybe he did have to leave but Dr. Walker snatched him up before he made if off the island. I could feel my heart squeezing with grief as I thought about how it might have all gone down. Did they beat him up? Did he feel anything when they cut off pieces of his body?

I felt anger. Angry because from the moment I met Dr. Walker, I knew he was up to no good. Why didn't I listen to my intuition? Maybe because all I wanted to do was eat. The hunger...it made everything else less important.

I came out of my thoughts and realized we had somehow made it outside and back into the jungle. Ian and I struggled to keep V balanced. We have lost some of our Zombrid strength since we hadn't eaten in while. V was almost unconscious, so having to hold him up above the ground seemed like an impossible task. But we were somehow managing. Sonny followed close behind, trying to get in touch with her daddy on the phone.

"He's in bad shape, Grace. How could a bite do this to him?"

"I don't know. We just need to get him back to the huts."

"Then what?" Ian asked, his voice strained from carrying V.

"Well, I'm not handing him over to Dr. Walker. Who knows what he'll do to him. I'll go to the Z lab alone. I don't think he'll do anything to me. I'll try to talk to him." I tried not to sound frightened. Deep down, I was. Obviously, Dr. Walker was capable of more than I'd imagined. A part of me already knew that when I found out he'd made Phoebe and Eric's deaths look like a murder-suicide. But I needed to find out what his end game was here. And I needed to figure out a way off this island.

"I can't get through to Daddy. But I can get on my computer when we get back to the huts," Sonny said behind us.

"Just do what you can, Sonny."

We hurried through the jungle as quickly as we could. It was late and the smell of a rainstorm was in the air. There was silence until we finally reached the beach. The sound of the waves crashing onto the shore broke up thoughts of what was going to happen next, and I let out a sigh of relief. We were finally as far away as we could be from the Spanish guys with guns back at East Cocos.

"Oh my! What happened?" Estelle stood up from the steps of the porch of the Laguna hut. She opened the door, and we stumbled into the first suite on the right and practically threw V onto the bed.

"Damn," Ian said between catches of breath. "That is one heavy man!"

I assessed his condition. He was still pale and sweating from every pore of his body. His lips were white, and he was shivering even though his head was soaking wet with sweat. I put my head against his chest to listen to his heartbeat. It was beating, but barely.

"Sonny, get on the computer and see what you can find out about transportation. Estelle, please grab some cold rags and anything you can find to clean up V's wound. I'm going to the Z lab."

I was in mission mode.

"What do you want me to do?" Ian asked.

"I want you to find a way out of here. You've been here a long time. Maybe you and Estelle can fill Sonny in on where a plane or helicopter can land if she gets one."

"You going to be okay by yourself?" he asked.

"I'll be fine." I rested my head on V's chest one more time, just to make sure there was still a heartbeat. When I backed away and stepped toward the door, he grabbed my wrist with a very weak grip.

"Grace," he grunted. "Please...be careful."

"I will be. Don't worry. Just hang on and don't go anywhere. I'll get you some help."

He didn't say anything, but his lips parted and the corners of his mouth curved, and then there they were—V's teeth. It was a pained half-smile, but it was a still a smile. And his teeth were pretty and straight and everything I'd imagined.

I smiled back and fought the urge to hug him.

"What's going on?" Maddi stood in the hallway, sleepily rubbing at her eyes.

"Maddi, why don't you go back to your room?" I said. I walked over to her, deliberately blocking her view of V on the bed.

"Where's Charlie?"

I smoothed her red hair. "She'll be here soon. She told me to tell you to wait for her in your room," I lied. I felt horrible for lying to this completely innocent little girl, but I couldn't explain what happened. As a matter of fact, I didn't even know if I wanted to ever tell her the whole truth.

I gently turned her back into the direction of her room. She was too tired to object and simply went back to bed.

"Okay, I'm going. I'll be back."

"Grace," Ian called as he walked over to me. He grabbed my shoulders and squeezed. "Be careful."

I nodded. "Ian, I don't know what happened to Charlie, but I'm sorry."

Sadness filled his eyes. "Let's just hope nothing terrible happened."

Ian might have been a womanizing little ass at times, but he was a good guy. And I knew he cared more about Charlie than he led on. I felt bad for him. He usually spoke without a filter and said whatever was on his mind, but it was clear that he was in denial. We all knew something terrible happened to Charlie and Destiny.

I walked down the steps of the Laguna porch and mentally prepared my questions for Dr. Walker. I had a ton of them and needed to get them sorted out before I busted into his office and began making accusations.

Drops of rain fell from the sky as I practically jogged across the courtyard. It actually felt warm on my cool skin. Familiar hunger pains shot across my stomach, which meant my heart rate will be slowing down below normal and my temperature was going to drop soon if I didn't get some food in me. I hadn't eaten in a few hours.

I searched for a Ziploc of snacks, dipping my hands into the bag that was still slung over my shoulder. I crammed the food into my mouth all at once and stepped up to the glass door of the Z lab. Damn it! I completely forgot that I needed V to get in. I pulled on the door to see if maybe it was open, but it wasn't. Great. How was I supposed to get in? I started pacing back and forth, trying to figure out what to do. But then, as if on cue, the door opened. Robin came out, holding a manila folder and her keys.

"Grace!" She flinched. "You scared me. What are you doing here?" She was dressed in sweatpants and a tank top, completely different from the usual business attire she wore for work.

"I need to see Dr. Walker. Is he here?"

"Yeah, he's upstairs. I just came in to get some paperwork that I forgot. Is everything okay? Where's V?" She seemed concerned.

"I can't talk about it now. Just get me in, please," I pleaded.

It didn't take much convincing. She opened the first door, then punched the code into the second. We walked into the waiting area.

"Grace, can you please tell me what's going on?"

"I really can't right now. Something happened tonight, and I really need to see Dr. Walker. I think you should just get back to the beach...to your hut and wait there." I felt guilty for keeping her in the dark, but I just didn't have the time to explain. I didn't know what was going to happen to V and he needed some medical attention.

Thankfully, she didn't ask any more questions. She just nodded and went out of the door. I made my way straight to the elevator and to the second floor. Beverly was not at her desk, which made sense because it was so late. This was good. I had a feeling she might ask more questions than Robin did.

I followed the same path I normally did when I had to come for testing. It was a ghost town. None of the other researchers and doctors were in sight. My stomach felt queasy. Not enough food and not enough balls to confront Dr. Walker.

I walked down the hallway all the way to the end. Dr. Walker's office door was closed. I knocked. Nothing. I knocked again. Nothing.

"Grace."

I turned around and there he was, in his white lab coat and gold-rimmed glasses. He was evil. And I knew it the moment I met him.

"Please, come with me."

He didn't seem like the same creepily excited Dr. Walker that I was used to. His facial expression was much more serious, and I wondered which was more frightening: the creepy, excited Dr. Mark Walker or the serious, doctory Dr. Mark Walker.

I was hesitant, but I followed him. We entered what seemed to be some kind of conference room. His aide, Kate, and three other men in lab coats were all sitting at a large, shiny wooden table.

"Please have a seat," he offered and gestured for me to sit.

"No. I think I'll stand." No way was I going to get comfortable. I didn't know these people well enough and I didn't know what they were here for.

"Very well," he said and sat down at the head of the table.

"What's going on?" I asked.

"Well, you tell me. You and your hut-mates decided to break into the East Cocos lab. You harassed one of my sick subjects and cost two of your hut-mates' lives and now one of my best guards is severely injured." He leaned back in his chair and folded his arms across his chest. "So, Grace, you tell me what's going on."

He just confirmed that Charlie and Destiny were dead. And that something was seriously wrong with V. My stomach churned. It was hunger and anger and worry all mixing together. I glanced around the table. The other four people watched me, waiting for me to answer. Anxiety kicked in, and I could feel the sweat pooling on my scalp. Or was it the hunger?

I thought of a million things to say, but nothing seemed like it would make sense once it came out of my mouth.

Finally, I settled on something. "How did you know about V?"

"Everlasting Paradise has cameras everywhere."

"Abby attacked Destiny and bit V. He needs help." Tears threatened to fall out of my eyes, but I needed to stay away from emotion at the moment.

Dr. Walker leaned forward, his eyes piercing mine. "My subject, Abby Johnson, is Destiny's girlfriend. She was sent to East Cocos, along with others, because she was severely ill. This morning, she was still not feeling well enough to even eat. You mean to tell me that Abby attacked her girlfriend while sick and from inside her cell?"

"Yes!" I was getting pissed. He wasn't there. He didn't see. "She practically ate Destiny's face off and bit V."

"Sir." Kate handed him a piece of paper from across the table.

"Oh, yes. Thank you," he said as he reached for it. "Grace, this is a letter written to Destiny from Abby dated about a week ago.

It states that she no longer wants to be her girlfriend." He slid the piece of loose-leaf paper over to me. "If you see here, it was written and signed by Abby. Now, here is what I think. Destiny was very upset about Abby's sudden change of heart and decided to confront Abby in her vulnerable state. Unfortunately, I wasn't there, but I can only imagine the hostility from Destiny. After all, she was a drug addict for many years."

I shook my head in disbelief. Was Dr. Walker insinuating that Destiny was the one who initiated this? And this letter had to be bogus. Just like the letter he said was written by Tristen. Or maybe he forced Abby to write it. By the way Abby looked tonight, there was no way in hell she could hold a pen to write a letter. Even if it was a week ago. Her state of deterioration had to have started more than a week ago. Abby's skin was practically curdling. And there was no way she'd always weighed that little. She looked like she'd been suffering for weeks. She couldn't even speak!

"No, that's not what happened. Abby attacked her and V."

"I have video cameras that prove otherwise," he responded. He leaned back in his chair. "And it even looked like Agent Vito was trying to hold Abby down."

The pain in my stomach intensified, and I could feel the outrage boiling inside me. My knees began to wobble. He was blaming Destiny and V? It didn't make any sense. How could this man be so evil?

"I was there. And so were Ian and Sonny. Bring them here and they'll tell you what really happened."

He brought his hands together on the table. "Grace, I'm sorry. I can't do that. From this point on, you will all be on lockdown—"

My eyes were getting heavier, and it was getting harder to understand what he was saying. I tried to focus on his mouth, to keep my mind off the nauseating feeling in my throat.

"—you will each have a guard that will stay with you at all times and—"

"What...about...V?" I mumbled. The words came out in a slur as I fought to hold back the bile. The room began to spin, and I clumsily searched for the edge of a chair to keep me steady.

"Grace? Have you eaten?"

I focused my attention on Dr. Walker, but he wouldn't seem to keep still. He was floating around and around, and my eyes followed. I looked up at the fluorescent lights of the conference room, which seemed to be getting brighter and brighter and burning my eyes. I scanned the room, trying to find something else to focus on. Something that would stop moving.

There was a man sitting at the table, right next to where I stood. He looked very young, but he had on a lab coat. He had to be a scientist or a doctor. I squinted at him as he furrowed his brows at me. Staring at his mouth, I thought maybe it appeared as though he was talking. I tried to read his lips, but nothing would register. It just sounded like noise.

"I...I..." I didn't know what I was trying to say. All I could see was a tiny red dot on his neck. I zeroed in on what was probably just a cut from shaving his face that morning. But my body and stomach knew it was much more than that. Underneath that tiny dot was a whole mess of veins and arteries and delicious meat.

My mouth watered at the thought of how he tasted. How the layers of his flesh would probably taste better than the crunchy, greasy skin on a piece of fried chicken. My stomach rumbled as I imagined his tender meat gliding down my throat and landing into the ravenous pit of hunger in my belly.

I bit my lip—hard—because I knew that what I was thinking wasn't the right thing. I knew that what my body wanted to do was against the vow that I made myself take. My mind was in the right place, but it wasn't about my mind anymore. My stomach was thinking for me, and now...I needed to eat.

He had no idea what was coming. I lunged at him so quickly that he didn't even have a chance to blink. Aiming straight for his neck, I opened my mouth and bared my teeth. From someone on the outside looking in, it might have looked like I was leaning in to give this man a hug and a kiss on the neck. But this was no kiss. I sucked in the smell of his musk cologne through my mouth before the aroma of that tiny speck of blood on his neck took over.

Then, I bit down.

Normally, I would black out at this point. Normally, I wouldn't remember a thing if I was sitting down and having a regular meal. But while I chomped away on his neck, I realized that that wasn't the case when I was eating something with a pulse. I remembered things so clearly when I ate Fluffy the Cat and Sonny's arm and my beautiful bestie. Phoebe's situation was more like a dream state, but I still remembered what I did and what she tasted like. Maybe it was because, instinctively, I needed to be fully awake and lucid to be able to keep hold of my prey. Because, let's face it, I was a predator. A predator on the hunt for the freshest meat possible.

Using mostly my front teeth to puncture his skin, I twisted my head and pulled, which loosened the muscles in his neck. Blood began squirting out like a sprinkler, and I closed my eyes. I bit down again, this time ripping away a chunk and swallowing it whole. There was no time to chew. I needed more.

There was noise in the background. I could hear people shuffling around and my name being called, but I didn't care enough to look up from what I was doing. The euphoria of every bite took over everything else. All of my emotions. All of my worry. All of my guilt. All of my anger and all of my sorrow.

The blood gushed down the sides of my mouth, and I was actually pissed about that. I didn't want to waste one ounce of this guy. He was either too shocked at what was happening, or I was just strong enough to hold him down because it seemed incredibly easy. Maybe a little too easy. And I didn't remember this much blood coming from Sonny's arm when I bit her. Was something wrong?

I pulled away for an instant to sneak a peek at the doctor's face and what was going on in the room. I found myself practically sitting on top of him as if he were Santa Claus. He and I were completely covered in his scarlet blood, and I could feel it dripping off of my face. He was leaning to the side, almost falling off the chair. His head hung low, exposing the gaping hole in his neck. His eyes were somewhat open, but I could easily tell that there was no more life in them.

I had killed him.

Suddenly, there were hands underneath both my arms and I was being jerked out of the man's lap and onto my feet. My body went limp. I stared at the dead scientist sitting motionless in the chair. He was gone. And I had killed him.

My feet shuffled as I got hauled away from the blood-spattered conference office and down the hall. I was taken into an examining room, where my body was slammed down onto a metal examining table. I stared up at the ceiling. My arms and legs were spread apart and strapped down. Two straps were slung over my torso, locking me into place.

I had killed another person. The body count was growing. Ian's back-story suddenly came to mind. How could he have killed all of those people and not feel an ounce of guilt or remorse while he was doing it?

Death wasn't something I thought about before I turned. And killing someone wasn't something that I thought about beyond what serial killers did in horror movies. I loved blood and guts and Halloween and all things scary, but it wasn't something that I ever had a desire to see in real life. And now, I had killed two people.

I could never get used to this. I could never get used to the empty feeling it left inside of me. I felt heartless. Devoid of a soul.

I felt like a monster.

# THE VILLAIN

A MECHANICAL NOISE BUZZED under my butt and suddenly the ceiling started moving. The examining table repositioned vertically, and a second later, Dr. Walker came into view.

He sighed. "On top of what you did at East Cocos, you didn't eat the right amount of food today."

I didn't say anything.

"You have backed me into a corner here, Grace. I'm not sure what to do with you now."

*Just kill me.*

"You were supposed to be the role model. You were supposed to be my best subject. The face of Serum Z. You were the first to revolutionize this drug. If I hadn't injected you, I may not have ever injected anyone."

Would that have been a bad thing?

"You proved that my formula worked and encouraged me to further my research."

"Why are you lying about Destiny and V? You know they didn't attack Abby."

He sat down on a stool with wheels. "Insurance and liability purposes. It's much too complicated to explain to a teenager."

"What's wrong with Abby? What did you do to her? And why did those guys kill Destiny and Charlie?" I asked, desperation in my tone. There were too many questions to ask, and for some reason I felt like I had no time to ask them.

"Abby and the other subjects were part of an experiment I did to change the side effects of Serum Z. It involved changing the chemical components of the formula. I have created many different formulas over the years in an effort to eradicate the side effect that causes the subject to desire human flesh. Unfortunately, this particular experimental formula caused some unwanted results."

"How? Is that why Abby bit off my friend's face?" I wanted to yell and scream at him, but I kept my composure.

"The formula caused my subjects to become more aggressive. Stronger. Unable to control their hunger," he explained. "This is why Abby attacked Destiny. My employees were instructed to kill any subjects who escaped their cells. They didn't know Destiny and Charlie were not amongst those sick subjects."

"What's going to happen to V?" The thought of him being sick and in pain hurt me deeply. I never intended to put him in the middle of all this. He was a good person.

Dr. Walker stared at me a moment as if wondering whether or not to tell me.

"It seemed that the particular serum we used on those subjects mutated and developed a viral agent. The serum that you carry in your blood is not contagious. As I explained to you before, you cannot bite someone and make them what you are. However, the subjects who were sent to East Cocos can. They can infect another person. And they will attack anything and anyone. It doesn't matter to them, as long as there is a beating heart."

Holy crap!

"Are you telling me that they could cause a zombie outbreak? And that V could become one of them?" For months I felt like I was in a horror movie, and this confirmed it.

"Oh, he will definitely become one of them," he said, as if it were no big deal. "But you don't get it, do you, Grace? You think this is just one of your horror movie scenarios. That I'm the evil villain and you're all the victims. But I'm on the cusp of changing the world! Every one of my subjects that have been injected is able to live forever. Do you understand that this goes far beyond anything you can comprehend? Do you not understand that I have created a whole new meaning to life?"

He was so proud of himself. His eyes gleamed, almost sparkling, as he basically proclaimed himself to be the new God. But there was something else in his eyes. It was greed. There was an unspoken power radiating off him and dripping from every word that came out of his mouth.

"So, what? Do you plan on selling this stuff to people?" I asked. I tried to remain calm, but I was getting more and more pissed off at the sound of his condescending voice.

"Not the East Cocos formula, but the formula you have running through your veins. I tried, Grace. I truly tried to get rid of that...need. But I couldn't. So, it turns out the very first formula I made is the winner. And do you have any idea how many people I have already saved? Do you think you and the rest of the subjects here are the only ones that have been injected? I have spent years traveling the world, finding victims that have succumbed to death much too soon."

I was too dumbfounded to respond. The world? I tried to somehow use my math skills, but there was no way to accurately figure out exactly how many people we were talking about. I didn't have the right numbers in front of me. All I could do was take a wild guess and multiply that by his massive ego.

"I have been a savior to many and continue to be. With the benefits that Serum Z has—intelligence, strength, healing abilities—there is no reason why disease or accidents or murder should even exist anymore. Death will no longer be an option. At least, not so easily."

"But you're killing innocent people! You killed Sonny to make her a Zombrid. And I saw your Freezer of Death. You killed Tristen!

Why?" The wall blocking the flood of tears had breached and I was now blubbering as I spoke.

"Sonny was also another consequence of my research. She's missing an arm, but I can change that. And her family was more than willing to participate and be a part of it all. After all, the Westwoods could never turn down money. As for Tristen, Serum Z recipients have to eat, right? And when things settle down and the formula is on the market, we will be able to weed out the human donors. Eventually, we'll get to a point where we are only sacrificing people who don't deserve a life. Prisoners, homeless people... Our world has enough evil and useless people to feed everyone."

"But Tristen wasn't bad! He didn't deserve to die!" My heart felt as though it were being squeezed. It was my fault that he was dead. I trusted Dr. Walker and Tristen paid for it.

"I arranged for Tristen to come here."

He what?

"He was the perfect candidate for harvesting."

No. No, he couldn't have. He purposely had Tristen come to the island?

"Young. Healthy. Appropriate weight. He was everything a subject should have in their diet."

Diet?

"He was only going to be a distraction for you anyway, Grace. We are in the early stages of marketing. If you're going to be the ambassador of Serum Z and this company, I need you to focus." He placed a hand on my cheek. "He was mortal, and it would not have worked out between you two. But he served his purpose. He kept you well-fed. And you need the proper nourishment, Grace. As much as you might hate it, human flesh *is* the only way for you to stay alive."

Well-fed?

"What do you mean 'well-fed'?" I felt like I was suddenly losing my breath.

"The morning you woke up in the Z lab and had that amazing breakfast? It was provided by your boyfriend. Actually, *all* of your food is provided by humans. It's how you are even alive right now."

I could feel everything I had eaten earlier in the day begin to bubble up into my throat. He fed Tristen to me? He fed Tristen to me! "But you said...you said I didn't need to eat human meat," I countered. "You said none of us need it. That we can live on animals."

He chuckled. "Grace, did you really think we could live in a world where people eat people? I had to lie. I needed all of you to believe that you were 'cured,'" he said, using finger quotes. "You think I'm going to broadcast that I've been harvesting and feeding humans to my subjects? Lying to you all just a part of my plan. I won't be able to market a drug that has immortal properties with the requirement of ingesting humans. It's simply unethical. But I've been working on this serum for years, Grace. There is no way around it. You need human flesh to live a normal life."

It was one crushing blow after another.

"But over the past few months, we've finally been able to come up with a solution. It was simple, really." He shrugged.

"Yeah. As simple as lying," I snorted.

"Yes. Why does anyone have to know that you're eating humans? Why does anyone have to know *anyone* is eating human meat?"

"Um...because we would tell them!" I blurted.

"You're the only subject who would know." He stood up and stepped closer. We were inches apart, and he swiped my long curls out of my face. "And you won't tell anyone because you'd be working for me. And if you did tell someone, you'd be endangering people you love. You don't want that, do you, Grace?" he rasped.

I wanted to scream! I wanted to bust out of these restraints and choke the man to death before eating his entire body in one sitting! He was threatening me. He was threatening people in my life. My friends. My mom.

With every muscle in my body, I tried to somehow maneuver myself out of the arm restraints. I wiggled and thrashed, but there was no way I could get out. I had just eaten a huge chunk out of that scientist's neck, but it wasn't enough to give me the Z strength I needed. And I knew that with all of Dr. Walker's high-tech toys, these restraints were probably made of some ridiculously strong material or something.

Dr. Walker ignored my attempt to get out of the restraints and turned away from me. "You're only hurting yourself," he said over his shoulder.

"How do you expect to lie to everyone about eating human meat?"

"Z Meals," he answered plainly.

"Z Meals?"

He turned back toward me and exhaled, as if annoyed that I was asking. "Z Meals will be the pre-made nutritional packaged meals prescribed to subjects who have been injected with Serum Z. They will be made with the necessary special ingredients, a secret formula, if you will. It's a front, of course. My staff will continue to harvest humans, kill them and freeze them, and the Z meals will contain the human meat required to keep the subjects from becoming starved and crazed. The whole operation will be done on this island. The harvesting. The manufacturing of the meals. And the subjects won't know what they're really eating. I will be the sole distributor for the people who choose to have Serum Z as an end-of-life option. My drug will be ground-breaking. I will gain the credibility I deserve as a hardworking doctor and scientist. And money will continue to roll in. I suspect most of our clientele will consist of the wealthy. Something tells me they want to be smarter and have the ability to live forever."

This was crazy. This was all too crazy!

"So, how about it, Grace? How do you feel about becoming the Serum Z ambassador?"

"Are you kidding me?" I scoffed.

Kate came to the door. "Sir, there's a problem."

I learned over the past few months that the size of Dr. Walker's staff wasn't as big as you'd think. He had employees here and in the States, but he kept the number small. And it made complete sense now—he didn't want his secrets to come out. But his personal assistant, or secretary or whatever Kate was formally called, was *always* somewhere close to him. I only knew her name. We never spoke, just exchanged tight-lipped smiles and semi-friendly glances. I would have made more of an effort to get to know her, but she really didn't seem to be into making small talk. Her facial expressions were always contorted into some kind of an irritated glower.

Kate didn't look at me and Dr. Walker turned his attention to her. She whispered whatever the problem was into his ear. I moved my head to the side to see if maybe I could read her lips, but they were moving too quickly and she had tilted her head toward the floor. She probably knew I'd try.

"Why must you always disappoint me? I don't even know why I bother keeping you around here. You're as useless to me as those Zombrids back at East Cocos."

She bit her bottom lip and her right hand formed a fist at her side.

"Why are you still standing here, looking like a fool? You need to round up the rest of the guards and find him. Now!" he yelled. This was a side of Dr. Walker I had never seen before. He was menacing and belittling. It was truly awful, but not all that surprising. For some reason, I just knew *this* Dr. Walker was the *real* Dr. Walker.

Kate scampered out of the room. He took a breath and slid his hand through his hair before turning back toward me.

"Well, it seems that Agent Vito has disappeared. But not before costing yet another one of my subject's lives."

Oh my God. Who was it now?

"You and the other subjects will be going to East Cocos tonight. Since I cannot trust that you won't cause any more trouble at the moment, I feel that it would be safer to have you in a cell. At least until we get things figured out here."

"I'm not going to be a part of any of this!"

He stuck his hands in his pockets and stepped closer to me.

"Grace, if you don't do this—if you don't become a team player..." He narrowed his eyes at me. "...your mother will be your next meal."

"No!" I cried out. "Why are you doing this?"

"Wealth. Power. Reputation. Everything. And don't think you will just be the face of Serum Z, Grace. You know why Agent Vito protected you. Your blood is vital to this whole institution. I need your DNA in order to create the Serum Z formula. You're important to us, Grace. To the cause. We need your body for further experimentation. It was hard to do things to you that you were unaware of. I don't want to do that anymore. I want you to be a part of it all."

"Unaware of what?"

He tilted his head and frowned. "We put you to sleep for those checkups to analyze your sleep patterns. But you are a female. We must also examine the reproductive system of our female subjects. Surgical procedures were performed while you were asleep. But the beauty of it all was that with your healing capabilities, you simply recovered almost fully in just a few hours. And you never knew exactly what we were doing. We just didn't want you, or any of our subjects to feel unsafe. Unsure of living on the island. We needed all of you for research."

He was inside of me? Without my consent? It was the reason for all of the mysterious soreness after my testing. I felt so...violated!

Dr. Walker smiled and laughed. "Phew! It feels so much better to tell you these things. Now that you are aware, this can all be so much easier for all of us."

I couldn't believe what he was saying.

"We're still in the very early stages of all of this. But my ultimate goal, *our* ultimate goal, is to create a drug that will change the world. We could very well create a whole new race. A race of people who have the ability to live forever and who will be intelligent and strong. And once the serum is completely out in the world, you will see all the good it'll bring. Now, I have to get going. There is much to do. So many meetings and people to meet with. You wouldn't believe what it takes to get a new medical drug approved. Paperwork and inspections and a wide range of checklists."

What more could I say to this maniacal psycho? He clearly had a plan. He had multiple resources: money, power, a slew of people working for him. If he was able to make Phoebe and Eric's deaths seem like something it wasn't and hide this island and what he was doing on it for so many years, then he was pretty much capable of anything. I was surprised, but not really. I knew from the beginning that there was something off about him. And maybe after hearing everyone's personal story about how Dr. Walker saved them, I started to believe that I could have just been paranoid. He was so charming and compassionate. He even gave me an effects studio, for crap's sake!

But no. I was super wrong. I should have listened to my gut. Well...when it wasn't yelling at me to feed it.

How was I going to get out of this? He was threatening to kill my mother. I was still so angry with her about lying to me my whole life about who I really was, but I didn't want her to die. And I certainly didn't want to eat her!

He looked down at his watch. "I have to go. I'll have someone transport you to East Cocos."

"What about you?"

"What about me?" Dr. Walker asked.

"Are you going to become a Zombrid, too?" He could have already been a Zombrid for all I knew.

He grinned and his creepily excited look was back.

"That's a great question, Grace. You know, your father was just as important as you were to this drug and my research."

My father? What could he know about my father?

"If it wasn't for him, I would not have known that Serum Z could not be administered to a live human."

My brain. My brain was working at its full capacity. It was doing double time, trying to figure out what Dr. Walker was saying. Trying to comprehend the words that were coming out of his rambling mouth. I wanted him to just shut the hell up once and for all, but what he just said... My dad. What happened to my dad?

Dr. Walker's expression changed. It was more sincere. Empathic. "Jack was a good man. He loved you very much. You *and* your mother. It was truly unfortunate, and I was sad when he died."

"He..." The tears that had dried up from the anger of Dr. Walker's diabolical plan came rushing to the surface again. "He died? I didn't...I didn't know that. I thought he left my mom. I thought he left us."

"He didn't. He was my second subject. I injected him with Serum Z while he was still alive, and it killed him."

"Does my mother know?" I croaked. My throat had become so dry from all of this information.

Dr. Walker's eyes shifted to the ground. "She does."

My heart. My heart shattered. Crushed into a million jagged pieces. The tension in my body that I'd held taut against the restraints suddenly exhausted me, and the weight of his words forced my muscles to slump. Not only did my mother lie to me about the fact that I was a Zombrid, but she also lied about my father. How could she be so heartless? I could never forgive her. Never.

Dr. Walker glanced at his watch. "I must be going. But to answer your question, I will be turning. I have plans to become what you are. Unlike you, I believe that living forever is a gift incomparable to anything else. And I plan to take full advantage of the fact that it is an option. Now that I feel I have completed my research and we have found a solution to our side-effect issue, I am ready to become a...what do you kids call it? A Zombrid."

"But you have to be dead," I reminded him.

"Very good! Someone's been paying attention," he said in a patronizing tone.

Then, without another word, he left the room and it was suddenly quiet. And lonely.

My mother was a traitor. My father was dead. And Tristen had become my meal. I'd lost them all and I didn't know what I was going to do.

# THE ATTACK

I SHUT MY EYES and banged my head against the metal table in frustration.

I hated him. And I had always hated him. Why did I give in to his lies and promises? I would have been better off at home, feeding on the neighborhood cats!

I wondered if my mother knew anything about Dr. Walker's plans. If she knew about my dad. If she knew about Tristen... Did she know about Tristen? She helped get him to the island! My mother was a hypocrite. A crazy, lying, hypocritical mean lady who intentionally sent me to live with a homicidal maniac!

The straps around my arms, ankles, and torso were tight. I tried to wiggle out again but was not successful. How the hell was I going to get out of this?

Just as I began praying for some kind of miracle, Kate poked her head into the room. She glanced around before walking in and shutting the door behind her.

"Grace, I'm going to get you out of here," she whispered.

What? Totally out of left field.

"You're going to help me get off the island?"

"Unfortunately, I can't do that. The boat isn't docked here right now. Plus, Dr. Walker's guards won't allow it. But I can hide you until we figure out how."

She undid the straps around my body in a hurry and helped me down the table. I watched her as she typed a message or something in her phone. Her fair complexion was flawless, and she wore very minimal makeup. Her hair was pulled back into a sleek ponytail and she had on black slacks, a white buttoned-down shirt, and a blazer—reminding me of something a detective would wear. She couldn't be more than in her late twenties, and those feelings of familiarity came flooding back with her face so close to me again.

Did I know her from back home, or did she look like someone I knew?

"Where are you going to hide us?"

She opened the door just enough to peek out before closing it again.

"I'm friends with one of the natives who lives on the other side of the island. We won't be able to hide for long, but long enough to figure things out."

"Sonny's parents own a plane."

"A private plane would be perfect, but we can't fly off this island. It doesn't have a runway. But my friend has a small boat that can sail us to an island nearby that does have one."

"Did you find V?"

She looked back at me with sympathy behind her eyes.

"What? What's wrong?" But I was scared to hear what she was going to say. Dr. Walker mentioned losing another one of his subjects. I hoped that maybe somehow that was a misunderstanding.

"Grace, Estelle and Maddi...they didn't make it."

"They what? What do you mean they didn't make it?" This couldn't be happening. How could they not make it? We were immortal!

"We don't have time to talk about this right now. We need to get out of here before someone catches us."

I was going to lose it. Too much information and too many secrets were revealed tonight. Too much grief. Too much heartache and betrayal. I didn't think my brain could handle much more, and if she didn't tell me the truth about what happened to my friends this instant, I was sure that this woman was going to be my next meal. And not because I was starving, which I was. But because there were emotions inside of me that I couldn't even identify.

I grabbed her wrist and forced her to look at me. "No! You are going to tell me! What happened to Estelle and Maddi? Where are Sonny and Ian? And where is V?"

She snapped her wrist away, which was a bit shocking because I was angry and hungry—two ingredients needed for an aggressive Zombrid. Our zombie strength was weird. Serum Z itself made us stronger than the average person, but the ravenous times of gluttony made us weaker and more powerful at the same time.

Kate grabbed at her wrist. Maybe I did hurt her. "Sonny and Ian are in your suite right now. They're waiting for us. Agent Vito attacked Estelle and Maddi. He ripped them to pieces before he ran off into the jungle. We have agents out looking for him now. Can we go now?"

I nodded. A part of me felt guilty for getting physical with her, but I didn't care. I had two friends left and they were in danger. I was so worried about V, but that didn't matter at the moment. I needed to get to Sonny and Ian before something terrible happened to them.

She opened the door to take another peek before motioning for me to follow her. We rushed down the hall and to the elevator. No one was in sight, thankfully.

We reached the courtyard and passed the mess hall. That doctor that I took a bite out of didn't give my tummy enough of what it needed, and the hunger was coming on strong. Sonny and Ian hadn't eaten in some time, either.

I stopped in the middle of the courtyard. "Wait! We need to get some food. I'm starving and I know Sonny and Ian are, too."

"Grace, we really don't have ti—"

"Do you realize how dangerous it is to be around three starving Zombrids? We've all been through a lot tonight. With as much anger and sorrow as we all feel right now, mixing that with hunger could equal disaster. So, unless you're okay with feeding us your flesh, then I think it would be a good idea to go into the mess hall to get something to hold us over." I was so proud of my assertiveness. If she wasn't looking, I would have patted myself on the back.

She didn't seem perturbed, however. It could have been that she was so used to being around Zombrids. Either way, she didn't argue with me and we headed toward the mess hall.

Newport was empty. We ran into the kitchen and she helped carry containers full of whatever raw meat we could find. Tristen came to mind. I still couldn't believe I ate my boyfriend. And I felt even more ashamed when I thought about the morning I'd eaten him. The mouthwatering smell and scrumptious taste of...

*Stop it, Grace!*

I decided to leave those terrible memories back in the kitchen of the Newport hut as we rushed across the courtyard to my suite. Once we arrived at my room, I had to knock because it was locked. Ian opened the door and Sonny sat up on my bed. She lunged at me immediately when she realized it was us.

"Grace! I'm so glad you're okay!" She wrapped her arm around my neck and squeezed me tight but pulled away when she noticed I was carrying containers of food. Her eyes darted down to them. "You got food!" She nearly growled.

"I'm so hungry," Ian said, too.

"Okay. We need to hurry up and eat so we can figure out what we're going to do." I set the containers down on the floor and we gathered around them. I glanced at Kate, who looked a little uncomfortable standing by the door.

"Um...I'm sorry we don't have any food for you."

"Oh, it's okay. I'm fine," she said. She might have been silently praying we wouldn't attack her.

"Why don't you go wait outside?" I suggested. She nodded and stepped out of the room. Sonny and Ian had already started, and it took about a second for me to join them.

Before I knew it, my eyes opened to Ian and Sonny. Satisfaction shrouded their faces, and I knew I had the same look on mine.

"So, why is Dr. Walker's associate with you?" Ian asked.

"Kate is going to help us. Sonny, did you get in touch with your dad?"

"Daddy is away on business, but he's meeting with his team to come up with a plan. He just needs to know where to send the plane and when. Can she help us do that?"

"Yeah. She knows where the plane can land. She's going to hide us until we get help," I answered.

"You sure we can trust her?" Ian was skeptical, as he very well should have been. The thought of her lying about helping us did cross my mind, but it just didn't make sense. Why would she lie? What would she have to gain? Maybe she just wanted to get off this island, too. Maybe she was afraid of becoming Zombrid food now that V had escaped and was running around the jungle as a real, no-crap zombie.

"I think we can," I said hesitantly. I was a bit skeptical, too. I hadn't asked her why she was helping us. But, at this point, we had no other option.

"Grace, I'm sorry about Estelle and Maddi," Ian apologized.

"Why are you sorry? You didn't do it."

"It was horrible, Grace," Sonny said, terror in her tone. "V turned into this...this monster! He looked just like Destiny's girlfriend. He passed out and woke up, then grabbed Estelle and just started eating her. We had no time to react and she didn't even scream."

I knew why she didn't scream. Estelle was welcoming death.

"Ian and I knew there was no way we could take him down. He's just too big and we were too hungry. So we locked ourselves in your room. We figured Maddi would be okay because she was sleeping in her bedroom, but she had her door open and...then, we heard her yelling and...it was just horrible!"

I didn't say anything. I tried not to think about V in that state of mind. The state of mind where nothing else mattered. The one where your brain no longer functions normally and all you want to do is fill that empty void inside your stomach with whoever has meat on their bones and blood flowing through their veins.

The three of us lowered our heads as if to say a quick prayer for those we lost.

"We should probably let her back in," Ian said before opening the door. Kate came in and shut the door behind her.

"Where is Dr. Walker?" Ian asked.

"I just got off the phone with Dr. Charles. They're getting everything set up for the turn," she answered, thumbing through her phone.

"How long does that usually take?" I asked.

"Everything should be over within an hour. It doesn't take long."

"What are you talking about?" Sonny asked, confused.

She glanced at her. "The turn. Dr. Walker is getting injected. He's going to become a Zombrid."

"So, he's going die first, right? Like me?" Sonny asked.

"Well, yeah. That's usually how it's done."

Sonny was on to something. We all stood up and I could tell the wheels were turning in all of our heads.

"Sweetheart, who is injecting him?" Ian asked Kate charmingly.

"There are only two of his colleagues that he trusts enough to do it. All of the other doctors are back in the States preparing and dealing with Serum Z, which is why we can't take the boat."

"What about the guards? Where are they?" I asked, worried that they could be a potential problem.

"They're all out looking for Agent Vito and securing the East Cocos facility. He poses a risk to all of us. This mutated form of

Serum Z is dangerous, and no one is safe," she warned. "What is it? Do you guys have a plan or something?"

The three of us glanced at each other. Yeah...we had a plan.

# THE PLAN

I PEERED AT IAN and Sonny. They both signaled a silent okay, and I began to explain what we were thinking.

"Dr. Walker needs to die first before he gets Serum Z. In order to do that, he has to be injected with something to kill him, right?

Kate dipped her head in affirmative.

"Once Serum Z is injected, he will come back to life."

She studied my face. She was trying to figure out where I was going with this. Honestly, it shouldn't take a genius.

"Well, what if Serum Z doesn't get injected? What if we don't revive him?"

My mental health was in danger. I struggled with the fact that I was responsible for a few people losing their lives. Killing was never something that I intended on doing. It was morally wrong and heartless. But murdering Dr. Walker was the only way we were going to get out of this situation. If he lived and became a Zombrid, then persuaded America to buy into Serum Z, we would be saving more lives than he thought *he* would be. He planned to murder people for their flesh.

Granted, he claimed he would only kill people who deserved it, but it was still wrong. And what did he have planned for Ian and Sonny? I knew he wouldn't kill me—I was too valuable to his "cause." But would he get rid of Sonny and Ian? Or would he force them to be a part of the institution by threatening their families, too? In old folklore, zombies were technically slaves. Is that what we would become?

Kate stared into my eyes. She wasn't responding, and I began to fear that she wasn't on board with our plan.

"I'm sorry, what's your name again?" Sonny asked nicely.

"Kate."

"Okay, Clair, listen." Sonny suddenly turned into that mean girl from high school. "If we don't do this, Dr. Walker is going to turn us all into his bitch. So, we really need to know if you are going to help us or not."

"It's Kate. And what if I don't help you?"

Sonny wasn't expecting that. "Um...if you don't..." She straightened her posture. "If you don't, we will just eat you."

Ian pushed Kate out of the way and stood in front of the door, blocking her from leaving if she wanted to. Lovely. Now we were threatening the one person on this island who could help us. I wished V could be here.

Kate glanced at each of us. She didn't say a word. Instead, she pulled out her phone and held it up to her ear. Was she calling for back-up? Damn it! Sonny just had to ruin it.

"Dr. Charles, when exactly will the procedure take place?"

Okay. Maybe not.

"I see. Yes. I'll be there in ten minutes. Thank you."

"So?" Sonny was eager.

"He'll be dead in twenty minutes, give or take."

"Does this mean you're okay with not reviving him?" I asked. I had to make sure.

Kate was suddenly angry. "Let me tell you something. Dr. Walker is more evil than you think. For years, he has dragged me all over the world with him in search of innocent people to inject. Some he would have to persuade, and some he would just inject without their consent. He has included me in so many of his lies that I don't even know what's real anymore. I had to swear to never reveal what his true intentions were, which is to basically make the world his... how did you say it, Sonny? His bitch. I'm tired of lying. I'm tired of traveling. I'm tired of being treated like shit. I'm tired of working for that man. I'm done.

"We don't have to worry about the guards. They're all out in the jungle searching for V. And I have access to their channel of communication, so I'll know if they're coming back to the lab. As for Dr. Charles and Dr. Tamma, they should be easy to ambush. They're old and won't fight back much."

"Hold on, we have to attack them?" I asked. More killing? I didn't know if I was okay with this. And though I'd been here for about three months, I didn't quite know Dr. Charles or Dr. Tamma all that well. Dr. Walker was always in charge of my testing. But still, I didn't necessarily want to hurt them.

"Well, yeah. It's the only way. What else are we going to do with them? There's an hour window between the time of euthanasia and the time Serum Z is injected. After that hour, he's done. We don't want to risk those two cutting loose from us and finishing the job. Plus, they've been behind him for years. He signs their paychecks. They won't be okay with killing him."

"Grace, just look at it as our next meal," Ian suggested. There was a sparkle in his eyes, and I didn't know if that was disturbing or not. He was either itching to kill or itching to eat. Well, I guess the two coincided in our world.

I glanced at Sonny, who was also looking at me, awaiting my approval. Even though she seemed so broken with her missing arm and all, she was still so beautiful. I understood why Tristen kept going back to her. Beauty may only go so deep, but it's still beauty.

"Are you okay with this, Sonny?" I asked. She tilted her head to the side, probably surprised that I was asking her opinion. I pointed to her nub. "Your arm. If we let Dr. Walker die, he won't be able to fix your arm. Are you okay with that?"

She immediately grabbed on to what was left of it and peered over at Kate. "Won't there be someone else to fix it?"

Kate's expression wasn't promising. "Unfortunately, we have only done that type of surgery to a handful of Zombrids and he was the only one who has performed the procedure. I'm sure we can figure it out later, but I can't guarantee a time frame or even if anyone could do it for sure."

I could tell Sonny was mentally arguing with herself about whether or not she wanted to be okay with this. There was a long pause before she finally answered, "Yeah. I'm okay with it."

I knew it had to be a hard decision, but I was glad she understood this went deeper than her getting a new arm.

"Okay, dolls. We've got to get out of here. We're running out of time," Ian said.

We all agreed and headed toward the Z lab.

Being the Worry Bug that I was known to be, I fought with my uneasiness over the whole situation as we crossed the courtyard. So much could go wrong. The agent guys could come and ruin the plan and kill us. The two doctors could turn out to be stronger than we thought and kill us. Dr. Walker could come back to life and kill us. We were in danger no matter what.

We got inside the Z lab without any interruptions. I realized that the lab was empty. Dr. Walker sent everyone back to the States, which made total sense. He had plans to turn. He was anticipating no incidents. Just a quick, simple turn.

We reached the second floor and quietly made our way to the procedure room where Dr. Walker was preparing to die. Kate stopped outside the door.

"How are we doing this?" Ian whispered.

"I'll go in. Once the doctors have euthanized him, I'll text Grace. Then the three of you come in and do what you need to do."

"Why is it okay for you to go in? Doesn't he only trust those two doctors?" Sonny asked curiously.

"It's fine. I'm family."

She must have noticed my puzzled reaction to what she'd just said.

"I'm his daughter."

WHAT! She was Dr. Mark Walker's daughter? How did I not know this? Before I could even begin to comprehend what she had just revealed, Kate entered the procedure room.

"Holy shit! Dr. Walker's own daughter wants to kill him?"

"Shh! Sonny, we've gotten this far, let's not blow it," I whispered.

"So, when she messages you, the three of us are going to rush in. I'll grab one, and Grace, you grab the other," Ian ordered.

"Hey, what about me?" Sonny whined.

"Sonny, you can watch Kate to make sure she doesn't do anything stupid. We still don't know if we can completely trust her," I pointed out.

We sat quietly and stared at my phone. I clasped onto it tightly.

"It's because I have one arm, isn't it?"

"What?"

"The reason why you guys won't let me have one of the doctors. It's because I'm missing my arm. You think I'm weak," Sonny said in an accusing tone.

I shut my eyes in frustration. "No. It's not that, Sonny."

It was quiet again.

"Well, as long as you guys let me eat some, I'll promise to pretend it isn't about my missing arm."

"Two doctors should be enough for all of us," Ian reassured her.

My phone buzzed.

**Unknown:** Now.

"You guys ready?"

Ian and Sonny both nodded. I took a deep breath. Then, we busted through the door.

# THE NEWS

I BLEW THROUGH THE door to the procedure room with my crew in tow. The doctors immediately turned in our direction. Dr. Walker lay on the examining table, as if simply asleep, and his daughter stood next to him.

"Hey, you can't be in here!" Dr. Charles yelled.

Sonny hurried over to Kate's side. I kept one eye on her and one on the doctors. Ian dashed over to the closest doctor, which was Dr. Tamma. When the doctor saw Ian coming his way, he held up his hands—like he was surrendering to a gunman.

Ian took advantage of this and grabbed the doctor's arms, pulling them behind his back. In one swift motion, he locked the doctor into a type of wrestling move and buried his face into the man's neck. Dr. Tamma released a deep, agonizing cry, and I didn't have to watch anymore. I knew Ian could take care of the rest.

I turned my attention to Dr. Charles, who was too stunned from watching what was happening to his colleague to even move. I made the decision to steal Ian's moves and sprinted over to him while his focus was on his colleague. But he must have seen me coming in his peripheral vision because he turned in my direction right as I reached him.

I threw my weight into him. We collided and stumbled onto the ground together, knocking over the metal tray of surgical tools.

I landed on top of him and maneuvered my legs in order to straddle his body. We played slapped hands for a moment before I was able to grab hold of both his wrists and attempt to hold them down, but this guy was proving to have enough strength to at least hold me in place.

Dr. Charles then thrust his hips into the air, causing me to lose control and power in my legs. I bounced off him and he turned me over. Now, he was on top of me! Really? Why did I have to get the tough old guy?

He pressed my wrists into the floor, and I fought with all my might against him. I quickly glanced around, searching for anything that might have fallen off the tray and could be of use. I spotted Ian and Sonny hunched over Dr. Tamma. They were in their food trance. I looked over to my right and could see Kate's legs and feet. She was still standing near her father.

I glanced up at Dr. Charles. He was sweating and shaking, fighting to overpower me.

"Why are you doing this?" he asked through clenched teeth.

A twinge of remorse washed over me. Although he was subduing me in that moment, I had just eaten and knew I could have this guy's flesh in my mouth at any time if I really wanted to. But why *was* I doing this? I was going to kill this poor old man. Doesn't this make me just as evil as Dr. Walker?

And right before I could make any decisions on whether or not to spare the doctor's life, a needle was plunged into his neck. His eyes widened and he froze. I let go of his wrists, and his hands immediately grasped onto his neck. He fell on his side. I sprawled out on the floor and allowed my body to relax. The old man put up quite a fight!

Kate's head came into view above me. She held up a large needle and said, "Serum Z."

She had injected Dr. Charles with the serum, which would kill him because he was injected without being dead first.

"Thank you," I said between catches of breath. I didn't have to kill him after all.

After a few minutes of gathering my bearings, I stood up. The doctor was still lying in a fetal position, but now he was shaking intensely.

"Um...is this supposed to happen?" I asked Kate.

"Yeah. He's going to start convulsing pretty violently before he dies. So you might not want to watch. It's kind of disturbing."

A part of me did want to see it, but the other part felt too guilty to watch. I glanced over at Sonny and Ian, who were still in a food coma. As much as I wanted to get over there to have my share, I had to check up on Dr. Walker. He was still on the table, looking peaceful and serene, like he was sleeping soundly after a long, hard day of work. Kate stood at his side, staring down at him.

"Are you okay?" I asked, certain that she had to feel something for her father who lay dead in front of her.

She didn't look up. "Were you surprised to hear I'm his daughter?"

"Yes. I had no idea."

"No one really knows."

"He never mentioned you. I just thought you were one of his employees," I admitted. "You called him 'Sir.'"

She sighed. "I chose to call him that. And I'm not surprised he never mentioned me. Zack was all he cared about."

She lifted her hand and gently smoothed his hair. "Zack and I were playing with a red ball in the backyard. We had a pool, and we both knew not to get near it unless Mom and Dad were outside watching us. But the ball rolled into the water. I yelled at Zack because it was his fault. He didn't catch it. He was younger than me, and I was frustrated because Mom and Dad were making me play with him. I yelled at him to go get the ball.

"When he ran over, he slipped and hit his head on the edge of the pool before falling in. The water around him immediately turned red." She looked at me. "I didn't jump in after him. I didn't run to get my parents. I just...froze. By the time Mom and Dad came outside, he was just floating in the pool and it was too late. Turns out he was alive. He had just gotten knocked out. Had I helped him out, he would not have drowned."

I felt sadness for Kate. That must have been an awful memory to have.

"For years I struggled with the idea that I was the one who killed my brother. Mom and Dad were too distraught to comfort me, and they even blamed me on a few occasions. How could I have let him go near the pool when I knew the rules? Why didn't I go in after him? Why didn't I call for help? I was the oldest, I should have known better. I should have taken care of my younger brother.

"Mom ended up divorcing my dad and left us. I guess she felt like she no longer had children, since I let her down and Zack died. I never heard from her again."

Okay, this story was getting worse and worse by the minute.

"I was forced to stay with my dad." She glanced down at Dr. Walker again, only this time there was a different expression on her face. It was empty, as if she was looking down at a stranger.

"And all he did was work and treat me like the red-headed stepchild. There were so many nights I spent home alone. He was always working. Always at the research lab—sometimes not even coming home for days. He barely spoke to me. If he did, it was about the serum or Zack. I was forced to raise myself and felt alone for most of my life. Now, here he is. Dead. And I couldn't be happier."

Wow. Talk about family drama! Kate had years of hatred toward Dr. Walker boiling inside of her. I was afraid to interrupt her venting, but I had to ask. "Why did you start working for him then?"

"Because I thought that maybe if I became interested in what he devoted his life to, then he would at least show me something. Anything. But he didn't. He just got deeper and deeper into this whole Serum Z bullshit." She chuckled. "I actually started to feel like I wasn't his daughter anymore. Like I was just another employee he hired."

I could identify with her on some level. Her mother left her and never spoke to her again, just like my dad did. The feeling like you're to blame would never go away. It would always be there, lingering somewhere in the back of your mind.

Kate glanced at her wristwatch. "In twenty more minutes, Dr. Walker will be gone forever."

"Kate, I would understand if you change your mind. I mean, I didn't know he was your dad and—"

"Are you kidding?"

I didn't know what to say.

"Did you not hear anything I said? There's nothing I want more than to bury his ass once and for all. At least then, he can finally be with his precious Zack."

"Then it's settled. Dr. Walker remains dead," Ian said behind me.

I turned toward him and Sonny. They were both covered in blood, as if they had been playing in it.

"Grace! Aren't you going to eat?" She seemed drunk with satisfaction.

"Yeah. I just want to wait until this is all over."

We stood around Dr. Walker and watched his lifeless body in silence. I thought about remorse and the empty, heartless feeling I felt earlier when I killed that scientist guy. I thought about Phoebe and I wanted to cry my eyes out because of what I did to her.

But as I stood over Dr. Walker, there was not one ounce of me that felt repentance. There was no shame. No guilt. No regrets about what was going to happen to him in about fifteen minutes. He killed my dad. He killed my boyfriend and made me eat him. I was glad that Kate was okay with allowing her dad to die. I was more than happy to never see Dr. Walker's creepily excited grin ever again.

I watched Kate as the minutes counted down and prayed that there wasn't enough time for her to mull it over and vote to keep him alive. But there were no tears. There wasn't any kind of reaction. She remained stoic, and I fought against visibly exhaling a sign of relief when she glanced down at her watch and finally said, "Okay. That's it. The window has closed."

"Thank God! Who wants a drink?" Sonny asked.

"Let's go down to Newport and get some celebratory Z Juice," Ian suggested.

"Mind if I come?" Kate asked Ian.

"Sure."

"Wait! Grace hasn't eaten yet." Sonny. My keeper, ladies and gentlemen.

"Dr. Walker is dead right there. Go on, Grace. Take a bite out of him," Ian insisted.

I glanced at Kate. There was no way I was going to eat her father right in front of her. Even though she hated him, it would be disrespectful.

But she looked me straight in the eyes. "How ironic it would be? He wanted to feed you so badly. Well, he would be doing just that."

I'd guess that was her approval. My eyes shifted to Dr. Walker. What a satisfying ending this story would have? The heroine seeks revenge on the evil villain, then she eats his soul.

But it was too predictable. And I didn't want to have that man's flesh and blood inside of me.

"Honestly, I don't think he would even taste good," I said.

"Yeah, he's probably rotten." Sonny chuckled.

I smiled.

Ian walked over to Dr. Tamma, who was on his back, arms and legs spread out. His entire torso had been ripped open, exposing only the ribs Ian and Sonny had sucked dry. He was completely hollowed out. Nothing was left inside of him. Ian picked up one of the doctor's arms and twisted until there was a snap. He placed a foot on his hip, then pulled on his arm. One quick tug and Ian tore Dr. Tamma's arm clear off. He walked over to me and handed it over.

"Here you go. A little appetizer."

I didn't know if I should be disgusted or grateful for what Ian had just done. But the smell of the luscious blood dripping down to the floor helped me make up my mind.

"Thanks."

I devoured my "appetizer" within minutes and was ready for the main course. But I didn't want the others to have to wait. So I opted for us to go down to the mess hall without it. The arm was enough to hold me over for a while.

I glanced at Dr. Walker one last time before we left the room. It was finally over.

We walked out of the Z lab doors and I squinted at the sunlight. It was early morning, and there was an eerie feeling in the air. Everlasting Paradise was empty now. Dr. Walker was gone, his employees were away, and the rest of our crew didn't make it through the long and emotionally exhausting night. I was actually looking forward to finally being able to sit down.

We were entering Newport when Kate's phone rang. "Hello?"

I wondered who it could be. She had connections to all of Dr. Walker's minions, which could be beneficial to us while we tried to figure out what we were going to do next.

"Oh...I see. Okay, well, you had to do what you had to do. No. It's fine. Listen, Dr. Walker wanted me to give you and the others orders to stay at East Cocos. Yes. He will meet you there with the remaining subjects. Yes..."

She was attempting to keep the guards away from us. That was great, but my heart pounded over what happened to V.

"Yes. I will let you know. Okay. Bye."

We all walked up to the bar. I stared at Kate, waiting to hear bad news. She sat down on the stool.

"What happened?" I asked.

"I'm sorry. They had to take him down."

"Take him down where?" I was being coy, but I knew exactly what that meant.

"They had to kill him, Grace. It was either their lives or his."

My heart sank. I turned away from her and glanced down at my hands. He didn't deserve to die this way.

I felt a hand on my shoulder attempting to comfort me, but I shrugged it away. I didn't want to be touched. I didn't even want to be near anyone at the moment. All I wanted to do was go home. But even that didn't sound all that smart after thinking about it. For all I knew, my mother could be just as evil as Dr. Walker.

I was so pissed at all the things this stupid place had taken away from me. People I loved and cared about were dead. In the span of three months, I'd lost my naivete, my innocence. This wasn't something a teenage girl should be experiencing. I should be at home with my best friend, applying for colleges and finishing up high school and deciding if I should live on campus or in an apartment with my soul buddy. The idea of ever being a normal person again was completely thrown out of the window. Now? My mind was corrupted with images of dead bodies and blood and gore and a frozen boyfriend I would never get to see again.

Ian placed a bottle of Z Juice in front of me. "Drink up, doll. It will make you feel better."

I felt drained and void of any feelings. I was emotionally shattered.

"Do you want to talk about it?" Sonny asked in a small voice.

I shook my head. Talking about it would only make me feel like crying, and I didn't even know if I could.

"So, Kate, what's the plan?" Ian asked.

"Well, my dad might have hated me, but he had no one else to sign this place over to except me. I was with him when he made his Will."

"Didn't he know how much you hated him?" Sonny asked.

"Nope. I pretended to enjoy what I did. It was hard, trust me. He wanted me to take over Everlasting Paradise and continue his research if anything happened to him. Little did he know, I had my own plans all along."

"And what's that?" I asked, curious to know how she planned to get rid of the residual Dr. Walker wickedness.

"I want this place to be exactly what he claimed it to be. Everlasting Paradise. A place of sanctuary. A place for you guys to get the right treatment, the right food, and the right help that you need. No more traveling the world and injecting random people. No more newbies. It ends now. And I know you guys need human flesh to stay sane, but we will figure out some other way. I don't want to kill any more people."

Something had just occurred to me. "Did you know about the freezer and the harvesting?" I asked. If she knew about Tristen, I wasn't sure if I'd be able to control my rage. On her face. "Did you know about—"

"I didn't know about your boyfriend," she interrupted, placing a hand on mine. "I swear it. But I did know about his plan to secretly kill humans and about the Z Meals, and I can promise you that I was not okay with it."

I pulled my hand away. Not in an obvious don't-touch-me-because-I'm-skeptical-of-you way, but I would be lying if I didn't admit that there was suspicion. I still didn't know Kate well enough to trust her words. Not after finding out that she was the spawn of an evil man.

"So how are we going to get food if we can't live on just animals?" Ian asked. It was a great question, but somehow, I knew deep down he was thrilled about being able to openly feast on human flesh.

"I'm going to be honest with you...I really don't know," Kate answered. "It's something we'll have to work out. But for now, what's left in that freezer will have to hold you over."

"What about the other doctors and guards? Won't they wonder what happened to Dr. Walker? And will they even listen to you?" I asked.

"I'll come up with something about my dad and his death. For all they know, the turn didn't work. But as long as this place is mine, they can either join us or leave us. I run things now."

"I can help," Sonny chimed in. "Daddy can donate money and help get Zombrids here."

"And the other Zombrids? What happened to the group that was sent to East Cocos after the incident?" We didn't see anyone else but Abby and those two on the gurneys at the jail.

"Dr. Walker had all of them killed. They were too far gone. But now that they're all dead, we can focus on the ones that we can help. It's going to take a lot of work. We're going to have to travel and find everyone Dr. Walker injected, but I think we can do it." Kate was nothing like her father, I was beginning to tell.

"Ian, turn on the TV. Let's just chill for a bit," Sonny said before taking a swig of her Z Juice.

Ian walked around the bar and turned on the television. It was already on *CNN*.

"No news! Put on *MTV* or something."

I watched the pretty, dark-haired news anchor while Ian searched for the remote. It was muted, but underneath her was a headline that read: *Supermarket Epidemic Coverage.*

"Wait! Ian, turn that up," I demanded.

He reached up to manually turn the volume up louder.

"*...authorities are urging residents to stay inside their homes until further notice. A spokesperson from the Centers for Disease Control and Prevention has confirmed that given the time it took for the individuals that were all attacked at the supermarket to become ill, it seems this virus could spread at an alarming rate. They have also released a list of symptoms to look out for, which includes nausea, vomiting, diarrhea, bleeding of the ears, nose, and eyes, increased hunger, and aggressiveness.*"

A piece of paper slid across her desk and she glanced down at it.

*"Okay, it seems we are just getting word that there have been several attacks at the hospital where these patients are being treated. Uh...we're not exactly sure what's happening, but we're going to take a quick break and when we come back, we'll have our correspondent, Dan Michaels, who is at the scene in Tampa, Florida, fill us in with new information."*

Sonny, Ian, Kate, and I glanced at each other.

"An epidemic?" Sonny asked, wide-eyed.

"Kate, do you think it's because of Serum Z? The mutated formula?" I wasn't certain that she could even answer that, which was scary. Dr. Walker traveled the world injecting people with that stuff. And there were a bunch of different formulas. How could he have known which one would eventually mutate into a contagious virus?

I was hoping she'd say they never went to Florida to revive someone.

"Um...I don't know." There was fear in her eyes. "But we went to Tampa a week ago."

We all grew silent. Holy. Crap.

# ACKNOWLEDGEMENTS

To my husband, who *still* hasn't stopped believing in me after all these years. Thank you.

# ABOUT THE AUTHOR

J.Q. Davis is from New Orleans, Louisiana. She has a bachelor's degree in healthcare but chooses to pursue her dreams of being a writer. Her husband is a retired Marine (23 years!) who works with surgical robots. They don't have kids but spoil their pups as if they were real little girls.

Her other interests include exercising, listening to indie music, watching anything even remotely related to horror, and reading young adult novels. She is also a video gamer and secretly dreams about being a professional ice skater, volcanologist, and a stop-motion animator.

She is excited to continue this journey through writing and hopes that her readers enjoy her books.

Don't be shy. Leave a review!

Follow J.Q. Davis on:
Twitter: @JoJoQD
Instagram: @authorj.q.davis
Website: www.jqdavis.com